T0359332

THE
VERINDON
ALLIANCE

The Verindon Alliance

© Lynne Stringer, 2020

Published by Rhiza Edge, 2020
An imprint of Rhiza Press
PO Box 1519,
Capalaba QLD 4159
Australia
www.rhizaedge.com.au

Cover design by Carmen Dougherty
Layout by Rhiza Press

Print ISBN: 978-1-925563-99-3

A catalogue record for this
book is available from the
National Library of Australia

All rights reserved. No part of this publication may be reproduced, stored in a retrieval
system or transmitted in any form by any means without the prior permission of the
copyright owner. Enquiries should be made to the publisher.

THE
VERINDON
ALLIANCE

LYNNE STRINGER

rhiza edge

For my son, Kaden
—a never-ending source of love and
inspiration

GLOSSARY

Chumming – fat domesticated animal with paws and little hair. Farmed for its meat.

Commlink – visual communication channels

Grondal – heavily-muscled but stupid predator about the size of a leopard

Handspan – fifteen centimetres

Image caster – screen or monitor that displays still or moving images

Lerkek – small scuttling rodent that feeds on refuse

Maxispan – one hour

Microspan – one second

Minspan – one minute

One length – ten metres

One span – one hundred metres

One distance – one kilometre

Parcack – vicious predator smaller and much smarter than a Grondal

Ransim – small burrowing mammal sometimes kept as a pet

Remling – rodent similar to a lerkek but a little smaller

Roller – vehicle similar to a car

Snervel – tiny slithering creatures that swim in waterways

Vision taker – camera that records still or moving images

CAST OF CHARACTERS

The High Family of the Vendel
Chief Prince Liffon, the leader
Aliana, his princess consort

Their daughters:
Mestitha, the heir to the throne, who is bonded to Elloran
Lara, who is bonded to Ostin
Meeka, who is bonded to Rallace
Illora, who is bonded to Brexin
Vashta, the youngest

Members of the Vendel High Council
Kenon
Merlina, who is bonded to Xeran
Nelen

Vendel mentors, commanders and personnel
Blassin, senior scientist
Dorias, section commander
Elestin, a soldier and pilot
Erleph
Tremore, an official

Graduates and contemporaries of the princesses
Anam

The High Family of the Verindal
Overlord Dransen

His children:
Brandonin, the heir to the throne
Larinda

Members of the Verindal High Council
Motronis, chief of the council
Loora
Lady Mirkana

Verindal mentors, commanders and personnel
Edrison, platoon leader
Ivanna, chief scientist
Lissia, commander
Nestor, the armourer

Staff at the bunker
Tellaph, the archivist
Gisel, a guard
Mognul, a guard
Nenan, a guard

CHAPTER ONE

Vashta lifted her flier towards the Verindonian sky.

She soared above the palace, the rest of the city of Matarsiss coming into view. She could see the extensive and lush palace grounds with their wild skyflower-filled pathways and dense copses of trees. Further on, there was the city centre with its low hexagonal buildings painted white to reflect the brilliant rainbow hues of their sky.

As she flew higher, she looked beyond the city streets to the farms in the lowlands—farms for meat, for wheat and the most important ones—sugar plants waving in the breeze. Behind them was the mountain range that shielded their people from their enemy—the Verindal.

Circling back to the palace, she looked down on its four spires, the tallest barely four spans from the ground. She wondered why her ancestors had aimed so low when they'd built it. The Verindal palace was much bigger, or so her tutors had told her, their faces flushed with indignation at any superiority shown by their enemies.

But what would Father say?

'Vashta, don't be jealous of the Verindal. And don't hate them. It will only cloud your judgement. I want you to be above that.'

'But everyone else hates them. And we're at war … again! And have been for hundreds of years.' Possibly longer than that, but she had only misty memories from a history class where she'd spent most of her time asleep.

She knew her father too well to doubt the response. 'It's my desire that we would know peace. Please, try to think of how to help our people, not envy our enemy. The High Family of the Vendel must set the tone for our race.'

'Tell Mestitha that,' she hissed through her teeth, returning her attention to her flier and the enemy that shared the skies with her, although this 'enemy' was not a Verindal.

The flier coming towards her dipped and skittered to the side. That's right, she was facing Anam. This wouldn't take long. Not that she could take any skirmish for granted; even he could pull an occasional trick, although it was usually accidental.

The rattling around her honed her concentration. Considering how much she adored flying, she should be a little more respectful of the vehicle that housed her, but the engine's put-put-puttering was so loud it drowned out everything else. The Verindal fliers were better. The images Erleph had shown her had made her sick with envy. They had plans to steal one but stealing a flier was a lot harder than swiping something that could be slipped into a pocket.

She glared at the gun mounted on her nose cone. Their weapons fired projectiles, rather than the lasers the Verindal had developed. And her gun was only loaded with rubber ones. Standard for a final combat assessment, but it felt like an indignity. But if she passed, she might get to lead a squadron into battle against Verindal fliers. What a challenge that would be! Far greater than facing … who was it again?

Yes. Anam. *Pay attention, Vashta!*

He was practically begging her to fire on the flank he'd just exposed; his standard feint—get her to engage, then accelerate so he wasn't there to receive her strikes. She didn't know why he bothered with it.

Instead, she rolled before looping until she was behind him. He tried to find her, but she knew the time she'd spent out of his scopes would slow his response. And he wasn't allowed to transform in this part of the training—to go into the Vendel safe state, which made them stronger, sharpened their reactions and helped them win a fight. With a laugh, she launched a volley of harmless projectiles that left a red mark where they struck.

Her communicator crackled to life, making her jump. 'Her Highness, the Princess Vashta, has made the first strike.'

Erleph's voice was non-committal. Even after spending so many years studying under him, she still couldn't tell when he was pleased. Her father had laughed when she'd told him that. 'If you work it out, let me know. I never have.'

Anam turned, planning his own strike. *You may try.* If he made any points against her, she would leave this battle bitterly disappointed. He pointed his nose ahead of hers, counting on her trajectory to put her right in his path. Instead, she aimed at his flank, ready to release another volley of shots.

But although her weapon spluttered, no projectiles came out.

Her attack window was gone by then, so she slipped into the sky above Anam, trying her gun again in the air. There was noise but no projectiles pierced the sky.

Her weapon must have jammed. How could that be? She had checked and double-checked everything before she'd gone to receive her instructions from Erleph. She always ensured her flier was in perfect working order before taking to the skies.

Now what did she do? Have Erleph call off the assessment because she was no longer a combatant? She cringed at the thought of such a failure, especially in front of her family.

She gasped as Anam's flier swooped from above, releasing a volley of shots. One skimmed her nose. Damn it. He'd made a strike. That shouldn't be possible! She slipped under him and dived, spiralling down towards the ground, smirking at the thought of his frantic face. He would never attempt a manoeuvre like this.

Her radio crackled. 'Princess Vashta, disengage from that manoeuvre immediately!'

I can handle it.

But Erleph was adamant. 'Disengage *now!*'

She broke her descent and levelled off, again trying her weapon. Nothing. Not that it mattered, as her mentor's severe tone broke through the stuttering sound of her engine. 'Both fliers return to base *at once.*'

***

The base was one distance from the palace grounds. It was always being expanded, and new weapons and equipment appeared whenever they managed to steal some from Verindal lands.

The mastermind of these thefts strode towards her as she popped the cockpit and climbed out. 'Your Highness, why did you execute an illegal manoeuvre?' Grey wisps of Erleph's hair flew in disarray as he reached her.

Vashta could feel her face paling. She'd forgotten about that. She shrugged it off. 'It was a logical means to escape Anam's attack.'

He was unmoved. 'It's unusual for you to be caught like that.'

That wasn't her fault, although she wondered if he would see it that way. 'My weapon wouldn't fire.'

'Then you should have reported its failure.'

That was the key reason she hadn't. That one little word—failure. 'I didn't think of it.'

Erleph said nothing as Father arrived, his multicoloured cloak trailing behind him, his gait rushed. 'Vashta, are you all right?'

'Yes, I'm fine.' She kicked the flier's front tyre.

Pausing to bow, Erleph hauled his hefty form over to the faulty weapon where a team of shrugging maintenance personnel had gathered.

Anam chose that moment to hurry over. 'Chief Prince Liffon,' he said with a bow, before turning to the scarlet-flecked nose of Vashta's flier. Anam's grin stretched wide across his round face, his grey eyes triumphant. 'I knew I got you!'

She fought back a snarl. 'Barely.'

He pointed a long finger at the mark. 'That's more than barely.'

'Oh? How many shots did you fire? I bet there are a lot more marks on your nose.'

He shot a look at Father and straightened his flight suit. 'Only in the first strike.'

Erleph came back, his face foreboding. 'Making sure all weaponry

4

and equipment onboard your flier is functioning is part of the assessment.'

She could feel her pass mark slipping through her fingers like the wispy clouds lining their skies. He couldn't fail her for a mechanical issue. 'But I scored the first strike and landed more than Anam.'

'Yes, you did.' He looked weary. 'We will therefore declare this a draw and reschedule the flight assessment for a later time.'

Was that better than failing or worse? 'But I checked my weapon prior to launch. It was working perfectly.'

Erleph waved at the technicians. 'Locate the fault in Princess Vashta's weapon and make sure a detailed report is given to her.' With that, he stalked away, nodding a bow at Father as he passed.

Anam's fat lip popped out in a pout. 'I should have passed. I did everything right.'

'Except fly well.'

'Vashta!' Father scolded. 'You'll both have another chance to prove yourselves in a few weeks. Depart from Anam with respect for your rank and leave this for another day.'

She could tell when she'd pushed Father too far and felt she was balancing on the edge. She reached out and put a hand on her opponent's shoulder. 'Good work, Anam,' she said. 'I look forward to facing you again at a later date.' *When the result will be different.*

He returned her farewell gesture. 'Thank you, Your Highness. I look forward to facing you again as well.' She could see the sweat pouring off his face. A sign of nerves? The realisation that next time he wouldn't be so lucky?

She glared at his back as he walked towards the hangar.

Father frowned at her. 'Don't worry. I'm sure Erleph will pass you next time *if* you do as you're told. No more illegal dives.'

But she had wanted to succeed. Her sisters were sure to be laughing. And her father! Why did he have to be there to watch her fail? 'It's not fair.'

'I think it is,' Father said. 'Erleph could have banned you from flying for a few weeks. Then you would have missed the next assessment.

It's a mercy he hasn't done that.' A shriek from behind made him turn his head. 'But your mother is about to make up for that.'

Mother came racing around the corner, the other pilots scrambling to get out of the way while bowing at the same time. Her rainbow-hued gown fanned out in the breeze as she lifted it to avoid the fine coating of mud on the side of the runway. 'Vashta! Were you trying to get yourself killed? Spiralling out of control towards the ground like that. I thought you'd never survive.'

'Mother, I was never out of control.' The very thought was ridiculous. She knew more about flying than anyone in her family. She'd read every report they'd made or stolen on flying techniques, flier construction and the use of weapons in aerial combat.

'But what you did wasn't safe.'

She sighed. 'It is when you know what you're doing.'

Her hands were on her hips. 'Then why didn't Erleph pass you?'

She could take a lecture from her father or Erleph but not from her mother, a woman who didn't know how to fly, fire a gun or throw an opponent. 'Because we didn't finish the assessment. How could I, when I couldn't shoot?'

She stormed away, ignoring her mother's angry retort. She didn't care that she'd been rude. She didn't care that she pushed a path through her fellow graduates as they turned away, pretending they hadn't heard Her Highness, Princess Vashta, scolding the Princess Consort Aliana.

She marched off the airfield, back into the hangar. She didn't want to go up to the change rooms, but she needed to change out of her flight suit. And that meant walking past the observation deck. But there was no help for it. She'd have to face them sooner or later.

She clumped up the metal stairs, not bothering to keep quiet. It may have been childish for a woman of eighteen, but she wanted to take her frustration out on something, and the stairs were annoying her by the simple fact that they were there. That she was there instead of wowing everyone with her combat skills and making Anam look like a fool.

She took a breath as the door to the observation deck slid open.

Sometimes looking at her sisters was like looking in a mirror.

Many of the courtiers couldn't tell them apart with so many of the same features, all inherited from their parents—long blonde hair, tall and statuesque, blue eyes, attitude … although the minions that surrounded them would never say that last one in front of them. People had to dig further to find their differences. Most never got beyond the fawning stage.

At least the four of them were without their bond-partners. That made it slightly less humiliating.

Mestitha, her eldest sister, lolled on the plastic bench next to the observation window, taking a drink from the servant before her, dismissing him with a flick of her finger. The triumph in her expression stopped Vashta in the doorway.

Lara was sitting next to her but heaved herself off the bench with a resigned expression. Her hand supported her pregnant belly as disapproval settled on her face; an all-too-familiar look.

Meeka, the middle sister, was standing near the window, her face full of sympathy. At least Vashta knew it was genuine.

Illora was the sister she'd always felt closest to, given that only a year separated them. That had changed when she'd bonded to Brexin six months before. However, she was the first to reach her and gave her a hug. The affection on her face brought air back to Vashta's lungs. She didn't realise how much she'd craved Illora's attention while it had been on the man she loved.

'Don't worry, Vashta. It was just bad luck. You showed plenty of skill in what little time you had. Passing next time will be a formality.'

Meeka soon joined them. 'It's all right, darling. You did your best.'

Trust Meeka to miss the tragedy in everything. 'Thank you. I know it took you five times to pass your flight combat assessment.'

Heat passed through Meeka's usually mild expression, but she held her tongue.

Lara did not attempt to hug her. Vashta knew it was difficult, considering how pregnant she was, but that wasn't the real reason. She braced herself for the lecture.

'You've only got yourself to blame. You can't have checked your weapon properly before you took off. How can you expect to be trusted at the controls of a vehicle like that unless you do all the checks? Piloting a flier is about more than just the adrenaline rush.'

'I'm aware of that.' *Don't you think I checked? Don't you think I checked again? Don't you think I would have done* anything *to win?* She wanted to scream it, but Lara's lecture trailed off.

She turned away before Mestitha could join the chorus of disapproval. Not that it would make any difference. The fury rose in her blood as she waited for the biting words she knew would come.

It was worse than she feared. 'It's okay, *little* sister. We understand that you didn't make it. Nobody's perfect, right? You can't be expected to do everything we can do. It's too much to ask of someone so young.'

Don't turn around. Don't turn around. But her body disobeyed her.

Falseness was written all over Mestitha's face. Sympathy barely masked delight and her words were a pale shadow of true support. She didn't know how to support anyone but herself. 'Thank you for your kind thoughts, sister. Of course, we know you failed to even qualify for a flight combat assessment.'

Mestitha's eyes hardened into glittering blue orbs. 'That's because I don't think it's necessary for someone in my position to acquire a skill like that.'

'Of course, it's beneath the heir, isn't it? Why should she learn anything about battle strategy? She just needs to strut around on the front line and leave the commanding to the commanders.'

Her eldest sister's hand twitched, but Vashta knew she wouldn't strike, even though she wanted her to. She was itching to drop her to the ground with a well-timed leg sweep. It would be so easy …

She struck with her words instead. 'In case you would like to learn how it's done, sister, come to this evening's hand-to-hand combat assessment. There's little doubt I'll defeat my opponent there. You've given me such stellar practice.'

She spun on her heel and marched into the change room before the snarl of fury had left Mestitha's lips.

The room was empty, so she stripped off her flight jumpsuit and snatched up the elegant long dress that was her normal attire. She wracked her brains to recall her afternoon schedule. All her thoughts had been on the flight assessment and the hand-to-hand combat that night. Everything else was a haze of boredom. Resigned, she knew she'd have to check to make sure she didn't have an official engagement like a hospital visit with her mother or a school inspection; the usual mundane tasks offered to the fifth of five princesses.

Determined to avoid her sisters, she slipped down the service stairway. Whether their sympathy was genuine or manufactured, it was to be avoided at all costs.

As she walked along the corridor, she heard Anam's voice, quiet, but with the high-pitched squeal of nerves. 'How can you not be happy with that? She looked like a fool.'

Her back stiffened as she heard Mestitha's hissed response. 'You were supposed to beat her, idiot. You should have pummelled her flier with so many marks that Erleph had no choice but to fail her!'

Nerves cracked his voice again. 'Your sister is ... well, that's not always possible.'

'Why not?'

'Because ... because ... she's too good.'

Fire exploded in her sister's voice. 'She is not good. You'll beat her next time, but you'll need to do more than fix her weapon!'

Vashta felt an explosion building up inside her, but she couldn't interrupt them yet. Who knew what else she would discover? Her hand shook, desperate to thwack across Mestitha's face.

The sound of retreating footsteps sounded in the corridor. Damn it, she was too late. She turned the corner to pursue Mestitha, only to run straight into Anam. His face blanched at the sight of her. 'Vashta! Where did you come from?' He swallowed.

She couldn't stop the tremor of rage that tore through her. Did she take him apart then and there or do it publicly?

A forceful step sounded and Erleph appeared. He glanced between them. 'I think it's time that both of you retired and prepared for the hand-to-hand combat assessment this evening.'

Colour returned to Anam's face. 'Yes, Mentor Erleph. That's very wise.' He began to scamper off, calling over his shoulder. 'When do we find out who we're fighting?'

'You can find out now, Anam. Given that your session this morning was interrupted, I think it's only fair that you fight Vashta.'

She thought he was going to faint. 'Oh? I guess I'd better ...' He bolted down the corridor, no doubt to find Mestitha and plead for help.

Vashta looked at her mentor. The glint in his eyes told her he'd heard everything.

The evening's event was bound to be entertaining.

***

Vashta could see Anam's knees knocking as she entered the training room. He was dressed in a service jumpsuit like hers, the light bringing out its pinkish gold colour as he rotated his arms to warm up. The suit was a startling contrast to his face, which looked so white she expected him to pass out before Erleph called them to start.

The room was half a length squared; each wall covered by one-way glass. Vashta wondered who was observing her this time. Father? Illora? Would Mestitha come in the hope that she would witness her defeat?

If only she would.

The intercom crackled to life. 'Trainees, this is your hand-to-hand combat assessment. You will transform on my mark. Fighting will last as long as you are transformed. If you have not bested your opponent by the time you leave that state, victory will be awarded to whoever remains transformed for longest.'

So she had about ten minspans to lay Anam flat on the ground. If she hadn't done it in two, she would be furious with herself.

The mark sounded and, in a flicker of concentration, she felt a grey haze descend over her vision. She watched the transformation on Anam's face as his bottom jaw extended, his skin became tougher and his eyes receded into his skull, their black sockets lit by a pinprick of red.

Even transformed he looked more terrified than terrifying.

Now that her abilities were enhanced, her transformed state

10

whispered his moves to her before he enacted them. She knew he'd receive information about her too, so it was down to who was the most effective and quickest at utilising it.

She expected the spark of thought that came just before he shoulder-charged her with all his enhanced strength. It was easy to side-step, sweeping his feet out from under him as he passed.

He scrambled to his feet, fear evident in his face and stance. He charged again, this time changing direction just before the moment of impact. Unfazed, she smashed her elbow into his face, and he fell back onto the mat-strewn floor.

There was no way he was getting up again. She leapt on him, straddling him and placing her forearm against his windpipe. He tried to buck her off, but even with his enhanced strength, he was no match for her.

'Match to Vashta.'

She rose and came out of her transformed state, not even sparing a glance for Anam as he stood, his shoulders slumped. He grabbed her arm. 'Vashta, please,' he whispered. 'She threatened me. Don't tell your father.'

She slapped his hand away and marched into the corridor. Did he think she would run crying to Father? He'd spent too much time with Mestitha.

Through the numerous doors to her left and right, she could hear grunts and the sound of bodies hitting floors as other trainees endured their assessments.

She reached for the sugar drink that had been left for her. Within the first two gulps, she felt her strength returning as it replenished her system, drained of sugar during the transformation. She turned to Erleph. 'How did I do?'

His face was mirror-smooth. 'You should have had him in one minspan, not two.'

She smirked. 'Maybe I was feeling merciful.'

Erleph turned to glance at Anam as he slunk away, not even courageous enough to hear the words that pronounced his sound defeat. 'However, your technique was sound, your moves on the mark and your anticipation exemplary. You have passed this assessment.'

She gave him a coy glance. 'With full marks?'

He did nothing more than raise an eyebrow. She would have pressed him had her father not entered the room with his two guards. With the thrill of victory in her veins, it was difficult to remember to bow. 'Father.'

The look he gave her took her back to her childhood. Hiding under the table when guests were eating so she could put holes in their footwear. Escaping to the gardens to play fight when she was supposed to be taking deportment classes.

And forgetting protocol. 'I mean, Your Great Highness.'

Father's expression smoothed. 'Princess Vashta, I came to see how your hand-to-hand combat assessment was progressing.'

'I hope what you saw was … acceptable.'

At times, reading his face was almost as hard as reading Erleph's. 'It was quite interesting. However, I'm relieved you're finished. You have another appointment. If you will excuse us, Erleph?'

Erleph bowed again as Vashta followed her father's lean form, trying to work out what she'd done wrong. He didn't seem annoyed—that was a mercy—but 'appointment' was usually a code word for 'lecture'. Why was he so quiet and grave after what she'd just achieved?

'Father?' her voice was tentative.

'Yes, my darling?'

'Have I done something?' It was best to assume the worst so she wouldn't lose any privileges. 'This isn't about the flight combat assessment, is it?'

His voice rose in surprise. 'No. And I must congratulate you. I was pleased to see your fight. I hadn't realised how much your skill had grown under Erleph's tutelage.'

She basked in his praise. 'I was highly motivated.' Should she tell her father about Mestitha? It was disgraceful that his heir had asked someone to sabotage her youngest sister's flier. While it didn't sound like she'd intended anything more than utter humiliation, intentionally damaging a flier could prove fatal if you didn't know what you were doing, and Anam wasn't a technical genius.

But she couldn't do it. It seemed so petty. And Mestitha would deny it anyway.

They left the training sector and headed through a quiet corridor that led to the royal residence. Her father's double guard led the way, their standard uniforms gleaming in the light. They were the same hue as her jumpsuit but with sparkling red lining on the seams. That lining had always seemed a bit much to her. Maybe Mother had suggested it.

Each carried a double-barrelled projectile gun. It seemed a trifle excessive if they were just escorting her from the assessment. 'What appointment do I have?'

She didn't know why he lowered his voice. 'We have guests.'

'Who?'

'A party of Verindal.'

Bizarrely, she scanned her surroundings for danger before chiding herself. Was there going to be an invasion in this corridor? 'How long have you known about it?'

'They approached us this morning.'

'Why?'

He looked thoughtful. 'I don't know. They say it's a security issue. However, if that was the case, I would have expected a military engagement, not a diplomatic one. But it's a significant visit. Their heir is amongst the party.'

The man who would one day sit on the Verindal throne. 'Why would they risk sending him? Are any other royals with him?'

'I believe his younger sister is with him.'

That made sense. Female Verindals of the upper classes could tell when people were lying. Their powers were greater the higher they were in the line of succession. 'Why not just send her with a security detail? Why risk the heir?'

'I've no idea. I look forward to finding out.'

'Why am I required?' She had seen a few Vendel before—prisoners of war and the like—but never a member of their high family.

'Sir, we should hurry,' said one of the guards.

Vashta was intrigued at the thought of being able to study Verindal royalty up close at an official visit. She rarely witnessed audiences unless she managed to slip into the back of the throne room unnoticed. Why was she allowed to attend this one? Her mind was dizzy with ideas, but one kept returning like carrion-birds circling a battlefield. It made her heart drop to her toes.

She needed a bond-partner. She knew the Verindal heir was single. Was Father planning …?

Impossible. There was no record of any relationship between their two races. She knew her father wouldn't mind peace with the Verindal, but she didn't think he'd sell his youngest daughter as a prize for it.

Would he? Could such a thing unite two warring races?

And what about love?

Love was the most important thing in a Vendel bonding. Only a love match would have any hope of producing energy between the two partners—one of their strongest offensive capabilities. If she was to be sold as a bond-partner to this foreigner, not only would she feel like she was betraying her race, she would be forced into a loveless marriage. There would be no chance of her ever gaining the energy component of her skills.

Admittedly, she'd never been sure about it anyway—the idea of loving like that—as it would mean giving away every part of herself to a man. Though her sisters seemed to adore their bond-partners, the thought of bonding with anyone made her cringe.

By the time they'd reached the palace complex, she found it hard to look at Father. She didn't spare a glance at the atrium, its deep blue ocean-like calmness disrupted by courtiers rushing to and fro.

No sooner did her father appear than several ran up to him, babbling about the visitors. 'There are ten in the throne room, Your Great Highness. The rest—'

'The rest?' Father interjected.

'Yes, the security detail they sent with them. Ten more. They are in the waiting room. They refused to stay any further away.'

'I don't blame them.' Her father seemed unruffled. 'And who is in the throne room?'

'The heir and his sister. Also a woman named Loora, who is, I believe, an advisor.'

'Can she also identify lies?'

'Yes, Your Great Highness. The rest don't seem to be of political significance. Five of them appear to be a specific guard for the heir himself.'

Father held out his arm to her. 'Shall we?'

Training for battle had never been as hard as walking into that throne room. Her father's throne was the only unoccupied chair, the large lukis stone at its head catching the light, brightening the room with its swirling multitude of colours. Her mother's throne, right beside it, contained her tense form.

Three other chairs were occupied by the Verindal visitors. The remaining Verindal stood, taking in their surroundings, sure to have already catalogued all four arched entrances and on the lookout for a quick escape if one was required. She doubted they knew about the secret exit concealed by the drapery behind Father's throne.

Her father's own courtiers and council were gathered around, along with her four sisters and their bond-partners. Were they all there to say goodbye to her? But perhaps there was another reason. She could see that each sister had her fingers interlocked with her bond-partner. They were ready to produce energy should the gathering turn ugly.

She took her customary place on the dais behind Brexin, his hand linked with Illora's. As crowded as it was with all their family, she was left teetering on the edge. She nudged Brexin and he shuffled over to give her more room.

A courtier bent his head to Father, but she was too far away to hear what he said. Hoping to learn something, she turned her attention to their guests.

Although the three seated Verindal were unarmed, the other seven held long-barrelled sleek weapons. Laser tech, most likely. Her fingers itched to snatch one.

Not a wise thought in a room tensed for battle.

Father turned to the man Vashta assumed was the Verindal heir. 'My apologies for keeping you waiting.'

Before he could reply, one of the women leapt from her seat. She looked older than the heir, but her hair was still without a thread of grey, and cut short, unlike any woman in the Vendel court. Vashta assumed this was Loora. 'And may I ask, Vendel usurper, why you have kept a true prince of our planet waiting for such a long time?'

It was a loaded question, of course; Loora was trying to catch Father in a lie. But he seemed unbothered by her attitude. 'I wanted to fetch my youngest daughter before we began.'

Loora's gaze landed on her. 'To what purpose?'

Although her glare was meant to intimidate, her words brought relief. It seemed the party was not expecting her presence, which would be necessary if she was being given as a bond-partner to the heir. At least, she hoped so.

Father stared her down. 'I wanted to ensure the whereabouts of every member of my family before these proceedings began.'

Loora watched him for so long it was as though she'd frozen. Finally, the woman turned to the younger one, who nodded. Vashta assumed they were confirming that he was telling the truth.

The heir glanced between the two women before standing. Vashta reminded herself, while looking him over, that no Verindal could ever be considered handsome. They were a dangerous, conniving race and couldn't be trusted.

But if he'd been a Vendel, she would have given him a second glance. Probably a third and fourth as well. He was tall and broad-shouldered with an intelligent expression that showed no sign of fear despite being in enemy territory. She had no doubt she could take him down if they were ever in a fight but felt she would almost regret his defeat.

The sister seemed less significant. She sat quietly; her brown braids draped over her shoulders. Her gown was all imaginable shades of pink and was even more splendid than Mother's. She watched everything with thoughtful eyes, probably scouting for lies. While she seemed to be a thinker, Vashta doubted she was a fighter.

'Sir, my apologies for our wariness, although I think you both understand and share it.' The heir sent a smile in her direction.

Vashta felt the unaccustomed sensation of a blush. She fought it away. It wasn't an appropriate response for a warrior.

Her father acknowledged the heir's remark with the lift of a finger. 'I am aware of the ongoing disputes between our two races …'

'Long-running battles, you mean,' Illora said under her breath.

'And I had hoped that there might be a peace between us. However, recent activity on the border of Andramadiss has been of particular concern.'

At the mention of Andramadiss, one of Father's aides whispered to him. He turned back to the heir. 'I fail to see why you're concerned about Andramadiss. There has been no fighting there that I'm aware of.'

Loora leapt to her feet. 'You lie! Your soldiers slaughtered a platoon of ours!'

Father's face remained impassive, but Vashta knew his expressions well. He was searching his mind for a connection. If he found none, she was sure there was none to be made. 'Nothing has been reported to me. As far as I know, there has been no disturbance at Andramadiss.'

The heir looked back and forth between his sister and Loora. His sister nodded, but the latter looked uncertain.

That was enough to confirm it was the truth. 'Perhaps you are unaware, sir, of what your soldiers are doing in that area. I realise it has been at peace for some time but there is no doubt that we have suffered losses in that region.'

'And I say again that, if it is so, it has not been reported to me.' Father scowled. 'I will investigate to see if what you say is true.'

Loora jumped up again. 'How dare you accuse your true leader of lying!'

The heir held up his hand. 'I can assure you it is. And I doubt our people would kill some of our own.'

Father's lips lifted. 'Then perhaps you don't know them as well as you think.'

Loora stepped forward again, but the heir caught her eye and she sank back into her chair. 'Perhaps the truth is something else, then. The region is mountainous. Could it be hiding deserters or anyone who might want to see hostilities resumed in the area?'

Father considered that. 'It's possible, I suppose, although I can't imagine why.'

The heir leant forward. 'Sir, I don't seek animosity with you. As I said, I'd like to see peace between our two races once again. I have come here today because I want your permission to go through Andramadiss as extensively as possible without fear of provocation. Hopefully, I will be able to determine what caused the loss of the soldiers. Perhaps this would be of benefit to both sides and demonstrate our goodwill.'

It didn't take long to see that Father would agree. 'Very well. I will ensure that my people leave yours alone as long as none of our fortifies are touched.'

The heir seemed pleased. 'That's a reasonable request.' He looked at Vashta again. 'May I have permission to seek you out if we discover anything of note?'

'You may.'

'Then, with your permission, we shall return to our lands until we have news.' The heir bowed his head before signalling to his guards and companions to follow him. The guards went out backwards, weapons at the ready, until they were out of sight.

Once they were gone, Father turned to his aide. 'Ensure they return safely to their lands.'

'Your Great Highness, taking their heir as hostage would—'

'Be an unreasonable thing given that they came in peace and did us no harm.'

'That we could see,' Mother said, ruffling her skirts.

Father stroked his chin. 'Aliana, while I may not have their talent for lie detection, I pride myself on being a good reader of people.'

'You forget, my darling,' she replied, 'they are experts at lies, both identifying and telling them. There is no doubt in my mind that this weak story is a cover for their true intentions, probably to see how heavily fortified the palace is.'

Father turned to Mestitha. 'What do you make of this?'

Vashta had been expecting this question. As heir to the throne, Mestitha was often asked her opinion on political disputes. Her reply was no surprise. 'I don't believe it, Father. They seek to ingratiate themselves in some way. Perhaps they see strategic usefulness in Andramadiss and want to explore it unhindered to that end. They are aggressors who should never be trusted.'

'I think they'd say the same about us,' said Vashta.

Her sister was so predictable. She straightened her back so she could glare down at her, even though she was only just taller. 'We are nothing like them!'

'Vashta, please.' Father turned back to her oldest sister. 'Although she does have a point, my dear. And you heard from the heir himself that he is pondering peace.'

'If that was true,' said Mother.

'Yes,' said Mestitha. 'And you know full well that while he may desire peace, his father does not. He has been the strongest aggressor for all his reign, and *he* sits on the Verindal throne.'

Father looked tired. He turned to the council members. 'Make arrangements to send extra troops to Andramadiss, although they're not to engage the enemy unless the enemy engages them first. In the meantime, I want a full investigation of the region to see if what they say is true.'

'Yes, Your Great Highness.'

As the courtiers left the throne room and her family went back to their duties, Vashta glanced at her father's weary face. While she loved the thrill of a battle, she couldn't bear the marks it left on her loved ones.

CHAPTER TWO

Brandonin ran his hand along the soft metallic coating on his seat.

Flexible metal that gave under his weight, like a cushion. It was one of the new innovations his people had developed, although this one wasn't available to the general public yet. His roller was the only one fitted with it.

His sister, Larinda, sat beside him, with Loora across from them. She ran a hand over her hair. 'Those people are so unnerving. I hope they let us return.'

Brandonin wished she'd kept her mouth shut as he noticed Larinda stiffen beside him. She turned to him, her brown eyes darting everywhere. 'Would they do that?'

He opened his mouth before Loora could shoot off hers. 'Of course they wouldn't. We made an official visit arranged under a treaty. That treaty says that a delegation from each side can visit the other and leave in peace. It's been in place for well over a hundred years now and I've never heard of it being violated.'

'Not that it's been used often,' Loora remarked.

No, it hadn't. He'd wanted to use it numerous times to see if some sort of peace could be achieved, like the peace that had existed in the past. He knew his people were more tired of war than they were afraid of the Vendel.

And why were they afraid? The Vendel were so like them, they must have a common ancestor. While DNA meant they were officially considered different species, that term wasn't used often. There were more potent insults to slander them with. There was no doubt that Verindal and Vendel ate the same, drank the same, even loved the same.

Both races had the same variations in skin colour and tone, hair and eye colour, different heights, different weights. Ten fingers, ten toes. Every facet of their physical form was shared between them.

The place they diverged was in their special abilities. He knew how terrifying the Vendel were in battle when their faces became deformed and their skills super-human. 'Mutated' was the way many of his people spoke of it. And perhaps it was a kind of mutation, a variation between them on a cellular level. After all, in his race, royal females could detect lies, an ability that had never been documented among the Vendel.

So that seemed to be the sole difference between them; an insignificant one, in his mind. Away from the battlefield, away from the political sphere, they behaved and looked normal. More than normal, if the chief prince's daughters were anything to go by. He'd heard rumours of the five golden-haired beauties, but he hadn't thought much about them until he'd seen them for himself. It had made it almost impossible to concentrate on the reason for his visit.

It also made it hard to concentrate on swatting away Loora's constant doubts. 'They must have learnt to hide their lies,' she said.

That earned a snort. 'I've never known you two to be wrong about lies before, not when you're backing each other up.'

'Nonetheless,' Loora replied, 'they've obviously found a way to do it.'

It was hard not to lose his temper with her. 'I don't think so.'

'What's the alternative?' Loora asked. 'That they were telling the truth?'

Brandonin turned to Larinda. 'What does your ability tell you?' He knew she was more reasonable.

And she was. The way she flicked a braid of her hair over her shoulder was a rebuke of the older woman. 'It tells me they were speaking the truth.'

'Impossible,' Loora declared.

'Well, without any further evidence, that's the conclusion we must come to.'

There was ice in her tone. 'You know what view the overlord will take.'

Yes, he knew all too well what his father would think. *A Vendel tell the truth? It's more likely that the sky will lose all its colours!*

Brandonin loved his father but he was immovable when it came to anything positive about the Vendel. And any mention of that dreaded horror—peace—was met with unbending resistance. It didn't help that most of their council did nothing more than nod whenever Father spoke.

He knew a number of them benefited financially from continued war so their failure to contradict him wasn't just because they loved their ageing monarch. On the contrary, some had already approached him about continued support for their efforts after his 'dear beloved father left them forever', hoping his talk of peace was the whim of an idealistic young man.

Brandonin looked out the window at the buildings surrounding him. The Vendel didn't build anything higher than a few spans but at least their buildings reflected their sky, just like the ones at home. He had only seen images of Matarsiss before, many taken from their fliers with brand-new long-range vision takers. The Vendel had no idea how much information they'd gained with their most recent tech.

As they pulled up at the final Vendel checkpoint, he watched the enemy guards as they tried to see him through the one-way glass. He wondered if curiosity motivated them or if they just wanted to know who to shoot on the front line.

Even when they were through the checkpoint and back in Verindal territory, no one in the roller relaxed. It wasn't until they'd reached the borders of Intersiss that everyone sat back in their seats.

The palace's beautiful spire was visible even from the city's outskirts, reaching up into the sky in a gentle curve. Brandonin often marvelled at how the builders of the past had managed to create it without the benefit of modern technology.

The buildings in their streets were taller too, although none as high as the palace. They were bustling as usual, as his people went about their business, buying, selling, working, living. He watched as several workers chatted on the side of the road, their colourful clothes flowing around them as they relaxed between shifts. He loved the splashes of colour that every Verindal wore.

At least the Vendel High Family also dressed that way, although there was something distinguished in the golden uniforms of their military and security personnel.

Loora sighed. 'It's nice to be back in civilisation.'

'The Vendel aren't primitive, Loora.' But he had to admit, it was easy to tell how much more advanced the Verindal were. Computers, image casters, vision takers, faster rollers, faster fliers, more sophisticated weaponry—these were all Verindal initiatives. His military division had even drawn up plans for a flier they hoped could reach the stars. What an achievement that would be! They had recently sent up capsules with tech in them so their scientists could find out more about what it was like beyond the sky. It intrigued him, especially since the meteor shower that had hit the mountains east of Intersiss the year before. He and Larinda had used one of the new long-range vision takers to watch it.

As they pulled up at the palace, Motronis, chief of the council, hurried up to him, his face tight. 'My Lord, Overlord Dransen wishes to see you.'

'I'll come at once.' *Best get this over with …*

Upon re-entering the throne room, Brandonin was drawn to the similarities between it and the one he'd just visited. So much of it was almost identical, from the lukis-encrusted throne—several of the rare colour-laden gems sparkled on its armrests—to the plush and colourful décor. It spoke of a shared history that he knew should be revisited.

Father had a select group of his councillors with him, but they weren't the ones Brandonin had hoped to see. As Loora joined them, they turned to him, their gloomy pall throwing darkness over the room.

He bowed before his father and reached out to touch his left shoulder; the traditional greeting of their people. His father returned the gesture.

'My son.' The overlord gave him a thin-lipped smile, the expression pulling at the wrinkles on his face, although his faded brown eyes still had all the strength he needed. 'I hope your visit was free from peril?'

He thought Father was hoping for a negative response, so Brandonin made his own smile broad. 'We were well-treated and respected.'

Father's pout was comical and his councillors muttered as they turned to Loora. She looked sceptical. 'I wouldn't call our treatment respectful.'

Larinda spoke up. 'Considering we have been at war for years I think their treatment of us was courteous.'

Father seized on this. 'So they were wary?'

'Just as we would be if they sent envoys to visit us,' Brandonin said. 'But we were heard in a fair manner.'

'However, there is concerning news,' said Loora. 'There's reason to believe that the Vendel have learnt how to lie to us.'

He suppressed a groan as shock clouded Father's face and the other councillors bent their heads together in foreboding consultation. 'There's no reason to believe that.'

Loora glared in his direction. She didn't have the nerve to look him in the eye. 'There is every reason. We all know they were responsible for the trouble at Andramadiss, but they claim they did nothing!'

The rumble of conversation echoed around the room.

'And it appeared to you as truth?' Father glanced at Larinda, who nodded. 'That's concerning. How could they develop such a talent?'

'Some say that their technical prowess has increased over the past few years,' said Motronis, one of Father's closest confidants. 'They may have found a way to block our gift.'

Time to rein them in. 'Or perhaps they were telling the truth.'

Everyone looked at him, amazed, except Larinda. She gazed at him calmly, always his support. 'Isn't it at least something we should consider? What if another force destroyed those stationed at Andramadiss?'

Father's frown furrowed his brow. 'How could that be? The intel we received … Motronis, what did it say?'

Motronis mimicked the overlord's expression. 'That a platoon had been slaughtered by the Vendel, my Lord.'

'They mentioned the Vendel specifically?' Brandonin asked.

'Why wouldn't they?'

'Did they mention them or not?'

The old man seemed perplexed. 'I'm sure they did.'

'Does it matter?' said Loora. 'We know it had to be them.'

'Yes, it matters. What if we blame the Vendel and miss danger coming from somewhere else?'

Loora spread her hands wide. 'There *is* nowhere else.'

Again, Larinda came to his defence. 'Weren't there rumours of rebels in the north? Deserters? Those who choose to live away from society? Andramadiss is mountainous. That would provide ample surroundings for those who wish to hide from the world.'

'To what purpose?' Father said. 'There are no lukis mines or anything valuable in that region.'

'Perhaps seclusion is all they desire,' his sister replied. 'Perhaps they felt our presence threatened it.'

The mutterings between the council members faded away as Father gazed up at him. 'Brandonin, I can see by your face you have a course of action in mind.'

'I do. I propose going to Andramadiss.' The chorus of disapproval made him raise his hands, seeking silence. 'I will, of course, take the necessary precautions and security details with me, but I feel that this case requires review at close range. Father, would you allow me to do so?'

It had been a long time since his father had given him that look—one both disapproving and proud in equal measure. He wondered which emotion would triumph.

His father was old but not unreasonable. He could not fail to acknowledge that there could be more to this than Vendel trickery. And if there was another significant danger, he would want to know. 'Very well. But please take the utmost care. You are the future of this planet, my son. Don't take unnecessary risks. Use your wisdom to sense danger and remove yourself from it.'

Brandonin felt like blocking his ears to drown out the councillors' objections but his father waved them away. 'Enough of this for now. We will convene again tomorrow at the council meeting and discuss the full details of the heir's visit. Motronis, make sure you have a complete and accurate transcript of what we know about the events at Andramadiss by that time and Loora, contact the base there and let them know that they will soon host ...' Father turned to him again. 'No, we won't tell them yet, not about Brandonin. Try and think of another excuse. The fewer who know he is attending the better.'

They left the room in a clamour of noise that gradually died away. Loora lingered behind as if to say something but must have thought the better of it, for she turned and hurried after the others.

Once they were out of sight, Father slumped in his throne. 'Those people can be exhausting.'

Brandonin knew it was no use pointing out that many of them mirrored their overlord's feelings.

Larinda patted her father's hand. 'They have served you well and I'm sure they will do so for some time yet.'

He squeezed her fingers before looking at his son once more. 'Are you sure this is a wise idea?'

Brandonin tried to hide his desperation to go. He knew something wasn't right and he felt sure he could find it. 'I don't think there's much choice.'

'Yes, yes. If you say so. You don't have to tell me that you'll be the one who's impartial. I know that too well.' He chuckled. 'Always longing for the truth. Always longing for more information. Always longing for peace.'

Then the look of the leader he had been entered his eyes. 'But remember this, son, although I don't want the Vendel found at fault if they are not, nor do I want them excused simply because you wish to see peace come to this planet. If you are to go, you will find out the truth, not your version of it.'

Brandonin bowed his head. 'I will be thorough, Father. I will do whatever I can to find out who's responsible and bring them to justice. I seek that as much as I do peace.'

The frosty mountain air rubbed his face raw as he clambered up the path behind his guide.

At least, they'd called it a path. He was doing his best to discern anything that looked like marks of passage. All he saw was dark grass which sometimes squelched under his boots and at other times sunk him in mud almost up to his knees.

His five-pronged guard had insisted on following him up the mountain; hardly surprising, given they were entering the area where the slaughter had occurred. He could hear their muttered curses as they fought with the ground. At least their scarlet tunics made them easy to spot against the snow.

He used a tree branch to pull himself up, resisting the urge to ask how much further it was. The squat, wrinkled Verindal who was leading them said little and didn't stumble, even though he never once looked at the ground in front of him. He wasn't clothed to combat the cold of that altitude either.

Finally, he grunted and turned back to them. 'Here.'

The trees thinned to reveal a plateau with several large buildings. Barracks for the men stationed there, he'd been told.

As they emerged from the forest, a man stepped forward to greet them and bowed, his winter officer's uniform creating a bright slash against the snowy backdrop. 'My Lord the Heir?'

Brandonin nodded. 'Yes. You are?'

'Platoon Leader Erdrison, my Lord. My platoon was sent to take over this outpost once the fate of the other was discovered. Please come this way.'

Erdrison insisted they take food and drink before they saw the site of the disaster. Brandonin accepted it, as he knew the man was making sure they had what they needed to withstand the cold. It wasn't long before he was led out of the barracks and further up the mountain. Ten members of the platoon accompanied him and Erdrison, with Brandonin's own guard bringing up the rear. The wiry guide led the way.

'This is it,' the platoon leader said.

'It' was another plateau, this one with a few stunted trees. The cold had made the air thick with swirling white, so it was difficult to see much. 'Why did the platoon come this far up the mountain?' It seemed too remote to be of use to the Vendel as an entry point into Verindal lands.

'They used it as a training area. It helped them adapt to the worst conditions.'

'How much do we know about what happened?'

Erdrison shook his head. 'We don't know where the Vendel came from and we don't know what weapons they were using. It must have been something new because the marks on the bodies …'

'What were they like?'

'Some of them seemed to have been taken down by lasers, and although I haven't seen every kind of laser we've developed, I'd never seen injuries like that. And no sign that the Vendel possess such a weapon. Others had been disembowelled. Our surgeon examined them and said that those soldiers were still alive at the time.' A slight twitch in the man's eyelid was the only sign of emotion.

Brandonin peered through the snow. 'What's at the end of this plateau?'

'Nothing, my Lord. It ends in a cliff. We have no idea how the Vendel got up here. There's no path down that side. Even the locals,' he nodded at the guide, 'can't go that way.'

Brandonin pondered that. 'How did they manage to take the whole platoon unawares?'

Erdrison found that easier to answer. 'Their transformed state would enable them to be more effective in these conditions.'

Yes, that was true. The famous Vendel safe state that every one of his soldiers feared even as they mocked it. 'But you know they can't stay in that state for long without sugar to replenish them.'

'Long enough to slaughter them.'

'Yes, but why the disembowelment? And why do it while those soldiers were still alive?'

One of the platoon spat. 'They are savages, my Lord.'

'But it's not consistent with their usual tactics.'

'Perhaps it was their way of throwing us off their trail,' said Erdrison. 'A deception to confuse us.'

He felt that there was more to it than that. His guards shuffled around, leaving increasing impressions in the snow. 'We'd better get back.'

The platoon leader and his force looked relieved. 'Yes, my Lord.'

'Did your surgeon leave detailed notes on his autopsies?'

'Yes, my Lord, complete with images. I have them prepared for you.'

'Good. I'll want our medics to see the full report.' He looked around as they returned. 'I'll also talk to the overlord about whether we need to maintain a base that's so remote. Have there been any confirmed reports of Vendel trying to enter our lands by this route?'

'No, my Lord.'

So it was a waste of resources put in place by his father. 'I think there are more important areas to guard. I'll see what we can do.'

While the younger platoon members seemed relieved at his words, their leader's face remained impassive. 'Thank you for your interest, my Lord. We will serve you wherever you see fit to place us.'

He knew that. He also knew he wasn't going to let these men and women end their lives needlessly.

It was clear there was some danger in the Andramadiss Mountains, even if it wasn't the Vendel who'd attacked. Should they stay there to combat it? The trouble was, the other platoon had stood no chance. Why should a new one be any different? It was imperative that they discovered more about how these soldiers had died and who or what had killed them.

***

Ivanna held the images up to the light. 'They made a mess, didn't they?'

Were all scientists the same? Brandonin had already seen the images of the bodies a number of times and felt nauseated every time he did. However, every time any medical or scientific personnel saw them, they were either enraptured or made light-hearted remarks.

They weren't just a mess, those bodies. There were organs all over the place. That was another reason he was following this up instead of his father. As far as the overlord was concerned, the Vendel had decided to have fun carving up some of their victims.

At least he'd seen a shudder come from one or two of the junior staffers who stood at their workbenches, testing samples, making notes on a variety of different experiments that Ivanna was running. She was always working on something. His father supplied her with all the new tech they developed. Her lab was sleek, clean and full of every piece of equipment a senior scientist could desire.

Ivanna coughed a little as she sat down and examined the autopsy files again, her petite frame bending over them as she crossed and recrossed her legs. She seemed lost in a world of her own, one filled with dismembered corpses. He waited.

And waited.

And waited.

Eventually, he had to interrupt. 'Ivanna?'

She started, rose and bowed. 'My apologies, my Lord, I'd forgotten what I was doing.' She looked lost as she glanced shamefacedly at him and back to the report.

'Does it tell you anything about what killed these soldiers?'

'It's interesting that they were killed in different ways, and so quickly, too. The culprit is fast, that's for sure. A fast mover and a fast learner, I would say.'

'What makes you think that?'

'Assuming the results of these autopsies are accurate—and I have no reason to doubt that, as I'm familiar with Altranin's work—the soldiers who were killed by laser died first. Although you can see from the shooting patterns,' she pointed them out as Brandonin tried to look at them through half-closed eyes, 'that whoever it was didn't know where to hit at first. They were shooting randomly. I would expect Vendel, even more so when transformed, to have been far cleaner in their killing.

'However, by the final victim,' she held up another image, 'the enemy was already well aware of where it needed to aim in order to kill.'

She turned to the worst images. 'In the disembowelled soldiers, the enemy targeted all the vital organs. According to the report, the first victims—the ones killed by lasers—were killed on the mountain peak, the second another two lengths or so further down. Now, what does that tell you?'

'That the assailant followed them.'

Her face brightened, reminding him of his tutors when he gave the right answer. 'Yes, and learning quickly as it, or they, followed.'

Something ominous was building here. 'What were they learning?'

She held up the image. 'About us. With the final victims, they knew where the vital organs were situated and, from what I can tell, they wanted to see them while they were still in action, so to speak. But that's not the most disturbing part.'

It wasn't? 'Then what is?'

She dropped the image back on her desk. 'Like I said, fast at everything. Fast learner. Also fast mover. The time of death between the first victim and the last appears to be a period of no more than ten minspans.'

That couldn't be right. 'So in ten minspans it killed a group, then followed the others and autopsied them while they were still alive?'

The look on her face was so academic. Didn't she realise what this meant? Not if her unflustered tone was anything to go by. 'It means that you're dealing with a creature that's incredibly fast and I'd say there's more than one of them. How many, I don't know. And it looks like they've worked out the most effective ways to kill us.'

Brandonin took a deep breath. He knew panicking would be useless. But there was one final thing he needed to know. 'In your professional opinion, is there any animal or creature on Verindon that could have done this?'

She shook her head. 'I've never seen anything like this before. No creature on this planet kills like this, and certainly none that could survive in the Andramadiss Mountains. And where do the lasers come in? Or the autopsies?'

'Could it have been the Vendel?'

She looked over the notes again. 'I suppose they could have developed a laser and used it. We also know they're fast, but why perform the autopsies? What did they have to gain by that? They already know our biology; it's more or less the same as theirs. And if it were the Vendel, their aim would be to kill quickly. I can't see a reason for it. No, I'd be surprised if they were the culprits.'

'Which means ...' Not that he needed her to say it.

'Whatever it is, it's stalking us. And I have no idea what it might be.'

CHAPTER THREE

Vashta felt her eyes close. Her mother nudged her and she snapped them open, but it was no good. Councillor Kenon was still talking about hospital funding, on and on, after more than a maxispan.

She looked around the boardroom. If they were going to visit the hospital, couldn't they at least have visited the patients? To see the real people doing their work and hear their stories? No, it was more important to sit in a room with a few primary colours to decorate it and listen to councillors shuffle papers and talk about how money would be spent.

If her mother had her way, this would be her future.

At last, Kenon ran out of spittle and sat down. Mother rose from her chair at the head of the long, rich red table. 'Thank you, councillor. I believe that your suggestion for the transfer of funds should be enough to cover the new hospital wing.' Her glance at Vashta held venom. 'I think we'll recess for refreshments before we continue.'

Vashta stood, shaking her feet to get the circulation going again, then wandered over to the refreshments table. Some of the old people tried to engage her with talk about the new wing and how much it would cost, but she could hear nothing more than *blah-blah-blah-blah-blah.*

The door opened and Erleph entered. Immediately, her whole body was on alert. Was there trouble? Did she need to command a flier? She had finally passed her flight combat assessment with full marks against her opponent. She was ready to take to the skies at a moment's notice.

Erleph approached her mother and although she couldn't hear their hissed exchange, she hurried over. 'Am I required?'

Erleph gave a tight smile as her mother seethed beside him. 'Your Highness, I'm required to visit a battlefield today and the chief prince suggested it might be good to get this part of your training out of the way.'

Mother tutted him. 'Erleph, this is an important meeting. You know Vashta needs to develop a career in court circles. A patron of the hospital is the ideal path for a fifth daughter.'

'Yes, Your Highness, but the chief prince felt that most of the proceedings would be over by now?'

Her mother looked around at the councillors as they chatted and argued and debated costings and the allocation of funds. 'I'm sure more is still to be discussed.'

'But my visit is required today so it seemed an opportune time—'

Mother waved a frustrated hand. 'Take her then. But she must be back in time for the patrons' dinner this evening!'

'Of course, Your Highness.'

Pivoting on a heel, Mother went back to the councillors. Erleph was unperturbed as he turned to her. 'Your Highness?'

He didn't have to say it twice.

***

The roller rocked from side to side as she prepared for what was to come. Erleph was beside her, looking alert in spite of the plush seat that nearly buried them in its comfort.

He said nothing to either her or their driver as they bumped along over the disused roads. Flashes of forest passed by on either side, broken here and there by a dilapidated hut. Relics of the Verindon of the past, these places were now the haunts for chummings and ransims, and maybe a few ghosts who lived in memory of the rare times of peace between Vendel and Verindal.

Although she knew he wasn't one for conversation, she couldn't maintain her silence. 'How did you do it?'

He seemed surprised to hear her speak. 'Do what?'

'Get Father to agree to this.'

His face faded it into its usual non-committal mask. 'Visiting a battlefield is part of your training. He knows that. And you know how pleased he was when you passed your second flight combat assessment yesterday.'

She tried not to think of the first and filled her thoughts with how proud Father had looked as she'd left the cockpit. 'But my mother …'

Then she saw a shadow on his face. Her heart sank. 'It's conditional, isn't it? Are we even going to a region that's still being fought over or is this just a pleasure trip?'

'We're going to Leeftak.'

It was worse than she'd thought. 'There hasn't been fighting there for months!'

He gave her the chiding look of a disappointed mentor. 'There are still enemy soldiers in the area.'

It wasn't enough to placate her. 'But I'm not going to be fighting them, am I?'

'Vashta, be reasonable. Although your sisters went to more active war zones, we didn't thrust them onto the front lines during their training. They weren't ready for that, and neither are you.'

She tried to control her pout. She knew it wouldn't change his mind. 'Yes, but I bet they've been on plenty since they were bonded.'

This time he gave her a long, searching look. She couldn't decipher what she saw on his face. It didn't seem to be disappointment, as she might have expected. It was more like compassion. 'Vashta, you know you have the potential to do everything your sisters can do.'

'*If* I find true love.'

'The power that's brought into being by two people committed to each other in every way is an amazing gift that we're privileged to draw on. Those who develop this ability are to be commended. But it's not something everyone finds or even needs.

'You have a great deal of strength when you transform. This is far more beneficial for someone who excels at flying, as you do. It may be better to focus more on that skill, even if you do find the right lover. Failing to be an energy producer doesn't mean you can't be a great fighter anyway and it won't make you less than your sisters.'

No, my age does that. But she had to admit he had a point. 'So you'll still think I'm a worthy fighter even if I can never produce energy?'

He seemed surprised at the direction of her thoughts. 'Of course. Your skill in your transformed state is far above the level of any of your sisters. You know that. Producing energy with their bond-partners is the best way for them to contribute to the war effort, but that's not necessarily going to be the case for you.' She could have sworn his face softened, but the expression melted away before she could decide. 'You don't need that skill to be a worthwhile contributor on the battlefield.'

She settled back in the seat. Something in her wanted to hang on to the idea of producing energy, but she knew why—she couldn't stand the thought of her sisters, especially Mestitha, being able to do something she couldn't, to again be the sister who was left behind, too young, too weak, too small. That had been the mantra for as long as she could remember.

But he was right. Her skills at fighting were greater than any of her sisters. She'd trained harder and worked longer and studied every technique she could find. Having this confirmed by Erleph, who wasn't given to exaggeration, told her that she might be taken seriously as a fighter.

But not soon enough to allow her to visit a decent battlefield.

***

The Leeftak base was larger than she'd thought, so that was something. As she stepped out of the roller, she saw ten of their standard low-set barracks—heavy structures made of grey concrete rather than the reflective white used for their residential properties. While there were windows set in the sides, they weren't the usual broad expanse in most homes, which were large enough to allow its inhabitants an unhindered view of Verindon's colour-filled sky.

She knew each building housed about one hundred soldiers. That was better than expected in a place where the fighting was dying down. Assuming they were all occupied, of course.

A woman strode up to them as they disembarked. The yellow-

36

gold lapels and stars of service on her uniform marked her as a senior officer, even though she didn't look much older than Mestitha. She and Erleph greeted each other, then she turned and bowed to Vashta. 'Your Highness. Commander Erleph. We're pleased to have you here. I am Section Commander Dorias. Please follow me.'

Vashta had been expecting to find the barracks almost empty, but at least half still appeared to be holding a full complement of soldiers. She could tell Dorias was watching her. 'I hope you're pleased with your troops.'

Does she think I'm going to say no? 'Yes, they look as dedicated as any others.'

The commander seemed satisfied with her response. 'I understand you're here because you've reached the battlefield section of your training. That's a great achievement for one so ... I mean for someone of your position.'

She'd been going to say, 'one so young'. And what she had said wasn't much better. 'Yes, I was so pleased to reach this goal. And at a younger age than any of my sisters.'

This time the commander caught her tone and her face paled. She shot a desperate glance at Erleph, but he gave no response. When she turned back to Vashta, she could see beads of sweat gathering on the commander's forehead. 'Err, yes, Your Highness. I'm sure your skill does you credit. And I'm sure the chief prince and princess consort are proud of all you've achieved.'

Vashta didn't approve of using her position to humiliate people ... usually. She let Dorias stumble through some awkward fawning without doing anything to stop her. Erleph, however, shot Vashta one of his rare expressive faces—one filled with disapproval—so she tried to feign interest in the facilities.

When the commander left them in the mess hall, her mentor leant over. 'That was uncalled for.'

'Are you talking about me or her?'

He frowned. 'You need to *show* people what you can do rather than punishing them for not realising it in the first place.'

She wouldn't let her heart soften. 'They shouldn't be so quick to judge.'

'And neither should you. Of course people aren't going to know what you're capable of until they've seen it for themselves. It's a poor reflection on your character if you take offence so easily.'

He'd said enough. 'I'll take offence when I like, thank you.'

But he refused to release her from his steady gaze. 'You'll never be the fighter you can be if comments like that prick your armour.'

That hit home, although she tried to hide its impact by tossing her head. 'I'll take that on board.'

She stared out the window as though he hadn't spoken, but his words ran circles in her mind, refusing to give her respite from their nagging accusations.

The commander soon returned, a file in her hand. 'I believe you wanted to see this information, Erleph?'

He took the file and, to her surprise, held it low enough for her to see it. 'What is it?'

She clenched her mentor's shoulder as she read what was in front of her. Erleph gave the closest thing she'd seen to a triumphant grin. 'The schematics and flying techniques for a Verindal jet-powered flier.'

She fought the urge to snatch it from his hands. 'Where did this come from?'

'From our spies, Vashta. Where else?' He laid the papers out on the table as they looked over the blueprints for the fliers. Then he handed her a thick wad which she began leafing through. It was an operational manual. She began soaking in every word, comparing it with their own fliers and adjusting her mind to the differences. What she wouldn't give to pilot one!

'Does this make our visit to such a quiet outpost a little more acceptable, Your Highness?'

She grinned. 'Maybe.'

***

Even though the flier manual was more interesting, Vashta needed to take a place on the front line to complete her training.

She looked at the troops guarding this section of the line—fifty foot soldiers hiding behind barriers while they waited to see if the enemy would attack. So inspiring. At least the past two maxispans she'd spent dissecting the flier's operational manual made up for it.

But the section commander was still determined to make her appreciate Leeftak for what it achieved in their fight against the Verindal. 'This is important work,' she said, her voice speeding up to breakneck pace. 'The Verindal have an outpost just over there. There's no immediate danger, though, or we would never have allowed a princess to come here.'

Dorias pointed to a pinprick of a building Vashta could see when she squinted. It had to be at least a distance away!

'So it's essential that we keep an eye on them,' the commander babbled.

Vashta was determined not to upset her this time. 'Yes, I can see that. I take it this was the site of a major battle at some stage?' Although there was a light sprinkle of grass in no man's land, there were also dips and jagged ground; a sure sign it had been broken up by heavy fire.

Commander Dorias nodded. 'If you had been here six months ago, these barriers would have been shielding our troops from the enemy's laser fire.' She sighed out her weariness. 'Even transformed, it's a challenge for us to combat the Verindal's superior weaponry, but our soldiers rose to this challenge and fought admirably, holding the Verindal ba—'

Vashta's head connected with the ground so quickly it took her a moment to realise Erleph had thrown her there. He lay on top of her as laser fire rained down on them. She hurried to the safety of the barriers, the commander and her mentor behind her.

Commander Dorias peered through a transparent screen, searching but showing no sign of finding the source. 'First wave, be prepared to transform on my signal.'

The soldiers, who had standard weapons firing steel projectiles, would be at a disadvantage against lasers. At least their transformation should ensure more effective fighting.

This was what she'd hoped for. She felt her blood pumping fast through her veins and readied for her own transformation. She pulled out her weapon—just another projectile-laden one—and glanced at Erleph, who looked stricken. She knew he would be scrambling for a way to get her out of there.

Not on your life.

The lasers kept raining down as Vendel bullets shot over the barriers. Vashta peered through them to pinpoint the enemy. Where were they? Could they still be a distance away?

She let out a strangled cry as a nightmare creature filled her vision.

It rose above the barrier in a single bound, hanging suspended in the air. It had a multi-sectioned body and eyes, almost like an insect, but it was far larger than any she knew of—at least ten handspans tall. And it didn't seem to have wings. It hovered there, regarding them, four shrivelled arms and two stumpy legs hanging crookedly off its body.

As it gazed down on them, an armoured section on its torso unfolded, revealing a circle of energy. The soldiers dived for cover as a laser beam tore along the ground, leaving a scorch of burnt earth in its wake.

Everyone transformed at the same moment, and all weapons rained fire on the creature. Owing to their enhanced state, every shot hit its mark. It ducked out of sight for a moment before rising to continue shooting. Most of its fire missed as the transformed Vendel moved too quickly to be struck. This seemed to confuse the hovering monstrosity.

A dozen others of its kind joined it.

'Get her out of here!' Commander Dorias said, her voice sounding muffled, as all voices did when Vashta was transformed.

'No!' But Erleph was already dragging her away. She refused to give up. Having reloaded her weapon, she let out another round of fire on the creatures.

Her senses warned her one was about to fire on her. Before it could, reinforcements arrived. They had heavier weaponry, but although it forced the creatures back a little, nothing seemed to injure them.

Just as Vashta reached the safety of the nearest barracks, she heard a cry and turned back to see one of the creatures pluck a soldier from amongst the others before bounding away over the ground in large leaps, the others of its kind flying through the air behind it. To the soldier's credit, she didn't stop fighting. Still transformed, she struggled and unloaded her weapon on it. Vashta knew she'd target every vulnerable spot it had.

It made no difference.

The remaining soldiers transformed back, heaving for breath as they reached for the liquid sugar canisters slung at their belts. Vashta had her own—a Vendel was never without one—and, sensing her transformed self fading away, she returned to normal and gulped down the contents of her can. She had to be ready to fight should the monsters return.

She scanned the horizon for any sign of them but soon there were too many soldiers in her way. Reinforcements raced around trying to obtain as much intel as possible on their assailants. Others loaded the injured onto mats and hurried them away. Vashta noted with relief that the only soldiers who seemed severely injured were those who had been caught in the first wave of the attack. The rest had used the skill and speed of their transformed state to keep them from serious injury.

She wanted to stay and be with the troops, to encourage them by her presence, but Erleph still tugged at her. 'Vashta, get inside, *now!*'

'But I can help.'

'The medics will take it from here.' He scanned the skies. 'We need to get you somewhere safe in case those things return.'

'Why should I be safe when they're not?' She pointed to the reinforcements.

Commander Dorias joined them. She had her hand clamped on her arm, blood seeping between her fingers. Her deference was gone. 'Why is she still in the open?' she screamed. 'Get her out of here!'

'But—'

She gestured to two stocky soldiers, who took hold of Vashta's arms and dragged her towards the barracks. 'Get your hands off me!' She considered transforming to teach them a lesson but knew it would be a waste of her power and theirs should the enemy return.

She let herself be seated in the barracks. She let the medics fuss over her, even though she only had a scratch on her arm. She let them waste their time with her when they had more severe injuries to deal with, as long as they let her sit near a window so she could watch for the creatures' return.

For the next few maxispans, soldiers and commanders ran in and out as reinforcements were brought in to strengthen their position. Vashta was forced to move further and further away from the scene of the attack until she could no longer gain any sense of what was going on. And no one would answer her questions.

She was at the outermost building, assuming she would soon be whisked away in a roller, when Meeka and Illora marched in with their bond-partners, Rallace and Brexin. They were in full uniform, the lukis-coloured lining sparkling in the light, ready to use their energy in battle.

Meeka ran up to her, throwing her arms around her. 'Sister, are you all right?'

'Of course I am!' Vashta spat. 'Now, tell me what we know. What were those things?'

Illora looked her over. 'It's not your concern. You're to re—'

'It is my concern when I witnessed the attack. I can guarantee I know more than you about what just happened, so I am of benefit here and you need to fill *me* in on what *you* know.'

Meeka gave her an indulgent look but Illora wouldn't bend. 'We can hear that from the section commander. You need to return home. Then you can tell Father what you've seen.'

She glared at the sister who used to be her ally. To see Illora pulling rank like this ... 'Why are you even here? Where's Lara?'

'She's in labour.'

'Already?'

'Yes, the baby's coming early,' said Meeka. 'You should go. Mother could use your help. You know how nervous she'll be while she waits for her first grandchild.'

They wanted her to hold Mother's hand and wait for the exciting

42

news of a baby so she could coo and fawn like some infant. 'You need me here. I witnessed everything.'

'No, we don't,' Illora insisted.

Brexin stepped in. He was more seasoned in battle, having been on the front line for a number of years before bonding with Illora. 'What did you see?'

'First, tell me what we know about where those creatures came from.'

'We know nothing,' said Illora, her words laced with frustration.

'They're just some abomination that the Verindal have created to slaughter us,' said Meeka.

'How could that be?'

'How do we know where the Verindal gets anything they throw at us?'

'They seemed impervious to all our fire,' said Erleph. 'I believe heavier weaponry might make a difference.'

'Heavier projectile weaponry?' Rallace asked.

'I don't think so. I think an energy surge might stand a chance, although I'm uncertain. I'm not sure what could take them down.'

'Strengths?' asked Illora.

'They're incredibly fast,' Vashta said. 'They can shoot lasers from their torso. They seem impervious to projectile fire, even at close range. They can hover in the air but have no wings to damage.'

Illora smiled. 'Thanks for your help, Vashta, but you need to go. Father will send a force to drag you away if you don't. He said so himself.' She turned to Erleph. 'Take her home.'

Vashta sighed at they walked off. 'I guess we leave now?'

'Yes, we do.'

But even as they boarded the roller that had been assigned to return them to the palace, she looked back at the chaos behind them. 'I'm not convinced the Verindal had anything to do with this.'

Erleph met her gaze. 'I agree.'

CHAPTER FOUR

Brandonin strode into the triage unit that had been set up at Leeftak to handle their casualties. He still wasn't sure what had happened. Loora had gone to find out.

The smell hit him as soon as he entered—cleaning fluid trying to cover the stench of destroyed flesh and blood. The room had been cleared of all equipment apart from mats for the wounded. At least fifteen soldiers writhed and moaned as medics hovered over them, murmuring soothingly while they administered treatment.

A minor official babbled in his ear. Her senior officers were lying on the mats in front of him ... the ones who were still alive. 'My Lord, the attack came out of nowhere. The only weapon we could identify was the lasers. I don't know how we combat that, my Lord. Combined with their ability to transform into monsters, that will make them invincible.'

A number of medics looked up in alarm, so Brandonin made his reply as smooth as possible. 'Captain, I'm sure we will learn to combat whatever the Vendel have unleashed in short order. This might be a setback, but we'll stand our ground.' He made sure his face was filled with confidence even though doubt gnawed at him. This attack was too different from all previous ones for any kind of certainty.

The young woman on the mat nearest to him drew his attention as the medic waved a probe over her. These were amongst their latest technology and helped pinpoint the source of the injury quicker than anything else. The medic removed the fabric of the soldier's uniform to reveal a welt, almost like a cavity, with bruised flesh around it, running down the woman's side.

'I've never seen anything like this,' the medic muttered. 'It's inconsistent with damage from our own lasers.'

But he *had* seen wounds like this before. On the soldiers killed in the mystery attack at Andramadiss. Was it really something new the Vendel had developed?

Loora appeared at his side. 'My Lord, please come this way.'

He was soon in the cool of the Leeftak Operations Room, with officers manning stations and relaying information. But the smell of the triage seemed to cling to him.

Loora nodded to a woman he recognised. 'Commander Lissia. It's a comfort to see you here. Were you on-site for the attack?'

The woman bowed, her greying head nodding before she returned her gaze to his. He knew her face well, as she had been serving their people as the leader of their military for the past ten years.

Her face was lined with concern and uncertainty; not emotions he was accustomed to seeing there, but her voice was still direct and unwavering. 'Unfortunately, no, my Lord. Leeftak has not been a scene of much action for some time so the highest rank here was a platoon commander.'

'Who is now dead?'

'Yes, my Lord.'

'Can you tell me anything about this attack?'

'I'm happy to say that we have vision.'

He'd heard that their military had been planning to roll out vision takers to all barracks but hadn't thought it had got as far as Leeftak yet. 'Vision takers had been installed?'

'Yes, my Lord, last week. It's a good thing they were on hand.' She led him to a control panel, motioning for one of the officers to move from their seat for him. He sat down and allowed the image caster to take his full attention.

An image appeared. It was grainy, but he could see some kind of creature, at least ten handspans tall, rising above their barrier. It had multi-faceted eyes and a sectioned body, and he couldn't see any reason why it was hanging in the air.

It began firing lasers on their people from some kind of opening in its torso. His soldiers returned fire with their own lasers. The creature dodged and weaved so quickly it was rare any of their shots found its mark, and although the creature seemed to jerk when struck, there was no sign it suffered any injury.

No sooner was fire returned than the creature was joined by ten others, all firing on his people. He tried to follow their movements, but they were so fast it made him dizzy. 'They're quick.' He could see how rarely his soldiers managed to hit anything.

However, when reinforcements arrived with additional firearms, the creatures retreated, even though they had suffered no apparent injuries. He seized on it anyway. 'They might have retreated because the heavier laser guns are too much for them.'

The commander conceded that with an inclination of her head. 'It deserves further exploration. My Lord, may I have your permission to submit this vision to our technical experts for their examination?'

'You may, Commander. I'll take a copy back myself. The sooner they start dissecting it, the better.'

He hadn't noticed that Loora had left until she returned, out of breath. 'My Lord, they have something else. Please follow me.'

She led him outside to where a flat-bottomed roller had been driven into the complex, its cargo tray covered. A foot soldier jumped out and started at the sight of him—not an unusual reaction—then bowed. 'My Lord,' he said. 'We wanted to get this back here immediately.'

He pulled back the covering to reveal an appendage made of flesh, but the flesh of no creature he'd seen before. It looked like an arm or a leg, although it was difficult to draw a comparison with any of their own limbs. The closest he could think of was a parcack's limb, which had three joints, but this one ended in a three-pronged stump, rather than a paw, and had an intermittent covering of coarse hairs.

Brandonin covered it again. 'Where did you find this?'

'In the forested section, quite deep. We were on a recon mission when we heard what was happening here. We were heading back to help when we came across this.'

Commander Lissia drew the covering back slightly. 'My Lord, you will want to return this to Intersiss as well?'

'Yes, Commander. I would also like a platoon to accompany us, one heavily armed.'

Loora shook her head. 'My Lord, that will draw too much attention to the convoy. We'll be begging for an attack.'

'I know that, but these creatures are still behaving covertly. They're feinting on inactive battlefields. I don't think they're ready to launch a major attack yet, and they seem to have some reluctance to engage with our heavy weapons. We need to take advantage of that, and we need to get this limb back to Intersiss for examination as soon as possible. I won't risk anything preventing that.' He turned to the commander. 'Please arrange it immediately.'

She bowed. 'At once, my Lord.'

***

The journey back to Intersiss was uneventful. Brandonin didn't know whether he should be worried about that and said as much to Ivanna as she examined the limb.

'Why would you think that a problem, my Lord?' It was a wonder she could even concentrate on what he was saying as she shone different lights on the limb and examined it at close range with her specs.

'They must have realised they were missing it. If they didn't, is it a sign that dropping a limb doesn't matter to one of them?'

'It's significant for us if we find useful data.' Pulling out a pair of tweezers, she plucked a tissue sample from the flesh.

He watched as she lowered the sample onto her microspecs. 'Yes, but then I thought perhaps they left it because they realise there's no useful data to be found.'

'Hm, if they think that then I doubt they're as dangerous as we fear.'

He leant forward. 'You've found something?'

She turned towards him, squinting as she removed the specs, putting them on the bench before her. 'No, my Lord. It will take some time to work out what we have, and even longer to work out if we can do anything to combat it. But we will.'

Her words brought another thought to mind. 'Maybe they know that too.'

'What, my Lord?'

'That it's too late.'

'Too late?'

He looked around Ivanna's lab. It had all their cutting-edge equipment—microspecs with computer components that transferred data to their computers. Infrared lights to aid in examinations. Every piece of chemical, biological and technical finery their greatest minds had brought forth was in this room, and if it wasn't here, it was in this building somewhere. She was right. If there was anything to find, they'd find it here. 'Maybe they know that whatever we find, it won't be soon enough to stop them.'

He could see Ivanna digesting that and some of her assistants looked disturbed. She snapped her fingers. 'Then we must work fast.' One of her aides came to her side and she barked out orders. Round-the-clock shifts, constant work, different teams assigned to different areas.

She turned back to him. 'You can report to your father, my Lord, that we will not cease working until we have something for you.'

But would the enemy have thought of that too? 'Thank you, Ivanna. That's a great comfort.'

CHAPTER FIVE

'Must we be so convinced that it's a Verindal attack?'

The week after the attack at Leeftak had been a flurry of meetings and debriefs, not to mention gossip and increasingly bizarre stories about what had happened there, all pinning the Verindal as the culprits. Vashta had detailed the event several times, pleased that her opinion seemed to be taken seriously.

At least, she thought it had been, until this council meeting.

Father had convened it in the conference room, asking her and Erleph to attend and give their firsthand account to the councillors. She knew it was a privilege to be in the ancient room with its high-domed ceiling, old brocade drapings and lukis-lined engravings. It had been the seat of discussion for the wisest sages her race had produced for as long as anyone could remember.

But her awe at gaining entrance to such a breathtaking location faded because no one would listen to her.

Nelen, an old wizened figure who'd been on the council longer than Father had been alive, nodded as she spoke. 'Of course, we understand how stressful and confusing this event must have been for you, Your Highness. Such events tend to addle the brain.'

Vashta could feel the temperature in the room rising. 'I am not addled in the slightest. I'm just wondering at the wisdom of assuming these creatures came from the Verindal.' She turned her glare on her oldest sister.

Mestitha had been attending council meetings since she'd turned sixteen, sitting on her father's right-hand side. When Vashta had entered the room, she'd looked as if she'd just been told her sister was usurping her.

And she loved to blame the Verindal for everything. 'Of course it was them, little sister.' The words were spoken with clanging judgement, as if such a suggestion could only be decreed by one so young. 'Or do you have some intel that would indicate otherwise?'

Vashta's mind filled with visions of beating her eldest sister in combat over and over again. Mestitha claimed she'd been going easy on her because she was young, but she never lost a battle willingly. Vashta could sense her sister's fear at her presence breaking through that smug smile she wore.

Vashta would wipe it off, just as she had every other time. 'From one who *witnessed* the event, rather than just hearing it second-hand, I can tell you that this creature looked nothing like anything the Verindal have brought against us before.'

Mestitha clattered her nails against the table in a steady tempo. 'So, they have something new. It's not unusual for them, is it?'

'But something *so* new?'

Mestitha raised her gaze to the ceiling. 'What does it matter if it's new or *so* new?'

Father must have reached the limit of his patience. 'Enough, daughters! If you can't speak civilly to each other, you will be silent. We are here to work out what occurred and what we can do to prevent it from happening again.' He turned to Erleph. 'What is your assessment of the events at Leeftak?'

'I agree with Vashta.' At his words, she tried to hide her sense of victory … a little. 'The Verindal have always hit us with new tech— machines or equipment. This creature was organic, made up of flesh that looked nothing like our own or anything we've seen on this planet. Why would the Verindal change to assaulting us with a living being? Where did they find it? Did they create it? Why not just keep creating tech?'

'What are you suggesting?' Merlina, one of Father's contemporaries, shifted her heavy form. 'Where could this thing have come from if not from our forests or from the Verindal?'

No one seemed in a hurry to respond to her question so Vashta

50

decided it was time to speak again. 'Could it have come from another world?'

'Ugh!' She wasn't surprised to hear her sister express her disagreement first.

Father also shook his head. 'We have no evidence of life on any planet other than our own. Why would this thing be from out in space? Why attack now?'

'Why not now? If they're out there, they will come at some point. So why is now the wrong time? Why, if they exist, must they have come before this?'

There were whispers and murmured conversation and she glanced at Erleph. He didn't seem to agree with her, as far as she could tell.

Mestitha whispered in Father's ear, flailing her arms around as if she'd taken up wave dancing. He nodded at her words. 'I think it's a bit premature to blame a creature from space for this. However, I will also say that Vashta has a point. This attack is significantly different from anything the Verindal have been known for.' There was more whispering from Mestitha before Father continued. 'But, considering the history of our planet, we must acknowledge that they're the most likely culprits.'

Vashta couldn't deny the logic in that, even though she wanted to.

'With this in mind, we need to consider our next move.' Father looked around the council table.

Mestitha leant forward. 'Professor Blassin has been working on something for some time—'

Father cut her off with a sweep of his hand. 'I'm not interested in Blassin's proposals, Mestitha.' Although he kept his voice low, Vashta could see his eyes glittering with rage. Who was Blassin? What was he proposing that angered Father so much? 'Does anyone else have any ideas?'

'Capturing one of these things might help,' Merlina ventured.

'I think that will be a challenge,' Erleph said.

'Still, it would be useful,' said Father. 'Having a body to assess would be a great help in working out where these things come from and what can be done to combat them.' He turned to Erleph. 'Do you think capturing one is a possibility?'

'The difficulty is knowing where and when to …'

His voice trailed off as a guard entered the council room, bowed to Father, and handed him a message. 'The heir of the Verindal is requesting that I or an authority from our people visit him.'

That set the grondal amongst the ransims. Everyone spoke at once, all voicing their objections, until Father raised his arms in protest.

'I understand everyone's fear and trepidation,' he said, 'but the heir himself visited us without incident.'

'To lull you into a false sense of security,' said Mestitha.

'Possibly. But the man didn't seem unreasonable. Nelen, didn't you say that there was a report of some disturbance on the Verindal line at Leeftak?'

The old man was sitting straight and still, as though frozen in fear at the idea of anyone going near their enemy. 'Yes, Chief Prince. I believe so. There's no direct word on what happened there but there was activity noticed just after the attack on our barracks at Leeftak.' He handed Father a report.

Mestitha nodded as she read it over. 'There would have been activity as they received the creatures back onto their line and decommissioned them.'

'It also says a vehicle was seen in the forest,' Father said.

'That might be where they hide or launch them.'

Father didn't seem convinced. 'Only one vehicle was seen there. I would say they'd need more than one to manage so many creatures.'

Vashta could see the tell-tale twitches that showed Mestitha was struggling to show their father the respect he deserved. 'There may have been more out of sight.'

'Perhaps. But if they have these creatures, why not just launch them on us? Why ask to see an authority at all?'

'Because they're not ready yet.'

'Why send a half-finished prototype? And even if that's the case, they can't be far away from being ready and, in the meantime, we know nothing about these creatures or how to combat them. What can we do to stop them? Why ask us to attend them in this way?'

Father sighed as objections to being at the Verindals' beck and call died down. Vashta could tell he was frustrated and didn't blame him; her ears were still ringing from the echoes of discontent that had rebounded across the room.

But as ever, he remained reasonable. 'I will contact the heir and see if they can guarantee our security.'

'Your Great Highness, you cannot go yourself!' said Merlina. 'And none of your family—'

Father cocked his head. 'Can I ask any member of my family to do something I am too afraid to do myself?'

Mestitha rose to her feet. 'I am not afraid to go, Father.'

Vashta knew that her sister wouldn't have offered if she hadn't been sure of the response. The rumbles in the council room confirmed it. 'Your heir cannot go,' said Nelen. 'She can't be placed at such risk.'

The look Father gave Mestitha meant that he agreed with the old councillor. As expected, they wouldn't let either of them go. But when his gaze passed over her, Vashta's heart soared with hope. 'I do need to send at least one member of my family, though. Their heir came himself and with his sister. That demonstrated a huge level of trust—'

'But his sister came because she would have been the best at detecting lies!'

'The danger has now increased beyond the level it was during their visit!'

'Why wouldn't they both come if they knew they had these creatures to call on?'

Father put both his hands flat on the table. 'As I was saying, I must send at least one member of my family. I do acknowledge, Merlina, what you said about the danger being greater now, and I feel the heir would understand if the eldest of my children did not attend him. I believe Illora should go with her bond-partner. Merlina, you and your bond-partner are also strong energy casters and I think you should lead the party. You have the highest level of experience with diplomacy and should be able to aid in the protection of the group. We will also send a platoon of soldiers containing other energy-casting couples.'

Vashta noticed Mestitha's relief when she heard Father's decree. But in spite of what he was saying, Father's eyes kept turning to her. Did he want her to go? If so, why didn't he say so? She felt her frustration rising. 'We should send some people who are skilled at transforming as well, as that can be performed by an individual.'

'The platoon will also contain our best transformers,' said Father.

She could see Mestitha's amusement as her sister realised what she was trying to do. It was hard not to make it obvious to everyone at the table, especially Nelen, who sometimes needed to hear a statement three times before he understood it, but Erleph had taught her it was best to be direct. 'Why can't I go, Father?'

He opened his mouth but everyone else spoke first.

'We can't send a child like Vashta. What will her mother do if she loses her youngest?'

'We should be able to manage without having to put little Princess Vashta in danger.'

'A smaller party would be easier for the platoon to keep safe. We can't ask too much of them.'

Their assessments of her raked like cuts to her skin. Would they ever stop viewing her as a child? But she knew pouting and protesting wasn't going to make Father decide in her favour, so she waited quietly, looking at him. He returned her gaze and again, she was hopeful until he spoke. 'I believe that what I have suggested is our best option. I shall liaise with them to work out the details. We will draw this meeting to a close.'

Vashta tried to control the anger that threatened to explode. Getting out was the only option. She headed straight for the training rooms. They were deserted at that time of night, so she sat in the corner of one, leaning against the wall. She wanted to transform and slam into the side of the room with all her strength. Maybe she'd leave a Vashta-shaped dent.

She knew she'd been there a while when the automatic lights

switched off. She continued to sit there in the dark, wondering why no one came looking for her. Erleph would have realised where she'd gone. Why didn't he come to help her work through her rage? Why weren't any security looking for her? She might be the youngest, but she was still a princess.

The lights snapped back on and she squinted in the brightness, her jaw dropping in surprise as someone entered the room.

It was Father. His expression was difficult to read, and she only realised what he was doing when he took off his outer cloak. 'I'm told sparring is the best way to work out our frustrations.'

She decided to speak with her actions and threw herself at him, transformed. He'd changed by the time she'd reached him, and he sidestepped her. She turned and stopped, allowing her senses to locate his weaknesses and anticipate his next move.

She knew he was doing the same thing. She also knew she'd received her ability to fight from him.

She didn't charge him again, instead feinting to the left. He was ready for her when she slipped closer and defended against her strike with a counterstrike that she likewise deflected. He stepped away and tried a kick, but she slipped under his leg and struck him in the back of the knee. He buckled and fell, but although she tried to pin him down, he was on his feet before she could.

She knew how often he'd watched her training sessions, but he didn't know she'd studied his fighting style. So when he ducked under her strike and tried to immobilise her right arm, she knew how to slip out of his grasp and twist his arm back, slamming him against the wall.

As he spun around and tried to pin her, she leapt over his head. He tried to grab her, but he was too slow and was still grasping at her as she landed and swept his leg out from under him, pinning him down by the shoulders.

They both came out of their transformation and she could see a number of emotions on his face—bruised ego, surprise, amusement, but also pride in her and what she had accomplished. Her father had won medals for fighting in his youth and, although she'd taken advantage of the fact that he was older, she knew just how formidable his skills were.

She let him stand up and he chuckled. 'Erleph was right about how good you are.'

'He told me you weren't bad either.'

They both left the training room and downed a couple of sugar drinks. Father looked at her. 'You're a good fighter, Vashta, and not just in there. You're good at fighting for what's right and keeping on fighting until the job is done. You also know it's not about your strength. It's about your brain and how you use it. You think. You use everything in your arsenal to win and you don't take things for granted.'

She grimaced. 'Except for my first flight assessment.' Was this the moment to tell him about what Mestitha had done? 'But I still can't go to Intersiss with the others.'

He rubbed his eyes. 'I don't want any of you to go. I trust the heir more than I'd trust many other Verindals. I don't think he'll allow anyone visiting to come to harm. But the fact is, he can't control all his people. His father still rules and, even if he's an old man now, Verindal forces will still listen to him over his son. If someone else whispers in the old man's ear …

'I know Illora and Brexin's abilities. I know Merlina and how diplomatic she can be. She has a great deal of experience and can cast a considerable energy field with Xeran.'

'But I can—'

'Yes, you can. I know you can.' He glanced at the door. 'I have therefore decided that you will go too.'

She leapt in to hug him. 'Thank you, Father. What made you change your mind? You won't regret this!'

He put a finger on her lips. 'I didn't change my mind. I intended from the first that you should go, but I knew the objections I would get in the council chamber and didn't feel like wading through them all, especially since Mestitha would have gone straight to your mother to report it.

'Keep this quiet. You are going as my special envoy. I want to use your eyes and ears and do your best to keep your lips closed. You need to tell me what you see, as you see the same way I do. Please do this for me.'

'But why not tell the others? Even if they object, what you decide is law.' She could already see the fury that would cross Mestitha's features if she knew. Nothing should glorify her youngest sister.

He shook his head. 'This is not the time for petty one-upmanship, Vashta. I will tell your mother because I have to. I know she'll object, but I hope she'll understand my reasons.' He pulled her close to him again and stroked her hair. 'I want you all to hurry back, safe and unharmed, hopefully with something that will help us in this fight. I fear it will be a greater challenge than we have ever faced.'

CHAPTER SIX

Brandonin hefted the weapon in his hand. 'Are you sure this will work?'

Nestor rubbed the bridge of his nose. His shock of white-blonde hair fanned out over his face and he pushed it back. 'We have thrown it together quickly, but the information we obtained from Ivanna's autopsy was a great help.'

Ivanna's team produced a breakdown of the limb's cellular structure within forty maxispans. The results had been distributed throughout the infantry, armoury and technical departments to see what they could come up with. Much to Brandonin's delight, the armoury had tried to match the science department in the speed with which they'd produced their results. They didn't quite make it, but five days had to be a record.

He looked around Nestor's toy room. Every weapon they'd developed had a place on the walls, whether large or small, encompassing the history of the Verindal's weapon development. Some of his favourites were there, including the first-ever laser pistol, which the armourer had developed a decade before. It hung next to their long-barrelled projectile thrower, several other projectile models of varying sizes and shapes, and some explosive launchers from historic battles.

Alongside them were Nestor's most recent inventions—laser shooters and blasters. Then there were the double-barrelled 'pingers', that had got their name because of the sound that echoed when they were fired. There was also a representative of every laser gun Nestor had designed. Brandonin could still remember when his father had first let him train with one. *'Hold it steady, son. There's no kickback, remember? Be prepared for its absence.'*

Nestor walked to the far end of the funnel-shaped room and

pulled a covering off the target that stood there. Scratching his head, he lined it up before his shuffling walk took him back to his heir.

Brandonin grinned at the sight of the alien creature that had been recreated on the target. 'Does this have the same biological makeup as the limb?'

'No. We didn't have time to rebuild actual tissue. This model is far weaker but we're confident that what you're holding in your hands will still cause significant damage.'

Good enough. 'May I?'

With a quick nod, Nestor scurried out of the way. Brandonin lined up the target in his sights and pulled the trigger. The echoing cacophony produced by the gun made him cover his ears. 'Can you do something about the noise?'

'Given time, I'm sure we can.'

He chided himself for being so impatient. They'd managed to develop a useful weapon within a week of the attack and he was whimpering about a loud bang?

He looked at the target. The figure lay in shreds, half a torso still on the stand with strings of flesh hanging down in tatters. 'Effective.' He handed the weapon back to Nestor.

'As I said, the target isn't the same as the real thing. We are working on developing something to ensure that the weapon will be devastating. But that will take at least another few weeks.'

'I'd like you to start producing this one anyway and send it out into the field. The sooner our troops have some way of defending themselves, the better.'

Nestor nodded. 'Yes, my Lord. We have already developed another.' He indicated a second weapon lying on his workbench. 'More will be put into production immediately.'

Brandonin's timepiece chimed. 'I have to go to my meeting.'

'With the Vendel?'

He was glad that Nestor didn't seem disdainful, as many others in the palace were. 'Yes. I'm certain they've also been attacked by these creatures. I want them to know we're not responsible and that we're doing what we can to combat them. It might bring about a change in relations between our two races.'

There was a heavy dose of scepticism in the noise Nestor made. He looked contrite. 'My apologies, my Lord.'

'I know it's unlikely,' he conceded, 'but the last thing we need is for the Vendel to increase hostilities because they think we're responsible for this. Maybe this creature is avoiding an outright attack because it's hoping we'll kill each other first. Then it can take over without resistance.'

The armourer's expression clouded. 'Do you think invasion is its goal?'

'No idea. But I can't think of any other reason why it would do this. And if it's not native to Verindon, well …'

Nestor bowed his head. 'Good wishes, my Lord. I hope that they'll listen.'

'So do I.'

***

Father was waiting at the door of the throne room, which made Brandonin hesitate. He'd been hoping his overlord would leave this to him.

'Son, do we need to tell the Vendel what we know about this creature?'

How many times do I have to answer this question? 'Father, you know how unlikely it is that the Vendel have been able to develop something like this. Everything our intel says declares they don't have the technology. They're in as much danger as we are from these beings.'

'They could still use this to their advantage.'

'I know but they could also persist in their attacks, which will mean we're fighting two enemies instead of one. Don't you think it's better to enlist their help in defeating it?'

The lines in his face drooped. 'Loora isn't happy.'

Is Father overlord or is Loora? He'd wondered that a lot of late. 'I'm sure she isn't but we need to be more progressive.'

These days it was easier to get Father to follow his advice. 'If you think so. But I will excuse myself from meeting them.'

The overlord walked away, his five-pronged guard standing close by. For the first time, Brandonin noticed his father's legs shaking. Was it stress or something else? He could feel the weight of the succession on him like the heaviest of cloaks.

He knew his father was old, unwell and listened to senior councillors and Loora a little too much. At least he allowed his son to have his way most of the time. It was a relief, especially since he knew what would happen if Father presided over this meeting with Loora by his side. They would be lucky if anyone left the room alive.

Brandonin went through the entryway, his own guards around him, and wondered again about the wisdom of holding this meeting in the throne room. He had favoured a meeting chamber—he felt it would be less divisive—but his father had insisted because the throne room had several secret exits should anything go wrong. It had seemed unwise to debate it.

However, he had made a concession. He knew two of the Vendel princesses were in attendance and he had insisted on thrones for each of them. They were smaller than his, granted, but it was a courtesy that had almost caused Loora to have an apoplectic attack. He had banned her from the throne room for the duration of the meeting.

As he entered, he was pleased to see that all three of the women were sitting calmly. The third woman in attendance—a Vendel diplomatic counsellor—had been given a gilded chair rather than a throne, her large form encompassing it.

An aide came up to him. 'My Lord, in attendance are the Princesses Illora and Vashta, and Councillor Merlina. These princesses are the chief prince's youngest.' He looked down his nose at them. 'The two men standing behind their chairs are the bond-partners of Princess Illora and Councillor Merlina. They are energy casters, my Lord.'

Which made them doubly dangerous, especially in an enclosed space. Some energy casters' beams could spread throughout a room, destroying those hemmed in by walls.

He recognised Princess Illora's bond-partner from his visit to Vendel lands and though Councillor Merlina was familiar, her bond-partner was not. He must have come for security purposes only. As for the princess's bond-partner, Brandonin had to admit he looked impressive—face set in a mask of severity atop a gold and lukis-lined uniform.

A large contingent of Vendel guards was with them. He had agreed that the Verindal guards should match the Vendel guards in number, which meant there were more hostile faces casting furtive glances at the opposition than there were members of the aristocracy.

He brushed all thoughts of that aside and took his own seat. The Vendel didn't rise or bow as he did so but followed his movements with heavy-lidded eyes.

'Welcome, princesses of the Vendel, councillor, your consorts,' he bowed his head at each in turn, 'and your security forces. I greet you in the spirit of goodwill and cooperation.'

Councillor Merlina responded. 'We thank you for your greeting but find ourselves at a loss to guess what goodwill or cooperation you speak of, given the recent events that have befallen our armed forces.'

Straight to the point. It was better than dancing around pleasantries, something that would be a waste of time. Her voice had seemed tremulous, though. 'While strikes between two warring nations are not an unusual occurrence, I can assure you that there have been no out-of-the-ordinary attacks from my people.' He wanted to draw their attention to unusual activities but would avoid specifics until he was sure they had suffered in the same way.

The woman and the princess on her left exchanged glances. 'Yet you mention out-of-the-ordinary attacks as though you expect us to have had them.'

Whoops. Now he'd made them suspicious. Best to be as honest as he could without saying too much. 'We suffered a recent attack of that kind at Leeftak and our intel led us to believe you had suffered in the same way. This is one of the reasons I sought out this meeting.'

The youngest princess, who sat to the left of Princess Illora, fixed him with a burning gaze. Her lips opened as if to speak before her older sister turned her head and the girl shut her mouth.

The councillor spoke again. 'So, you would have us believe that you were not responsible for the attack on us at Leeftak?'

'We were not.'

'Why should we believe that when all previous attacks have come from you?'

He held her gaze. 'I think there are already many doubts about its origins, aren't there?' There were hints of it in her voice and expression. True, he had to work hard to hear them, but they were there.

The youngest one smirked and her gaze flashed to his, revealing something he hadn't expected. Could she be his ally?

The councillor leant towards the nearest princess and conferred. The youngest didn't even bother trying to overhear. She interested herself in looking at the colourful engravings decorating the walls.

The two women continued to confer and came to no result so Brandonin decided it was time to speak again. 'Can you tell me why you think this attack came from us?'

Princess Illora spoke for the first time. 'Because it was an attack.'

He could almost hear the words *you grondal-head* tacked onto the end. Dumb question. 'Why do all attacks have to be from us?'

Again, the same scepticism. 'Who else would be attacking?'

'That's the crux of the matter. But I would hazard a guess that you have seen what attacked you and are aware there's no evidence of Verindal involvement.'

Merlina opened her mouth, but Princess Illora gestured for silence. 'I take it you have an idea of what happened to us, Verindal, so I suggest you stop waiting for us to say what we know and tell us what you know. *You* are the one who sought this meeting. If it's information from us you seek, we're reluctant to give it to our enemy unless we have reason to believe we'll benefit from this exchange.'

Brandonin felt deflated. 'Fair enough. A month or so ago, a force of ours at Andramadiss was wiped out by an unknown assailant. At first, we assumed you were behind it. However, an examination of the bodies revealed laser weapons had been used which, I understand, you still haven't successfully developed.' He hurried on, especially since the councillor straightened up and seemed about to launch into a tirade on the glory of the Vendel race. 'Also, some of our troops had been disembowelled.'

The youngest one spoke up. 'Disembowelled?'

'We believe whatever killed them was performing an autopsy on our forces, probably to find out our strengths and weaknesses.'

This resulted in a flurry of hissed whispers from the youngest to the others.

'Last week, our troops at Leeftak were attacked by a creature we have never seen before.' He pressed a control on the arm of his throne and watched the Vendels' amazement as the image caster unfurled behind him. An image they'd captured of the creature was beamed onto it.

There was recognition on their faces, no doubt about that. And if this thing had now revealed itself to both sides ... 'I take it this form is familiar to you?'

The councillor looked stunned. 'We aren't responsible for it.'

He held up his hands. 'I don't believe you are. As I said, this creature attacked us at Leeftak, and I believe it attacked you as well.'

This time the bond-partners joined in the flurry of whispers as all three women left their chairs and conferred. He could read scepticism in their tones but there was uncertainty as well, except perhaps from the youngest. She seemed sure and her hissing was forthright, even while her doubting companions shook their heads at her.

She seemed about to address him herself when the councillor took control. 'We refuse to confirm or deny whether or not we have experienced an attack from these creatures, but we find your experience with them interesting. Are you certain that the attack at Andramadiss and the attack you claim to have experienced at Leeftak were both committed by this thing?'

'Subsequent examination of the wounds on troops from both events presented compelling evidence.'

'Is this evidence you would be in a position to share?'

He'd gone far enough in his sharing and had got nothing in return. While he wanted her trust, he still wasn't prepared to give everything up if she wasn't even going to acknowledge the attack. 'I think it's not unreasonable for me to expect confirmation from you in exchange. Let's call it a trust exchange.' He tried not to laugh at her indignant expression. 'After all, if you haven't been attacked by these creatures, why do you need this knowledge? Perhaps they're only interested in us.'

The youngest seemed ready to bellow at the councillor but smashed her lips together instead.

'Very well,' Councillor Merlina said. 'We will consider this information and will return with an answer in seven days.'

'With all due respect, I believe these creatures are a real danger to both our peoples. I don't think we can wait seven days to start discussing this.'

She seemed annoyed but after another conference with the others, she assented. 'If we may have access to the grounds of your palace, we can discuss things at length there. Would that be an acceptable compromise for the moment?'

His shoulders relaxed. If they stayed, they might at least make a little progress. 'I'm more than happy to agree to that.' He signalled to a small contingent of guards. 'Please escort our guests into the gardens and give them some privacy.'

Once the Vendel party had left the room, Larinda entered. It was a relief that Father had sent her rather than Loora. 'How did it go?'

'As well as it could have.'

Larinda was always rational. 'It's not surprising that they're suspicious.'

'No, it's not.'

He rose from the throne so she could sit. Some of the councillors in the room gaped at his gesture but he didn't care. While he might outrank her, she was still his sister.

She polished the rounded edges of the throne's arms with her hands. 'So now what?'

If his head would stop pounding, he might have the opportunity to work that out. Was a headache a sign of thinking too much? 'It depends on what they decide.'

'The youngest seemed open-minded.'

He looked up at the black border that ran around the ceiling of the room. His guests weren't to know what was behind it. 'Did Father join you in the secret gallery?'

'Yes, Loora was up there too.'

As he'd suspected. 'And what did they think?'

A weary look wandered over her face. He'd seen it there too many times lately. 'Do you really want to know?'

'No.' But he needed to know.

'Father's suspicious but I think it's out of habit. Loora's suspicious because she'll never trust a Vendel. It's too much part of her core to change it. And Father feeds off that.' Larinda looked up at him. 'You're sure they're not responsible?'

'Nothing suggests they are. And what they said is enough to tell me they've been attacked too.'

'It could be a trick.'

He chuckled. 'Was it, my dear lie-detecting sister?'

'No, it wasn't.'

He went to the window, half-hoping he'd be able to see the Vendel women. Larinda followed him, also scanning the garden. They couldn't see much apart from the neat rows of colourful skyflowers, deep green hedges and grass.

She looked at the sky and breathed in its splendour. He relaxed his shoulders and did the same. It was amazing how looking at their beautiful sky could provide relief to ruling minds when they were assaulted with the most severe of problems.

'As much as I think you're right about them, I will confess they still make me nervous.' She screwed up her nose. 'I look at one of them and all I can see are their faces falling.'

'Falling?'

'Yes, you know, when they do that transformation of theirs.' She shuddered. 'It looks like their faces fall off and are replaced by something that's grown underneath. It's hideous.'

He hadn't realised she'd seen it firsthand. 'At least at an official visit they aren't going to appear so hideous.'

She examined his face. 'And who's caught your eye?'

What? 'Why would you think that?' He didn't like that triumphant expression of hers. It reminded him of too many childhood games when she would win by guessing his strategies from the look on his face, no lie-detecting required.

But this was worse, this knowing look. 'The princesses are attractive women, Brandonin, but they *are* Vendel.'

She couldn't be serious! 'Larinda, so I've noticed they're attractive. What does that mean? Nothing.'

He could feel beads of sweat on his brow and sighed with relief when she turned back to the window. That kind of thing would have only strengthened her suspicions, which were ridiculous at best. 'Yes, I guess that's true. It's not like you don't have a consort waiting for you anyway.'

'And one far more suitable than any Vendel.' He had ten different eligible females to choose from and knew he would have to decide soon … once everything had settled down.

One of the guards came to his side and bowed. 'My Lord, the Vendel have gone to the western corner of the garden.'

Far out of sight of the palace. 'Are they still engaged in their discussion?'

'I believe so, my Lord. Loora has requested that we use tech to record it—'

'Under no circumstances is that to occur,' he snapped. 'We can't expect them to trust us if we're going to use underhanded methods to overhear them. Go and put a stop to it at once.'

Larinda's eyes were on him again as he fumed. 'Loora.'

'She'll never change.'

He nodded. 'I'd better go and make sure that my instructions are obeyed. I don't want our guests to be treated with such discourtesy. Will you be all right here without me?'

She gave him a mocking look. 'I'll never survive.'

'Very droll. I won't be long.'

CHAPTER SEVEN

Vashta counted her good fortune. If Lara and her bond-partner, Ostin, had been included in their party, there was no way anyone would listen to her. But Lara wasn't there, and neither was Mestitha, who would have been worse. Meeka would have wrung her hands a lot.

Illora was more reasonable and, even though Merlina was meant to be the leader in this party, it helped that even Vashta outranked her. 'Don't you see, councillor? He's telling the truth about the autopsies these creatures carried out. There's no doubt in my mind that's why they took one of our own.'

She frowned. 'But what if the Verindal organised it all themselves?'

Vashta could tell she didn't believe that. 'Then why invite us here?'

'To gain our trust,' Xeran said. He was average in every respect—average height, average build, average intelligence. He wasn't even on the council. He had no business speaking up. He was there as an energy-caster, nothing more.

But he was Merlina's bond-partner and Vashta could tell by her face that she was listening to him. 'But why go to such elaborate lengths to do it? And for what purpose?'

'To hold us hostage.'

Vashta looked around. 'I don't see any guards waiting to drag us into cells.'

No, all that surrounded them were peaceful gardens, full of dark thick shrubs, with skyflowers, leapblossoms and other blooms lining the path they walked on.

'What are you suggesting, Vashta?' Illora asked.

'He's only asking for us to tell him what happened at Leeftak,' she said. 'We don't have to give every detail, but we can tell him the similarities between the two attacks.'

'What if he wants more than we can say?'

'We don't tell him more. But we need to tell him something.'

She was pleased when Brexin supported her. 'Vashta's right. I'm sure we're more likely to benefit from the intel than they are. We don't know much more than they already know, judging by what they've told us, and I bet they've got plans in place for defeating these creatures. Maybe even specialised tech.'

That caught Xeran's interest. 'Weapons?'

'Yes. Remember who we're dealing with here. They're bound to be creating tech for battle and if we can gain access to something like that …'

Merlina, thankfully, was a reasonable woman. 'That's true. I think we do have more to gain.'

She stood to return to the palace but Brexin put out a hand. 'Let's not be too hasty. They'll get suspicious if we race back in there and tell them everything. We should seem reluctant. Then they'll do more to convince us to talk.'

Vashta felt her shoulders drop. 'Why waste time playing games like that? These creatures are a real threat to our people. Every microspan's precious. We need to start working out how we're going to defeat them, not dance around for the sake of political intrigue.'

'Another maxispan isn't going to make a difference, is it?' said Brexin.

'It might.' Who knew what they were up against?

But Merlina nodded. 'Prince Consort Brexin is right. We don't want to seem too eager. I know there's a refreshment table they've set up for us. Our outer guards will have already tested the food. Let's go and partake first, then we'll talk to their heir.'

'Councillor—' Vashta began, but she was already drawing away, talking with Illora about how they should proceed. Brexin and Xeran also had their heads together, discussing strategy, followed by their guard.

Vashta smirked. Being the youngest had its advantages, especially since their group had been hastily thrown together. Although all of them had been assigned guards, each one had a dual purpose, which was why she found herself alone. Father would be appalled when he heard. Mother would probably faint.

She walked across the grass, unsure where the Verindal guards were posted. It was likely they were being watched but she didn't know how closely. The unfamiliar territory put her at a disadvantage if anything should happen, but she was prepared.

She headed back towards the base of the palace, slipping between the hedges. There probably wasn't a lot she could do—someone would soon catch up with her—but the mention of specialised Verindal weaponry had excited her. To heft that kind of laser in her hands, to test it herself, feel its weight and be responsible for unleashing a power that might destroy their new enemies ...

'Your Highness?'

Vashta stopped short of falling into a bush as she turned to the source of the voice. She didn't know whether to feel ashamed or angry when she saw it was the heir himself, complete with the five guards who followed him everywhere.

Erleph would have told her that fear was a good thing to feel when faced with the enemy. However, she had no fear of the heir. He'd already demonstrated that he was as eager for peace and cooperation as Father was, unless he was the greatest deceiver their kind had ever known. And she could see no sign of deception in those deep, beautiful brown eyes.

What did I just think?

'Err, yes.' She struggled over what to call him. His servants called him 'my Lord', but she was far from one of those. However, he had just called her 'Your Highness' and he had no reason to do that.

Was she going to stand there debating it all day?

'Are you lost? We have refreshments laid out on the terrace for you. The rest of your party is there. Perhaps we can escort you?'

He put out his arm—an unexpected degree of courtesy. She didn't miss the start of surprise from all five of his guards at his gesture. But he didn't seem to care so neither did she. Normally, she would have glared at an arm proffered like that, but in this case, she felt there was more to gain by taking it. She did so, aware that this might be the first time in at least a hundred years that two individuals from competing high families had touched.

She could feel the muscles flexing in his sleeve. He wasn't just some lazy courtier who left the fighting to everyone else, like Mestitha. She wondered what kind of training they gave the royals in Verindal circles.

'I hope your conversation with your party was productive,' he said, as they walked along.

He was fishing for information. Given the conversation she'd just had with Illora and Merlina, she knew what would happen if she was the one to divulge something. 'It was, thank you.'

He glanced at her; trying to read her expression, she thought. 'I hope you realise that we're offering a hand of friendship. These creatures are a threat to both our races. Working together may be the only way forward.'

She tried to remain enigmatic. 'You may be right.' Was that vague enough? 'However, it will take a lot for our two races to believe that we're not each other's biggest problem.'

She could see the outer wall of the palace a few paces away and slowed. She was enjoying assessing the heir's reactions. It was enlightening to converse one-on-one with him like this.

A familiar and terrifying whooshing sound was the only warning she got. She tackled the heir to the ground before he realised how much danger he was in. His five guards moved to restrain her, failing to see what was behind them.

'Look out!' Her warning came too late. Two had time to draw their weapons and one had time to fire. He got off a single shot at the three hovering creatures before he too, lay dead beside them.

Vashta had transformed the instant she'd launched herself at the heir and had drawn her own weapon, although her senses told her it was futile. However, her shots pinpointed the creatures' eyes, which seemed to confuse them, giving her time to lead the heir over to a copse of trees. The shrubbery there was thick enough to offer some temporary shielding and she again fired shots, diving out of the way as her transformed senses warned her where they would shoot.

But she had nothing to fight with. Her gun was as good as useless. The only reason she could dodge their shots was because she was in her transformed state and she couldn't stay that way for longer than ten minspans. And once she came out, she would be almost as helpless as the heir.

She reloaded her weapon, wishing for more than just projectiles. Without it, they would die.

CHAPTER EIGHT

Brandonin knew there was going to be a lump on the back of his head from the crack he'd received when they'd landed in the bushes. He wondered if he'd live long enough to feel its full effects.

It had taken him too many precious microspans to realise what was happening. He'd thought the worst at first, when the princess's face had 'fallen' and she'd launched herself at him. It was the same mistake that had cost his security team their lives.

She hadn't been attacking him. She'd been saving him.

She crouched above him and he kept his head down so that the shots whizzing in their direction didn't strike him. She avoided every single one, sometimes moving so fast she was a blur. In spite of that, he could see her face with its sunken eye sockets and pinprick eyes, jutting jaw and textured skin. It was the closest he'd been to a transformed Vendel.

But enough of that. They needed to get out of there. More than that—they needed the new weapons. They might be prototypes, but he knew they would be better than anything else they had.

Except for one thing. The girl—Vashta; was that her name?— twitched her head towards a sound just before he heard it. He exhaled as her sister entered the copse with her bond-partner.

Brandonin was sure they'd been expecting trouble but by the looks on their faces, this wasn't what they'd expected to find. There was a fraction of hesitation before they linked hands and the woman raised her arm and shot a vast energy field towards the three attackers.

The creatures cried out in pain and slid back across the ground, one slamming into a tree trunk, stunned. But they leapt forward again, bouncing over the ground in long jumps, avoiding another blast of energy, sending their own lasers at their attackers, throwing both of them back in a hail of fire.

The princess and her lover went flying, the man's head slamming into the wall of the palace with a vicious crack. His limp form slid to the ground. The girl slumped beside him, but she twitched. There was still life in her.

Some of Brandonin's own forces appeared and began firing at the invaders, but they were using standard lasers. The three creatures were joined by two more of their kind and his troops were soon mown down.

Vashta came out of her transformed state, unclipped a can from her belt, downed its contents and her face fell once more. She dived on two discarded lasers and began firing. Every shot landed but had no effect. Only her speed kept her alive.

They needed the prototype weapons. Vashta's sister sat up in a daze, her hand flying to her head. Keeping his head down, Brandonin raced to her side. 'You need to come with me.'

'Where's my sugar?' She tapped her belt, looking for the cans that should have been hanging there. They were strewn on the ground from the fall, their contents seeping into the soil.

'I have sugar. I also have weapons that can kill these creatures,' he said. 'You have to come with me now.'

'But Vashta … and Brexin!' For the first time, she noticed her bond-partner.

More Verindal troops came racing around the corner and Brandonin was sure the distraction saved them as the creatures began defending against oncoming fire. Vashta was a good few spans away from him, still transformed, and the troops around them wouldn't last long. Unless they had a weapon that would destroy their attackers, the princess would die.

'Come with me!' He dragged her sister to her feet and raced back towards the palace. He ran into more troops on the way and they insisted he move to safety. He ignored them, waving them in the direction of the battle. 'Get over there and engage the enemy. The creatures are attacking our guests and our own forces!'

He pulled the Vendel princess along with him as she sniffed the air. 'I need sugar. I have to help Vashta. Get me sugar!'

'I will.' He knew the armoury contained cans they'd taken from fallen Vendel soldiers.

He burst in the door. No one was there but he didn't need help. The two prototypes were the only weapons that hadn't been commandeered for the battle. Hardly surprising, given that one still had a panel hanging by a thread. He snapped it in place and snatched up the two of them.

The Vendel grabbed several cans of sugar and downed one while attaching the others to her belt. He threw her one of the weapons. 'These will kill the creatures.'

'Are you sure?'

No. 'Yes.' They'd better.

They bolted back towards the clearing, Brandonin leading the way. He cradled the weapon in his arms, feeling satisfaction rise within him. The Vendel might have their speed and strength, but the Verindal had tech, and this tech was going to save them all.

He burst through the bushes, sighing with relief to see that Vashta was alive, although just about everyone else on the field of battle was a corpse. Even as he watched, the young princess raced from her vantage point to another, firing a few shots, but she was tiring quickly.

There was no time to lose. He dived behind a retaining wall, charged his weapon, leapt up to get a prime aim, and blasted two of the creatures. He could feel the smirk on his face as both of them shrieked and fell to the ground, dead.

He took aim at two more and fired. However, they were too quick for him, both moving before the strikes could connect. He got off a few more, but his quarry bolted to the side to avoid them before they could find their mark. Then he had to dive for cover as return fire came from the creatures' torsos.

A can of sugar flew over his head and the weapon was snatched out of his hand. In the time it took to turn, Vashta transformed back to normal, drank the sugar, transformed back again, and caught the weapon her sister threw to her.

Both Vendel women stood back to back, their shots flying over the field, and every single one of them found their mark. The two of them moved faster than he could see, every speck of concentration engaged on the enemy. Once alien bodies started raining to the ground, he realised how many of the creatures had appeared. The Vendels' aim was unerring and both of them knew where to move to avoid the blasts that came their way. Their movements were so fluid, so precise, that Brandonin strained to watch every microspan.

But more of the enemy were coming. He could hear them. A strange whooshing sound accompanied them. Perhaps some kind of tech? Was that what allowed them to hover without wings? And he knew the girls would need to come out of their transformed state soon. They would be vulnerable then. He would be of no use—he wasn't fast enough.

Movement closer to the palace caught his eye. It was the councillor and her bond-partner, along with some of the Vendel guards. Aghast at the sight of the weakening princesses, the two of them clasped hands and sent a wave of energy at the creatures arriving to join the fight. Although the wave only threw them back, the surviving creatures retreated, leaping away and disappearing over the edge of the palace garden, leaving the area littered with bodies of aliens, Verindal and Vendel.

Vashta and her sister came out of their transformation, heaving with the effort, and reached for sugar cans. As soon as they had done that, the older girl raced to her stricken lover, where the councillor and her bond-partner were cradling his body.

The shriek of anguish that rose when she realised he was dead tore through the gardens. Brandonin knew that the energy they produced was powered through a bond of love. It was hard not to block his ears to shut out the agony gasping from the Vendel's throat. There was nothing he could do except move the body somewhere private, but he needed to go and make sure the entire city hadn't been hit.

As a new five-pronged guard came racing in and took up positions around him, he went to one of the Vendel guards and grasped his shoulder. 'Let your princesses know I will be happy to put their fallen in a place of honour in the palace whenever they're ready, but I must go and check on the state of affairs.'

The man seemed shocked at his words, but Brandonin couldn't stay to make sure the message was passed along. He hurried back to the palace, quizzing his new guard along the way. 'How bad was the attack?'

'There was a pocket of fighting near where the Vendel were taking refreshment and at other locations around the palace but nothing further afield as far as I've heard, my Lord.'

'So the overlord is all right? What about my sister?'

'Both were safe in the security area when we came looking for you, my Lord.'

The security area was below the ground floor of the palace. Brandonin was relieved to see a contingent of guards standing vigilant at the top of its stairway. They bowed to him as he descended the heavy stone stairs and walked into the main room. It was windowless, but that absence was compensated by the state-of-the-art security, including image casters that received a feed from the vision takers they'd installed around the palace.

Larinda raced up and held him, colour returning to her face. 'I am so glad you're all right. We could see what was happening ... well, some of it.' She gestured to the image casters.

Loora joined him, Commander Lissia by her side. 'Commander, I didn't realise you were here.'

'I had been reporting to your father about the situation at Leeftak and took charge. I sent troops to help under my best platoon commander. My apologies that they were so ineffectual.'

Ineffectual because they'd been mown down. The haunted look in her eyes bore testament to that.

A temporary throne had been set up for Overlord Dransen in the middle of the room. His face was as pale as Brandonin had ever seen, but Father reached out a hand to him. 'Son, I'm relieved that you're safe.'

He clasped his father's hand. 'Only thanks to the skill of the Vendel women.' He turned to Lissia. 'What's the state of affairs here?'

'The attack targeted four areas of the palace, one where you were walking, the other where the Vendel were taking refreshment, the front entryway and the terrace entrance.'

They'd been trying to get into the palace. 'There were no other attacks? None in the city? None anywhere else?'

'Not unless it was further afield, my Lord, no.'

'And the area is clear now?'

'Our assailants have fled.'

Brandonin wouldn't have put it that way. There was no sense of retreat in what the creatures had done. It was the essence of tactical withdrawal.

Nestor raced over. 'My Lord, the weapon appears to have been very effective.'

'I don't know if I'd use the word "very", Nestor, but there's no doubt it was more effective than anything else.'

Nestor rubbed his hands together. 'A few adjustments should be all that's needed to make it invincible.'

'Yes, if you're as fast as a transformed Vendel.'

Nestor's face dropped. 'It's true, my Lord, that the creatures looked quite fast.'

They moved over to an image caster that was replaying the fight the female Vendel had had with the enemy. The recording must have been slowed down, as Brandonin could see what was happening. 'Again, Nestor, "quite fast" is inaccurate. More like blindingly or incomprehensibly.' He sighed. 'Unless you can make the wielder of the gun move at the same speed, I don't know how useful it will be.'

'But the laser itself is effective, my Lord. If it can be made wider, it won't matter if the aim is not precise. It will still kill the combatants.'

Brandonin was far from convinced. 'We'll see.'

The image caster returned to real-time and he could see the Vendel group standing around their fallen comrade. He turned to Lissia. 'Please go and set up a specific triage area for the fallen Vendel royal and then ensure his body is escorted there with full military honours.'

If she was surprised, she hid it well. 'Yes, my Lord.'

He looked around to see if there were objections to his honouring the fallen Vendel. Given how he would have been dead if not for what they'd done, he wasn't about to accept so much as a doubtful look from anyone, even his father.

CHAPTER NINE

Vashta held Illora by the shoulders as she sobbed over Brexin's form. It was heartbreaking that she would now have to go on without him. Merlina wandered around the scene of their battle again and again, watching as the Verindal moved the bodies of the aliens and their own troops.

No one had come to speak to them since the heir had left. Vashta could feel her rage growing at that. If not for them, he would be lying with the dead.

An official-looking Verindal entered the copse with a troop of soldiers and a gurney. She went to Merlina and bowed. 'My Lady, we have set up a temporary triage for the dead and, with your permission, we would like to move your fallen comrade and prepare him for transfer back to whichever location you desire.'

Merlina turned to Xeran and then to Illora, who said nothing. Vashta shook her sister's shoulder. 'Illora, they're going to move Brexin now.' Illora moaned but rose to her feet, stepping away from him and leaning against her sister. Vashta nodded to the troops. 'You may take him.'

'I will follow,' said Illora.

'Of course. We all should.' She was encouraged by how respectful the Verindal were towards Brexin as they lifted his body from the ground and laid it on the gurney. The troops had armaments but seemed to be holding them in some kind of official position, like a guard of honour. She felt ashamed of thinking that they wouldn't respect Brexin, although she was sure this was at the command of the heir.

However, as Illora moved off, Xeran grabbed Merlina by the arm to hold her back, hissing under his breath. Vashta felt her blood boil.

Was he going to accuse the Verindal of masterminding all this?

He signalled her closer with his eyes. 'Your Highness, we can't let them take Brexin away,' he said. 'They'll want to examine him, find out what they can to use against us.'

She couldn't believe what she was hearing. 'Xeran, we've been fighting the Verindal since our history was oral. Do you think there's something they don't know about us?'

He scowled. 'It's a risk. And after what we've just seen …'

'What? You mean that attack that was aimed at the heir of the Verindal, not me? If it weren't for me, they would be taking his body away too.'

'But we still can't be sure they're not behind all this.'

'If you truly believe that after what you've just witnessed, I'm sure these creatures are jumping up and down with glee. They'll love the fact that you're still looking away from them for the fight. If the rest of our people do the same, I'm sure their victory will be swift.'

Merlina didn't seem to comprehend their conversation. 'We must follow the princess. Make sure she's safe.'

Vashta frowned at that, but she knew the councillor was just echoing her bond-partner's prejudice. She knew if they could get back home and explain it to Father, she would be able to out-talk her. Xeran would be no trouble; he wouldn't be believed over her.

At least she could agree with Xeran as they moved off. 'We need to get home as soon as possible,' he said. 'Return Princess Illora's consort for a proper passing service.'

Vashta followed, her mind already running through everything that had happened. She had to convince Father she was right with a minimum of fuss.

But they barely had time to join Illora at the triage when the heir burst into the room. Merlina and Xeran linked hands as though he was a danger, but the look on his face was stricken. 'My apologies for the sudden interruption but we've just received word that Matarsiss is under attack.'

Home? Vashta turned to race for the door before realising that running headlong into an attack wasn't going to stop it.

She turned back to see Merlina babbling. 'What do you mean they've attacked Matarsiss? Do you mean the city or the palace? Do you mean both? Who's attacked it? These creatures? Or is it you? Is it both? Are you responsible for all this?'

The questions were asked so rapidly that all the heir could do was open his mouth and shut it again. The woman beside him, though, stepped forward, her lip curled. 'Or is this all something you have done to force your continued presence here, Vendel, in order to spy on us?'

'Loora!' the heir snapped. But the damage had been done. Merlina and Xeran both began trading insults with the Verindal woman. Illora sobbed and raised her hands to cover her ears.

The heir stepped in front of his councillor and Vashta stepped between him and her family. 'Enough! What good is screaming at each other? Vendel and Verindal alike have died here today. How can you still think this is just some subterfuge?'

'It could be,' spat the Verindal.

The heir's face turned purple. 'Loora, you will leave my presence instantly. I don't want you, your counsel or your prejudices.'

The woman stepped back, her face incredulous. 'May I remind you that you are not—'

'*Get out of my sight!*' screamed the heir. He turned to his guards. 'Escort Lady Loora to her quarters and keep her there until our guests have left.'

The guards dragged the woman from the room as she spluttered out her rage. 'You royal upstart! Your father will hear about this, then we'll see what happens to your power. You don't rule yet!'

The commotion had at least stopped Merlina and Xeran's accusations. They stared at the heir and his remaining guards.

He turned to Vashta. 'I am sorry for that. She doesn't speak for me or for our leadership.'

She wasn't sure that was true, but she let it pass.

He gestured to another set of guards who had been standing near the wall since they'd entered. 'This is an elite squad of my personal guard. They will escort you and your dead the quickest and safest way back to Matarsiss. I'm sorry that the journey might not be as fast as we'd like but given the danger and the fact that your fallen comrade must also be transported, I believe it's the best we can do.'

No one else seemed capable of responding so Vashta took on the responsibility herself. 'Thank you for your kindness, sir, especially amidst the difficulties you are also facing. We will ready ourselves to leave immediately.'

He bowed and left.

One of the guards approached and bowed to her. 'My Lady, we have a medic roller waiting outside. We will transport your fallen comrade to the vehicle, along with your fallen guards.' He looked around at them and the surviving Vendel guards. 'If you have everything you need, we'll leave now, as time is of the essence. While we believe we know a secure way back to Matarsiss, it could change at any moment.'

'Certainly.' She looked around at the others and was relieved to see they were gathering up their things without any snide remarks. 'We'll follow you at once.'

The heir's guards picked up Brexin's body with every bit of reverence she would have expected from her own people and led the way out of the Verindal palace.

***

When they passed through the streets of Matarsiss Vashta's heart lifted, for there didn't seem to be any damage at all. No indication of so much as a skirmish.

The medical roller was disguised as an average transport. It pleased her that someone had thought of that and she wondered if it had been the heir. She was certain he hadn't been lying when he'd said the guards who escorted them were elite. Their stealth and professionalism could be seen in their organisation—she, Illora, Merlina and Xeran were transported in the medical roller. Brexin was in a sealed transport tube with the other three Vendel dead. Their other guards followed in a roller behind them, with another troop of Verindal guards.

Although she tried to console herself that things might not be as bad as they'd thought, she knew the palace would have been a major target, just as the Verindal palace had been, and the idea that it had been passed over was ludicrous.

She was right. It was hard to recognise it when it came in sight. The front section was caved in and much of the top storey had disappeared. She heard the shock from Merlina and Xeran. Even Illora turned away from Brexin's casket and gasped.

The roller pulled up at what was left of the embarking bay and the transport door snapped open. Erleph's pale face peered inside, whitening further as he saw the medic transport tubes.

'Who?' he whispered.

'Brexin was killed, as well as three of our guard.' Vashta knew he could cope with the truth. Telling Father would be the hardest thing.

He nodded and gestured over to a couple of low-level troops. 'Take Consort Brexin's body to triage. Put him with the other high-borns. Take the guards' bodies and put them with the rest of the dead.'

Vashta glanced at the rubble around the base of the palace. Which high-borns had been lost?

Xeran looked around them. 'How bad was it here? Was it the creatures? Who have we lost?'

Erleph drew Illora under his arm. 'We must get you inside first.'

Vashta told herself that he was dodging the question because he was worried about an attack. Because it wasn't safe where they were. Because there was too much to tell. But she knew her mentor better than anybody. Mourning was etched into his face. He was a seasoned warrior of many battles. He wouldn't reveal that kind of emotion except in cases of the highest loss.

He led them through the left wing of the palace, which seemed the least damaged. Even then, they stepped on dust and pieces of wall that tripped them as they walked. Erleph urged them to take care but didn't stop, leading them to a large room Vashta had never seen before. It looked like it had been a meeting place for the servants, given the humble metal furnishings and simple, single-colour flooring.

It had been converted into a temporary throne room, the thrones belonging to both her parents standing in the middle, courtiers and councillors standing around. But it was not the hangers-on and their tears that drew Vashta's gaze. It was her mother, standing beside her throne, rather than occupying it, wringing her hands in grief. On her throne was Elloran, Mestitha's bond-partner.

Sitting on her father's throne was Mestitha, her face like stone. She turned her gaze to Vashta and the others as they entered, but her expression didn't change. 'My sisters, thank you for deciding to return.'

Vashta didn't realise she was screaming until she was standing in front of her sister. 'Get off Father's throne! Where is he?' She turned to her mother, who leant on the top of the throne in front of her and sobbed.

Illora paled to bone-white and looked in every corner of the room, searching for Father. She began wailing as the truth of it hit home. Vashta tried to draw breath to calm herself. She needed to think. She turned to Erleph. 'What happened?'

'The creatures attacked the palace,' he said. 'No weapons we had stood against them. Our energy-casters did their best, but the creatures kept out of range of their beams.

'Then they produced … we don't know what it was or where it came from. It seemed to come from the sky itself. After it had struck, the upper storey was no more. When the chief prince saw what they had done, he insisted on helping evacuate the wounded. We begged him to go to a safe location, but he wouldn't listen. As he searched, they blasted again. Your father fell, amongst others.'

'Where is he now?'

Mestitha's voice was cold. 'With the dead. Where else would he be?'

Vashta looked at her sister. She was a strong energy-caster when matched with Elloran, yet she sat there unscathed. Mestitha's steel gaze said it all. 'The chief prince was foolish to risk himself in that way. He was a fine leader and should have put his leadership first and foremost.'

The sobs from her mother increased, joined by Illora's loudest wail.

Never before had her sister been so openly disrespectful of their father.

'Of course,' Vashta spat. 'If he was wise like you, he would have hidden trembling in an inner chamber and let everyone else fall dead at his feet before he dared risk his own life.'

For the first time, Mestitha turned to her, rose from the throne, and backhanded her across the face. 'Silence, foolish child. *Little* one.'

She felt the blood collect inside her mouth. 'Is that the best you can do, sister? You strike like an infant.'

Mestitha drew her hand back again but Vashta caught it on the fly. 'Now, now.' She kept her voice low, in case she shocked the already stunned courtiers beyond what they could bear. 'There has never been a time you've beaten me in combat. I'd be more than happy to display that here.'

Mestitha snatched her hand away and sat back on her throne before turning to Merlina. 'What news of the Verindal menace?'

It took the councillor a moment to reply. 'While we were in Intersiss, their palace was also attacked by these creatures.'

'The palace was attacked?' demanded Mestitha. 'Or were you attacked?'

Vashta's heart sank. She knew how it would look but was sure it wasn't true. 'The heir himself was attacked and would have been killed if I hadn't defended him.'

At first, she was surprised she was allowed to complete her sentence, but it seemed Mestitha's mind had headed in a different direction. 'So you were with him? Isn't it possible the attack was on you?'

She set her teeth. 'No, I'm quite capable of telling where an attack was directed.'

'But I notice Brexin's absence.' Mestitha turned to Illora, who started sobbing.

'Brexin and Illora came to defend us and the creatures killed him.'

Mother's eyes widened as she turned to her second youngest. 'My darling, tell me it isn't so?'

Illora's face crumpled and she sank into her mother's arms. Vashta could hear gasps of shock from the courtiers.

Mestitha shook her head. 'Another one of our high-borns

destroyed by the Verindal.'

'The Verindal weren't responsible!' insisted Vashta. 'They were under attack just as we were.'

Her eldest sister's smirk was crueller than usual. 'Then tell me, dear sister, when is the funeral for the Overlord of the Verindal?'

So it was going to be that way. 'I believe he still lives.'

'And the heir? I take it you managed to save him?' Mestitha seemed amused at the thought.

Vashta felt her temper rise and struggled to keep her replies calm. 'He was alive when we left. I made sure of that.' Her sister looked surprised at her choice of words, but she was beyond caring what Mestitha thought.

'And his little sister?' she continued. 'I trust she is well?'

'I must confess I have no idea, although I admit I didn't see her body amongst the many Verindal dead.'

'Yes, but I'm sure all their dead were commoners. Foot soldiers.'

'People they can spare, you mean?'

'Enough of this!' Mother said. 'You two should not be fighting. We are family.' She came up and put her arm around Vashta. 'We are all on the same side. Remember your father.' Her voice trembled.

Mestitha looked her up and down. 'With all due respect, Mother,' her tone said she didn't have much, 'I am the chief princess now and I will conduct this investigation in whatever way I see fit.' She turned back to the courtiers. 'These creatures are the creation of the Verindal. We must strengthen every action against them.'

'You can't be serious!' Vashta was pleased to see that it wasn't just she who objected. Merlina and Xeran looked doubtfully at each other. Illora shook her head and a number of the courtiers began their usual soft mutters, ones laced with objection, but too quiet to be distinct.

Erleph stepped forward to support her. 'Your Great Highness, surely any hasty action is to be avoided. If these creatures are the product of the Verindal, we should use the intel we've obtained on them to develop tactics that will help us defeat them first.

'Every weapon we have, even our energy producers, are not strong enough to kill these creatures outright. And how can we defend against blasts from the sky? Taking hasty action at this point may spell our doom, rather than ensure our survival.'

Mestitha was unconvinced. 'While I appreciate your advice and all you did for my father, we all know the Verindal are responsible.'

'We do not!' said Vashta

Mestitha didn't even glance in her direction but rose from her throne and began stalking around the room. 'We have put up with this menace for too long. We must destroy them once and for all.'

Councillor Merlina stepped forward. 'Your Great Highness, would you destroy every man, woman and child?'

'We have no choice.'

Vashta felt a laugh bubble up within her. 'Do you think you're capable of destroying even half of them, especially if they control these creatures that are so invincible? You're just going to wave your hand and watch them fall?'

The most frightening thing about the look Mestitha gave her was its certainty. 'Believe me, sister, I have the means and, unlike my father, the strength to use it.' In spite of the protests and questions that rose from around her, Mestitha gathered up her robes and left the room. Silence descended after she'd departed, one that was broken by a whisper of conversation, which gradually grew into a tumult.

Vashta turned to Erleph. 'How could she do something like that?'

He cast a furtive glance around the room, took her by the arm and led her out into the corridor. He set off at a steady pace, heading for … she wasn't sure where. 'Now,' he said as they walked, 'tell me everything you saw at Intersiss.'

She made sure she explained all he needed to assess the situation. Erleph understood the science of battle better than anyone she knew. If the Verindal were responsible he would identify it. And she knew she couldn't dismiss the possibility that her sister was right.

But Erleph nodded. 'I don't see how the Verindal could have done this. While they're not beyond killing their own to deceive us, to risk their heir like that seems unlikely. They couldn't be sure you would have been willing or even able to save him, but he would be dead if not for your actions.'

'What if it was his idea and he commanded them to?' Every memory of the heir made it sound like a lie.

'He couldn't be sure of his survival unless you were good enough to save him. Would he risk himself with an attack that was deadly enough to kill those around him? It would make more sense if you'd been the target and he'd saved you, trying to earn your trust. Considering how much his people depend on him, I can't see any reason for them to go to such lengths just to convince a minor member of the royal family they weren't responsible.'

She flinched at that but knew he was right. Why waste lives on a charade just for her? 'Unless he felt I was the most impressionable.' Could that be true?

Erleph put his hands behind his back and frowned. 'Even if they thought that they'd have known your word wouldn't hold much weight in this court. Regardless of how much your father valued your opinion, he still wouldn't have taken it over everyone else's.'

Her heart clenched at the mention of Father. 'When is he to be laid to rest?'

He must have heard the distress in her voice because he slowed and put a hand on her arm. 'We were to do it as soon as you returned, but I imagine it will be a day or so if we have to organise a service for Brexin as well.'

'But now my sister rules.'

He sighed. 'Yes, that's a problem. I'd already concluded that these creatures were not a Verindal creation. I see no reason to change that opinion in light of this new information, but Mestitha's prejudices will not be swayed.'

'But what could she have that would destroy every Verindal?' Who in the Vendel court would have the technology to do something like that? But … what had Father said in that council meeting before they'd left for Intersiss? Hadn't Mestitha said something to him? 'Blassin?'

Erleph hushed her. 'Quiet.'

'Who is he?' she whispered.

'He's a man on the fringes of our society because he has no scruples and his hatred for the Verindal is so fierce many think he's insane. Unfortunately, he is also the most brilliant scientist we have ever produced and his work is unparalleled.'

'What has he got?'

'I have only heard rumours, but if they're to be believed, he has developed something that can seek out and destroy specific DNA signatures.'

She stopped walking, her blood freezing her brain. 'Like Verindal DNA?' What was DNA again? Molecular coding? 'Do you mean he could target an entire species? What if we're wiped out too? We're not that different.'

He kept her moving, looking around the now-deserted corridor. 'I'm not big on the science, but there's enough information in our molecules to target Verindals specifically. I don't know how advanced it is, if it will work, or if we could find a way to spread it across the planet, but if it's true, then I believe your sister could destroy all Verindals and there's no doubt that she would use it.'

As sick as it was to think that her own flesh and blood could do that, Vashta couldn't disagree with him. She knew how entrenched her sister's hatred for the Verindal was. 'So how do we stop him?'

For once, her mentor looked uncertain. 'I have no idea. But he needs to be stopped.'

'Then work on it.' She lowered her voice as she noticed some guards approaching. She expected them to walk past with a bow but to her surprise, the three of them stopped in front of her.

She felt unsettled. They were an official guarding squad of the kind that often hovered around her father and sister. She, as the youngest of sisters, usually only had a guard when going amongst the people or away from the palace.

The leader turned to Erleph. 'Sir, Chief Princess Mestitha requests your presence in the council room. She would seek your advice on a number of issues.'

Vashta stepped forward. 'If it has to do with what happened at Intersiss, I—' She was staggered when the woman put out a hand to prevent her from going any further. 'How dare you?'

Erleph raised his hand, signalling for calm. 'I would be glad to attend the chief princess as soon as I have escorted Princess Vashta back to her chambers. She is weary after being away for so long.'

'We are to escort the Princess Vashta to her chambers,' the woman said, 'where she is to be placed under house arrest.'

The shock on Erleph's face had to be as strong as the surprise that struck her like a slap. It was so like her sister to send her to her room like a child. But she sniffed. 'I'm glad to hear that my chambers weren't destroyed. I take it Mestitha's are still intact as well? Or did she use it as an excuse to throw Mother out of the reigning suite and move straight in?'

The woman's eyes flickered, but she too stayed calm. 'All the royal chambers are still intact, Your Highness, although some have slight damage.'

Vashta turned her gaze to Erleph. He looked as if he was about to face an opponent in the training rooms. 'May I ask why the princess has been condemned to such a punishment? After all, she's still my pupil and I need to know if we will continue our lessons.'

The guard looked uncertain. 'Hasn't the princess finished her training?'

Erleph's face remained smooth. 'These things always require work, as I'm sure you know.'

The woman's mouth was tense as she replied. 'The princess will be on house arrest until further notice. If you would like to know which, if any, freedoms she will have during that time, I suggest you ask the chief princess.'

Rage refused to let her stay quiet. 'Am I to be allowed to attend my father and brother-in-law's passing service?'

Again there was uncertainty. 'I will discover the answer to that.'

Yes, she'd better. *The idea that I should be kept from that would not look good for dear Mestitha.*

The woman turned again to Erleph. 'Please, sir. Your presence is required.'

Erleph flashed Vashta a guarded look. 'Of course. I will attend her immediately.' He bowed. 'Your Highness, I will see you soon, I'm sure.'

She knew that was a promise.

***

At first, Vashta accepted her banishment with nobility, marching into her room with her head held high, noting that the three guards stationed themselves outside the door. She couldn't resist mocking them. 'My sister always said I was too low to have my own guards, and now she's the one who gives me them. How nice of her to finally be accommodating.'

A quick glance around her chambers revealed that they had survived almost unscathed. Her sitting room was intact, although a fine layer of dust covered the couches and other furnishings. The brocades on the wall would also need to be cleaned of dust, although she was sure it would be a while before anyone could be spared to clean them. She tried to busy herself with some tidying just to give herself something to do, but she soon broke down, unable to bear the grief of Father's loss.

Illora appeared at the doorway and gathered her in her arms. When she was finally able to speak, her sister took her hand. 'I'm so sorry this has happened to you. Mestitha is being unreasonable.'

'Are any of us surprised?' Vashta flopped onto one of her two sumptuous couches. 'What is she doing?'

Illora's expression was hard to read. 'A lot of talking but no action yet that I can see.' She sat next to her; head bowed. 'We've made arrangements for Brexin and Father's passing service.'

Vashta felt a weight press heavily on her. 'I hope Mestitha's going to let me out for the service.'

Her sister looked up. 'She'd better, or the entire family will rebel. She knows full well she has no reason for confining you to your rooms.'

Vashta pushed the tip of her finger into the couch's fabric. 'But will anyone stand up to her?'

'How do they do that? She rules now.'

She gave Illora a questioning look. 'Erleph?'

'Erleph is obeying her …' She glanced back at the door. It was shut and the guards were outside. She lowered her voice anyway. 'For now.' Her voice dropped even lower. 'He's told me what Mestitha is planning. I can't believe it.'

'I can believe her capable of it. That we could develop anything so advanced is what I find hard to fathom.'

She leant forward. 'I've told Erleph I will listen for more. Mestitha isn't always guarded in the way she speaks to me. She considers me …' Her sister's face clouded with guilt.

'One of them now?' Vashta tried not to make her voice accusatory. It didn't work.

Illora looked heartbroken. 'I'm so sorry. I should never have turned my back on you just because I was bonded. You're still by far my favourite sister.'

Vashta leant over to hug her. 'You've no idea how good it is to hear that.'

Her sister's smile shone, but it was still tainted with grief. Vashta wondered if she would ever smile without its shadow in her eyes. She could feel the grief at her father's loss already covering her soul, even though she knew she needed to be strong and focussed if she was to stand up to Mestitha. 'So, the passing service?'

Illora swallowed back her tears. 'It will be in two days' time. Midday.' She took Vashta's hand again. 'I will make sure you're there, and I guarantee this ridiculous house arrest will be ended.'

'I'm not sure it will.' Not if she knew her sister. 'She knows I won't ever bow down to her, and if she goes through with what she's planning, I'll do everything I can to stop her.'

Illora looked thoughtful. 'That may be what we need.' She rose to leave. 'I'll make sure you're kept informed.'

***

Two days passed and Illora didn't return. A message was sent to say Vashta would be collected for the passing service, but nothing more.

A glance at her timepiece was enough to tell her it was almost time and, in the absence of anything else to do while she waited, she gazed out the window, taking comfort in the colours in the sky. She ran her fingers along the windowsill. The wood on the outside was pockmarked with shrapnel. There was more damage to the right, with a gaping hole a length or so beyond. It was amazing her chambers hadn't received significant damage. She had noticed some crumbling coming from the ceiling but had been told it would have no effect on her room's stability.

A knock sounded on the door, a guard entering and bowing. 'Princess Vashta, we are here to escort you to the passing service.'

There were only two guards this time. She wondered if the others at her door would follow, but they didn't.

Only two to guard me? My sister underestimates me.

It would be devastating to miss Father's passing service, but the best way she could serve her father and her people was being free to stop Mestitha. Erleph had taught her how to still her mind in order to take in her surroundings more effectively. It also prepared her for transformation by collecting useful information that benefited her heightened senses when in that zone.

She took a deep breath and began to focus her gaze on everything that passed.

A door to the right. I'm familiar with that route. But didn't the guards say it had caved in? The passage coming up on the left will take me to the kitchens. Given that there's a passing service, it's going to be busy with preparations, if it's still functioning.

She was in no hurry. She knew there were better options further ahead, as long as the attack hadn't destroyed them.

She almost ran into the back of the guard in front of her as the woman stopped. She opened her mouth to berate her when the one behind snatched at her elbow. Her transformation was halted by a whisper in her ear. 'We have an escape route planned for you. Erleph sent us.'

Erleph? That was possible. But was it also something Mestitha would have thought of? She would need to justify putting her in more secure accommodation, if that's what she wanted. But since when had her sister thought that far ahead?

Concluding that the message was true, Vashta quieted herself. She still maintained her watchful state but allowed the guards to lead her. Her head remained calm, although her heart's rapid beating unsettled her. She needed to get it under control.

There were others around them going about their duties, mostly servants organising the passing service feast. Soon they entered the more damaged parts of the palace. The guard she was following bent to remove debris from their path or to help her through a blocked entryway—help she refused.

The first guard pushed a door aside and there was Erleph, standing in what was left of the front base landing with one of the many rollers her family kept for their use. She barely noticed the vehicle, throwing herself in her mentor's arms.

'I'm glad to see you're all right,' he said, stepping out of the embrace.

She sniffed. 'Mestitha wouldn't dare do more than hold me, although I feared she might decide I belonged in less opulent surroundings.'

'You're right. We heard rumours that she was going to move you to the prison. We couldn't let that happen.'

'We?'

He led her to the roller and opened its door. 'Your sister, Illora. I couldn't have done this without her. She couldn't be here because of the passing service.'

Vashta tried to swallow the lump in her throat. As much as she knew she needed to leave, she would have liked to have been there to farewell Father and Brexin. 'You couldn't get me a flier?'

'I feared that would be a trifle too conspicuous. It also might attract the creatures' attention.'

'And what have they been doing? Have there been any more attacks?'

'I don't have time to go into that now. I must get to the service before I'm missed and before you are.' He gestured at what she was wearing—a fine, colourful gown to farewell her loved ones. 'Your sister packed clothes for you. I told her to only include serviceable ones. Make sure you change.'

She was sure she knew the answer, but she needed confirmation. 'Where am I going?'

'To Intersiss. To the heir.'

'At his request?'

'No, we haven't been in contact with him, but I see no other way. From what your sister said, they have tech that can fight these creatures. We can't win this war without their aid. We must enlist it and the heir is the most likely person for that. You trust him, don't you?'

She had spent much of her incarceration thinking about what had happened in Intersiss and had been irritated by how often the Verindal heir had entered her thoughts. She didn't know what to make of it. But Erleph was right—she believed he would help her and, by extension, her people. And they had weapons that worked. 'Is it safe to travel on the byways?'

He pointed to a device fixed to the front of the roller. 'This is a pathfinder. We stole it from the Verindal.' The box lit up as he touched it, displaying a map. 'I've programmed what I think is a safe passageway. I'm not sure it will stay that way, but it's the best we've got.'

He'd thought of everything, as usual. She nodded as the two guards settled in the front seats of the roller. 'I just hope this will work.'

'It's our only option. The guards will take you to the heir but will need to return before they're missed. I've rearranged duty schedules to cover for them. Goodbye, Your Highness, and safe trip.'

CHAPTER TEN

Brandonin wished he could put his feet up, but as he crouched over an image caster in the situation room, looking at the grainy scene playing on it, he despaired of ever having a moment to himself again.

Commander Lissia blinked two long blinks—the only sign of her weariness—before passing her gaze over the images and reports they'd been given. 'As you can see, my Lord, the creatures feint, fight and flee, feint, fight and flee, over and over again.'

'Are we any closer to discovering where they're coming from?'

'I may have something on that.' He turned to Ivanna, who wielded another report. 'This may be the key.'

She put it down on the table and Brandonin tried not to groan. Yet another thing to focus on. How many reports had he seen in the past few maxispans? But Ivanna seemed excited about it. 'Do you remember that aerial monitor we put up in the sky a year ago?'

'The one in the floating bubble?' asked the commander. 'The Vendel played target practise on it with their fliers, if I recall.'

Ivanna's mouth pulled into a pout. 'Yes, but they didn't get the *second* one. It's still up there.'

'Still providing useless information,' the commander snapped. A second sign of exhaustion; matching Brandonin's own mood.

Ivanna looked lasers at the commander. 'Well, it's no longer useless.' She pointed to a long stream of numbers on the report.

Brandonin looked at it up, down and sideways, scrambling to discover what it meant so he wouldn't look like an idiot for asking. But when he noticed that Lissia looked just as clueless, he shelved his insecurity. He was the heir. He could ask questions. 'Would you mind explaining this to us?'

It took her a moment to catch up. 'Of course, my Lord. The aerial monitor was deployed so we could gain more information about Verindon's atmosphere. For the last few months, the information it's provided has followed the same patterns. However, the information here was recorded at the time of the meteor shower a few months ago. It's the first time we've had a moment to assess it. It records the passage of the meteors into the wilds behind the Shatsee and Intersiss mountain ranges.'

He nodded. 'I remember that. Didn't a team check for any damage in the area?'

'Yes, and they found the signs of impact from some large meteors which *seemed* to have broken into rubble when they'd hit the ground.'

Did she mean what he thought she meant? 'So you're saying that there was something irregular about them?'

She held up the report. 'This shows a trend that doesn't match any previously recorded meteor activity. Also, it shows a pattern of ... disturbance, I think that's the best way to put it, passing through the atmosphere onto the planet in various locations. It started appearing before the first attack at Andramadiss.'

Great. 'So you believe these creatures are causing it?'

'I think it's a reliable assumption, yes.'

'Which means they *are* coming from off-world?' asked the commander.

'While there isn't enough data to confirm that, I think it's probable.'

The commander looked devastated. Brandonin was sure his expression mirrored hers. From space—somewhere they were yet to explore.

Commander Lissia managed to speak. 'Then how do we destroy them?'

'Nestor's weapon seems to be working.' Brandonin knew that wasn't what she was asking.

'Yes, but he can't make them fast enough to help us destroy these creatures! And how many more are out there?' She looked at the ceiling as if expecting them to burst through it.

He grasped at the positives. 'At least we have some idea where to start.' He turned back to Ivanna. 'Throw everything you can into this research. See if you can pinpoint the ultimate destination of this disruption.'

'I don't think we have the equip—'

'Then invent it!' He hadn't meant to raise his voice and felt a stab of guilt as Ivanna took a step away from him. He tried to settle himself before he spoke again. 'Do whatever you can. We have to find out more about these creatures if we're to have any hope of defeating them.'

But instead of the usual delighted gleam in her eyes, she looked exhausted. 'We're already stretched thin, my Lord, but we'll do our best.'

Of course she would. 'I know, Ivanna, and I appreciate what everyone's doing. But we need an answer that's more permanent than killing a handful at every skirmish.'

She gave him a quick bow and hurried away.

Commander Lissia's voice was unsteady when she spoke. 'You do realise that even if she does find out where they are, we may not be able to do anything about it. While we've gained a lot of theoretical knowledge about what it's like out in space, that's different from a practical engagement.'

Maybe the Vendel can help us. He could have sworn he'd said that to himself until he saw the commander's scowl. 'We know they've been attacked by these creatures as well. And they have flier technology.'

'Their fliers aren't as advanced as ours.' At least she didn't try and blame everything on the Vendel, as Loora would have.

Speaking of Loora … 'Please go and give my father a report on these latest developments.'

She bowed. 'Yes, my Lord.'

Brandonin threw himself into a vacant chair, watching the parade of military and scientific personnel racing backwards and forwards, delivering information, picking up orders and assessing damage from the latest attacks.

What would his father say about this development? Would he

believe it? What would Loora *make* him think? She would blame these atmospheric disturbances on the Vendel. After all, they had aerial capabilities too.

Could they be responsible? Everything in him said a resounding no. Yes, they had fliers, but theirs, although flown superbly, were inferior. He knew his people had achieved many heights that the Vendel could only dream of.

A breathless soldier raced up to him. This was rarely a good thing. 'My Lord!'

'Yes?'

'I was sent to inform you that there's been another attack.'

He tried to clear the fog in his brain.

'It was to the east of the palace, on one of the roads leading into Intersiss.'

He didn't have a report to hand over? A casualty list? There was something different ... 'Get to the point, soldier.'

'My Lord, the people were saved when some ... some Vendel defended them. Although they couldn't destroy them, they held them off until some of our troops arrived.'

'Vendel?'

'Yes, my Lord. It's been confirmed that one of them is a Vendel princess.'

He heard the sound of his feet hitting the floor. 'Where is she now?'

'She's being brought here, my Lord. I was sent to fe—'

'You've done that.' He marched past the man, back the way he'd come. 'Lead the way.'

***

He'd been worried they had put her in the cell bay. If so, he was sure Father would hear his protests from his safe room. Instead, they'd taken the princess to the throne room. It wasn't the location he would have selected, but it would do. And he wasn't going to insult her by taking the only seat, especially given its significance.

Princess Vashta was calm and seemed unharmed, except for some

99

minor wounds that an apothecary was treating. Her clothes, which were far less fine than the ones she'd worn on her official visit, were torn and muddied, but her deep blue eyes were bright as they gazed back at him.

Two wary Vendel guards stood at her side. Both were injured. He turned to his own guard. 'Take these two to the infirmary and see they're well cared for.'

The princess held out her hand. 'No, they need to return to Matarsiss as soon as possible.'

'We'll treat their injuries first, then escort them to the border.'

The two women glanced at the princess as Brandonin's guards approached them, but she nodded at them and they left without complaint.

Once they had gone, she bowed. 'My Lord.'

It was a courtesy he hadn't expected and wouldn't have demanded of her. There was only one way to respond. He too bowed before her. 'Your Highness. I'm glad to see you haven't been seriously injured.'

She looked at her arm. 'It wasn't worth anyone's time.'

He looked around at the Verindal who surrounded her—his people. While they seemed to be trying—and failing—to give the impression that they were there to serve her, she must have realised they were guarding her. She too glanced around but seemed undisturbed. And unafraid, if the calm way she'd dismissed her guards was anything to go by.

But why had she left her people's lands and come to Intersiss? He gestured to her attire. 'I can see this isn't a state visit.'

'Not at such a time.'

Down to business. He liked this woman. 'Your people have been hit by these creatures as well.'

Something passed across her face that he couldn't decipher. 'Yes, they have struck our heart a savage blow.'

His own heart felt like a rock within him. He hadn't heard anything about a personal loss to the Vendel High Family, apart from the one that had occurred during their visit. 'I'm sorry. Can you tell me what's happened?'

Surprise flitted across her features. 'It seems your spy network isn't as extensive as some of my people have led me to believe.'

He snorted. 'I think both of our spy networks are stretched a little thin at the moment.'

'True. Then it is my … duty to inform you that my father, Chief Prince Liffon, has passed on to the next life.'

No tears fell, nor did her brow knit. But her grief was plain to see. 'I am so sorry.'

She gave a stiff nod. 'I'm sure.'

'But you haven't come all the way to inform me of that.'

Doubt clouded her face. 'No. I … I know you have weapons. We have nothing that can do more than temporarily drive these creatures away, and that still takes everything we have. We need something we can use to destroy them.'

Brandonin was aware that everyone in the room was listening to their conversation. Did the council really feel the need to spy on him? He would tell the overlord everything … once he'd worked out the best course of action. 'So your eldest sister is ruling your people now. Did she send you?'

Another glance at her—the clothes, the desperation she was holding at bay, and he knew the answer. 'No. My sister is no friend of the Verindal.'

He nodded in understanding. 'I have my own problems with that, believe me. But that doesn't make it easy for us to help.'

She looked at the people milling around them and was sure she would reach the same conclusion as he. She let out a breath, then her body slumped and her eyes closed. He had no clue what was happening until a tear slid out from beneath one of her long lashes.

His heart swelled. She was grieving the loss of her father and her sister's bond-partner and yet she had taken it upon herself to come to get help for her people.

But it was hopeless trying to make an ally of the Vendel now. If the new chief princess was interested in their help in defeating this threat, she would have sent her sister with multiple advisors, guards, commanders and who knew what else. She had made her own way to Intersiss and, while he felt she wasn't being entirely honest with him, he had no doubt that her fear for her people was real. And she was bearing it alone.

His fingers flexed with the desire to reach out and touch her, but he had no reason to think that his touch would comfort her and he could almost hear the gasps of horror that would burst from every onlooker if he did.

But what should he do? Perhaps there was only one thing until she was ready to tell him the whole truth. 'You've had a dangerous journey to get here. Why don't we take you somewhere so you can rest? It might be a while before we can work out the best course of action, so we should give you somewhere to stay ... for now,' he added when he heard the pause in everyone's step.

Her face told him she'd heard it too. 'Thank you. I appreciate your kindness.'

He looked around, trying to find someone he could trust to care for this woman decently. He ignored the more senior staff and called a junior runner over. 'I would like you to take Princess Vashta to my sister. Tell her she is assuming refugee status and I would like her to find her some quarters and see to it that she is attended to.'

Whatever his personal feelings as he looked the princess over, the boy bowed in deference. 'At once, my Lord.'

The princess gave him a small bow. 'Thank you, sir.'

He returned the courtesy with a nod of his head. 'Take some time to recover from your trip. I'll send for you after I've seen the overlord and figured out the best course of action.'

'I'm grateful.' She turned and followed the runner out of the room.

The bustle that had softened to a hum while she'd been there returned to its fever pitch. He could see some minor officials leaving the room, to report the conversation to his father, no doubt.

And as much as he didn't want to, he knew he needed to discuss this development with him. He began running through the objections to her presence, and there would be many, not least the fact that the

Vendel were now being ruled by someone openly hostile towards them.

He went over to an information station and the attendant bowed. 'My Lord?'

'Find all the intel you have on the heir to the Vendel throne and bring it to me as soon as possible. I will be in the council room.'

She bowed again. 'Yes, my Lord.'

CHAPTER ELEVEN

Vashta felt shame bite into her. She had come to Intersiss to warn the heir about what her sister was planning so why had she failed to tell him? He had been standing there, as sympathetic and open as he'd been the previous time they'd met, and she'd stopped her mouth from saying the words.

I believe my sister has a weapon that could wipe out your entire race.

She tried to tell herself it was because of the many listening ears. It was ridiculous to think that every Verindal in that room was as open-minded as the heir. If any others had heard, it would have caused more havoc than the invasion. But she had no idea how she would get the words out even if they were alone. Was it because she realised how it would sound? That would at least be a reasonable excuse.

Was it out of some misguided loyalty to her sister? No. Mestitha was an underhanded fool who desired Father's position for all the wrong reasons and she had no interest in peace with anyone if it didn't suit her. Any of her sisters would have been better on the throne than her.

But what did Vashta do now? Did she tell the heir the truth? He would have to tell his father. How would the overlord react? From what little she knew of him, Overlord Dransen was no friend to her people and had grown weak and feeble in the past few years. It was a good thing the overlord had a son he could depend on to give good advice, but Vashta was sure he wouldn't be the only one advising the leader of the Verindal.

And his sister. What was she like? She tried to remember her from that brief visit, but she'd done little to attract Vashta's attention. She wondered what kind of woman she would encounter as she was led up into the higher levels of the Verindal palace, up spiral staircases, past works of art that bore testament to the luxury her hosts enjoyed. This part of the palace, at least, remained untouched by the invasion.

She followed the attendant into a room which they entered after he rapped on the door. The interior looked like a waiting room and contained comfortable couches and a table, everything decorated in varied colours. Three women were seated inside, all of them turning as the door opened. The attendant bowed to a woman who Vashta recognised. 'Lady Larinda, this is the Vendel princess, Vashta.'

The other two women scrambled away, holding their skirts up, but the heir's sister looked curious.

'His Lordship, the Heir, asked me to escort her to you. She is a refugee and will need lodging with us for at least one night.'

The other two ladies' faces held terror as they whispered in Lady Larinda's ear before leaving the room. They made sure they didn't even cross Vashta's shadow. How pathetic.

After a murmured command from Larinda, the attendant bowed and left. The heir's sister looked more casual than she had the last time Vashta had seen her. Her dark brown hair was down around her shoulders, rather than woven in elaborate braids as it had been during their visit. Her dress was a simple blue brocade that had few embellishments. Vashta wondered how old she was. Would it be impertinent to ask? And it wasn't essential information, so she kept her mouth shut, watching to see what she would do.

Lady Larinda came forward with no noticeable hesitation, holding out her hand. 'Princess Vashta?'

'Yes.' Vashta stifled her impatience. The woman had just been told who she was.

'I was just checking. There are five of you, all beautiful, all with equally splendid names. I wanted to make sure I had the right one.'

Vashta floundered for something to say. Small talk had never been her forte. But Lady Larinda didn't seem offended.

'I'm sorry to hear you've been forced to accept our company for a time. I asked the attendant to prepare a room for you. If you'll follow me, I'll take you there.'

It seemed unusual that the heir's own sister would guide her to the guest quarters. Wasn't that a servant's job? But maybe they did things differently amongst the Verindal. Or maybe she had a reason for doing it. 'You've had to flee your own lands? Because of the attacks of the creatures? How are your people faring?'

So it's a fishing expedition. 'As well as can be expected against an enemy that's invincible.'

Lady Larinda grimaced. 'Yes, it seems so.' She looked around before lowering her tone. 'My brother thinks we can defeat them if our races work together.'

Straight to the point, just like her brother. But Vashta still wasn't sure she trusted this woman. And she had to remember that she was talking to a lie detector, so she needed to be careful. 'That may be the only way forward, but I don't know if it's possible.' That was true enough.

'You may be right.' Lady Larinda sighed. 'I just hope it doesn't mean the end of our planet.'

It seemed a little soon to be jumping to that conclusion unless she knew something about what Mestitha was planning. If she knew, the heir did too, and he had shown no sign of such terrible knowledge when they'd spoken.

Larinda opened a door to reveal a room that was both regal and relaxing. The attendant and a couple of servants bustled about in the living area, where there was a couch and a small table already set with refreshments. There was an opulent bed just behind that, with colourful brocades and fabrics decorating the walls.

No window. She wondered if that was to keep her from discovering any of the secrets they kept on the palace grounds or to keep her from escaping. Or both. But it was comfortable and more than she would have expected, given what she was.

She wandered over to the table and noticed that there was a sugar bowl beside the drink they'd left out for her. She looked up in surprise.

Larinda didn't seem disturbed. 'I imagine that was supplied at my brother's direction. Have you used your ... abilities recently?' Her voice trembled on those words. It was the first sign of fear she'd showed. But Vashta was amazed. To give her, the enemy, what she needed to be at her strongest. It was ludicrous.

It was a sign of trust.

She stirred the sugar into the drink, willing her mouth to say the words that would return that trust.

Larinda didn't seem to notice. 'I think you'll be comfortable in here.'

'And how long will I stay?'

She floundered. 'I'm not sure. You're not a ... We wouldn't ... Of course you're free to leave when you like. But I assume you came here for a reason?'

Apparently exhausted from her fluster, Larinda sat on the couch with a thud. Vashta joined her there. 'It's all right. I'm not concerned.' She glanced at the cup in her hand. 'It's a bad idea to give me this if I'm meant to be a prisoner.'

'There are many who would prefer it that way, I assure you. But my brother and I are not amongst them. May I ask what brings you here?'

There was no accusation in the enquiry. But Vashta knew that the longer she took to answer it, the more she would create distrust between them. She couldn't do that. She needed to be honest. That was why she'd come. 'I'm here because I refuse to believe your people are responsible for what's happening. There's no way they can be. My views meant that I was forced to ... find alternative means of serving our planet.'

Larinda cocked her head. 'But your father, the chief prince, struck me as someone who was accepting of an alliance between us.'

'My father is dead.'

It was impossible to remain seated and keep her grief locked inside so Vashta rose and wandered to the other side of the room. She wished she could see the Verindonian sky. The colours in the room were magnificent but paled in comparison with the rainbow hues in their atmosphere. But then, if she could see the sky, she could also see the battle-ravaged ground and the scars that told of a war still being fought.

She didn't realise that the heir's sister had risen and come towards her until she felt the woman's hand on her shoulder. Her whispered 'I'm sorry' shattered what was left of Vashta's resolve.

The tears came unbidden, and once they'd started, they persisted in tracking long trails down her cheeks. She had rarely allowed herself to cry since she'd heard of Father's passing. But here, surrounded by unfamiliarity and enemies who just might turn out to be friends, she didn't have the strength to stop herself surrendering to her grief.

Larinda placed her other hand on Vashta's arm and that awoke the princess's self-control. She breathed in and halted the tears before any more could come. As much as she wanted to like this woman, she couldn't accept sympathy in a moment of weakness, so she moved away. 'Yes, my eldest sister rules now, and she's not looking for allies from your people.'

'She believes we're behind these attacks.'

'It's not an unexpected conclusion, is it? I'm sure there are many downstairs who assume I've come to spy on you, to learn how we can make the attacks more devastating.'

Larinda looked down. 'Yes, I'm sure there are.'

Vashta set her mouth. The woman's sympathy had broken down the last of her reluctance. 'My people have a weapon they want to use to destroy you. It's not these creatures. It's something else, and its effect will be devastating. I have come here because I want to stop it. I would persist in believing this even if you were responsible for all this. But my sister has no sense of mercy or restraint. She will use it if she thinks it will end the attacks.' *And probably regardless of that.*

Larinda turned to the door. She approached Vashta, her voice low. 'What does she have?'

'Something that can wipe out certain strains of DNA. I don't know how real it is or how ready, but I know she's prepared to use it.'

Ashen-faced, Larinda stepped back. 'Tell this to no one else.' She turned and hurried out of the room.

Vashta sank onto the couch. Saying that had been a mistake. There was no way her people could have developed something like

Blassin's device, regardless of what Mestitha thought. And what would the Verindal do if they knew such a thing existed? The entire Vendel race might well be enslaved for this.

And what could be done while these creatures were attacking anyway? The Verindal forces were already stretched thin. *The only thing they can do is hate me for it.*

But the tale was told and there was no going back.

CHAPTER TWELVE

Brandonin rubbed the bridge of his nose, wishing he could cover his ears.

Loora's continual portents of doom rained down on the overlord as he sat at the head of the council table, reports on the attacks in front of him.

'All this is what the Vendel are responsible for, my Lord. They have done this to us with these creatures. It's by their design that we're suffering. And now one of them has come here, and your son wants to offer it food and lodging? The only thing we should be doing to this *princess* is interrogating her to find out what she knows.'

Father blinked a few times, then skimmed over the pile of documents Loora had presented. He let out a long sigh and shook his head. 'She's not even Larinda's age. What could she know that would justify using such harsh methods on a child like that?'

As shocked as he was at his father's unexpected softness, he breathed a sigh of relief.

Loora's face turned red but Brandonin could see she was trying to bring herself under control. 'My Lord, she's here to spy on us. We need to know why. We need to know what the enemy knows. She *can* tell us!'

Others at the council table nodded in agreement, although most of the mutterings he could hear suggested that interrogating a minor princess wouldn't achieve much more than enraging the Vendel.

It was time for him to speak. 'My Lord, I understand your concern at the young woman's appearance here, but remember, the Vendel are under siege just as much as we are. Is it surprising to discover a refugee from the Vendel High Family on our doorstep at this time?'

'With her sister now on the throne?' Loora spat. 'She may accuse us of kidnapping her. And why did she come here for sanctuary? Perhaps to escape her sister's fury. Perhaps she knows something significant. We need to find out.'

'How can we assume that? There are invasions all over Vendel lands. It may have been impossible for her to go anywhere else. And helping her may gain us allies amongst the Vendel.' He had to be careful how he spoke; there were a number of lie detectors in the room with varying degrees of skill and he knew the new chief princess wouldn't care what they did to her sister. He filled his mind with the belief that other Vendel would. That would make his words ring true. 'I think it would further our cause to aid her, rather than treat her harshly.'

Loora's eyes flashed. 'Of course the heir would seek to save a beautiful young woman from justice. It's to be expected.'

Never before had she sunk so low. The councillors fidgeted at the sound of her words, looking at each other, him and his father. Brandonin waited for his father to defend him.

He did not. His chin stooped to touch his breast.

Time to step up. 'I'm surprised that Lady Loora could see any beauty when she's so blinded by prejudice, something that leads to poor decisions and unwise judgements.'

This time Father responded, but it was not what Brandonin had hoped to hear. 'Now, now. You know Loora meant no offence.'

So Father *had* heard.

Loora gave him a triumphant look. 'Of course, my Lord,' she said, turning back to Father. 'Your word is always right.'

He tried to hide his dismay as she stroked Father's hand, his face turning up to hers with trusting eyes. Nothing would be gained by fighting at this table. Brandonin's only hope was to get Father alone. But when was he alone? Loora was always with him. And even if he managed to see his father in private, the words the overlord said in this room held weight, and Loora was a councillor, present for every decision.

He resumed his seat. 'Very well, my Lord. I'm sure we all appreciate your decision to treat the girl well on account of her youth and innocence.'

Loora's face faltered. His submission had thrown her. Anything that unsettled her would help him.

'So then, my Lord,' Brandonin said. 'What course of action should we take?'

His father's gaze returned to Loora. It was she who spoke. 'My Lord, may I suggest that it's time to resume attacks on the Vendel? They are taking advantage of our lapses, I'm sure.'

Lady Mirkana smothered a snort. She was the most skilled lie detector present. She shot him a look, but he turned away.

'Oh, if you think so, my dear. Does everyone agree with that course of action?'

Everyone in the room swivelled to meet Brandonin's gaze.

'Whatever you decree, my Lord.' It killed him to speak like that to his father, and he knew every woman, including Loora, would realise he was lying. But even she wasn't game to call him out in this company, probably because he had never been caught in a lie before. He was sure she would try to figure out what he was planning before she reported his deception to Father.

Any delay was beneficial, for Brandonin knew what he had to do. It might mean that his father was lost to him forever, but he had no choice. The future of their planet depended on it.

Never had he been so relieved to get out of the council chamber. He hurried away before Loora could extract herself from Father's presence to see where he was going, although he was sure she had spies amongst the servants.

His sister stepped into his path. 'We need to talk.'

'Larinda, I don't have time for this now.'

She glanced at the councillors pouring from the room and leant closer. 'Then make time.'

As she was walking in the direction of the command centre, he followed her. If anything, it would help alleviate suspicion if he was seen having a conversation with his sister. Spies might not realise his intention.

'I've settled the Princess Vashta in her quarters.'

'We'll need to move her,' he whispered. 'She isn't safe here.'

'We need to do more than that.'

To his surprise, Larinda headed out a door and into the gardens. Once there, she slowed her pace, examining a patch of skyflowers. She glanced at a group of servants cleaning up after the recent attack and moved away from them. 'Look here, Brandonin.' She pointed to a violet creeper and held up a bloom for him. 'The princess says her sister has access to a device that could see the genocide of every Verindal. I'm sure that's the real reason she's come here. To warn us.'

He felt a stab of disappointment. Why had Vashta told Larinda and not him? He chided himself. Why would she tell him? She had only just arrived and had probably been disorientated. And given the severity of this information, it would have been unwise to speak up unless they were alone.

A weapon that could destroy them all … 'She was telling the truth?'

'She was, although the information she heard might not be correct. I can't imagine the Vendel having technology like that, can you?'

'No, but anything's possible.'

A servant crept closer. Coming to inspect flowers hadn't been the greatest idea as a cover story for their conversation. 'Father is listening to Loora more and more.'

'Do you want me to speak to him?'

'You can try. I don't know if it will do any good.' Although Father loved Larinda, he thought of her as a delicate bloom, as their mother had been, rather than the capable woman she was. He wouldn't defer to her opinion over Loora's.

'Maybe not.' She flashed a dangerous glance at the creeping servant and he retreated a few steps. 'What will you do?'

Was there an easy decision to make at this time? He couldn't think of a way forward. 'I don't know. We can't move the princess yet. It will be too obvious. At the very least, we'll need to wait a few days.'

Larinda nodded. 'And hope they don't do anything to her in the meantime.'

Another day, another screen to peer at.

Yet again, their enemy was attacking various places around Intersiss. Brandonin watched the nearest on one of their image casters in the situation room. Commander Lissia was on location. She had insisted on going but was also trying to stay close to the palace. And this fight was a bit too close for comfort.

Larinda appeared; the first time he'd seen her that day. She gave him a weary smile. 'Good morning.'

'Morning. Been busy?'

She sank into a chair. 'No, I just needed a break.'

Father and Loora spent most of their time now in the safe room they had below ground. Larinda often joined them there … for as long as she could stand it. 'What are they saying now?'

Clouds gathered in her eyes. 'Father simply parrots whatever Loora says, and I'm sure I don't need to tell you what that is.'

'Vendel menace! They're responsible! We must wipe them out!' Brandonin said, mimicking the councillor.

'Variations on that theme, sure.' But her face only held a frown as her voice dropped lower. 'I'm worried about him, Brandonin. He doesn't seem to be there anymore.'

He knew she was right. Father's vacancy was a problem, given his increased dependence on Loora. It could be a help too though. After all, both of them seemed to have lost interest in Princess Vashta.

He looked up towards the princess's room. She didn't venture out much; her presence drew too many eyes. It meant they'd been unable to move her, or for him to put his own plan into action.

'My Lord, Commander Lissia for you.'

He held out his hand for the communicator. 'Yes, Commander?'

'My Lord, are you still watching?'

Unfortunately, he'd dared to be distracted. What had he missed? The frantic activity in the room told him something was wrong.

'The fighting is coming your way,' Lissia said. 'I'm using all the troops I have to keep the enemy here, but I fear it will not be enough.'

'Thank you, Commander. We will ready for an attack.' He handed the communicator to an aide. 'Send the alert throughout the palace. All fighters to their stations.'

He heard the siren sound and turned to Larinda. 'Go back to the safe room and look after Father.'

She gathered up her skirts. 'Not on your life. I'm going to get Vashta. She's our guest. I need to ensure her safety first.'

Larinda was right. Brandonin followed her out into the hallway, dodging the troops racing by. 'Where will you take her?'

She looked lost. 'No idea. Where is safe?'

Was anywhere in the palace safe anymore?

A blur caught his eye as it moved down the staircase, following the troops. Instinct made him dive left and he managed to catch her ankle and bring her to the ground. They bounced down the stairs together.

It was Vashta, her face fallen. She snarled at him. 'Do not stop me. I will fight them.'

He had never heard a Vendel speak in that form before and was surprised at how deep and slow her words were. But he wasn't letting go. 'You can't do anything. You don't have a weapon and you know being in this … state of yours won't help you forever.'

'I have sugar,' she slurred, holding up three cans Brandonin had given her, which she had strapped to her belt.

A blast shook the floor. The enemy must have arrived. A glance outside confirmed it.

'My Lord, the safe room!' someone yelled. But an explosion in the passageway rocked them on their feet, blocking their way.

'Upstairs!' Brandonin tried to think of a safe refuge. But the palace's construction was thinner the further it rose. If its foundations were destroyed, it would topple. Was that their plan? He glanced back at Vashta, whose face was back to normal. She downed the contents of a can of liquid sugar as she raced to a window they were passing, her eyes flickering in all directions. 'Is that a flier bay?'

He looked at the level just above them. 'Yes.' They had never used their fliers to battle these creatures before as the only weapons that could destroy them had yet to be mounted on the nose cones. And would they be fast enough?

She glanced around. 'Will they take three?'

'I believe so.'

'Get me to one.'

He strode up the stairs two at a time, Vashta keeping pace and Larinda just behind. A level and a few turns more and he slammed open the door to the bay. A maintenance server was working on a three-seater. Vashta went straight to it and leapt into the cockpit. 'Has this been prepped?'

'Yes.' The man looked at Brandonin.

'The palace is under attack. Get to battle stations.'

'Yes, my Lord.'

As they settled in the cockpit, Vashta examined the controls.

'You know how to fly?' asked Larinda. He could have been mistaken about the flash of envy in her eyes.

Vashta's face lit up. 'It's my favourite thing in the world.'

He put out a hand. 'These fliers don't have our new lasers and I don't think they can move fast enough to get around these creatures.'

'But they've never been piloted by a Vendel before,' she said, putting on a helmet and handing him another. 'And they weren't piloted by *me*.'

'But they aren't just propeller-driven. I don't think you understand the difference—'

'I know enough.' She flicked the starter and the engine whined. Her hands continued to move over the controls as if she'd sat in this cockpit scores of times.

Larinda looked at him. There was nothing for it. He strapped his helmet on.

They lifted away from the bay in under forty microspans. 'I know I can't fight them in this, so I'm going to get us somewhere safe,' she said, 'but if they attack, I'll have to transform. Don't worry if that happens.'

'I know. You're safer when you're in that zone.'

She turned to face him, her gaze steadfast. 'As are you when you're with me.' She had hardly turned back when three creatures began hovering around them. 'Hold on,' she said, her voice slurring again.

The swarm around them scattered as Vashta flew straight at them, diving at the last moment, rather than hitting them, and sliding underneath. He looked for any sign that she was having trouble controlling the flier. Were her movements choppy? Perhaps just a little.

It had taken him several flights before he'd mastered even the most basic of manoeuvres. What she was doing was way beyond that. He tried to stop himself from hanging on to the side of the flier, unused to the power she unleashed simply by her mastery of the controls. Why couldn't his own people fly like this?

But their enemy didn't give up. They again gathered around the flier with an angry buzzing. Vashta rolled out of their way before they had a chance to do anything. She flew further away from the palace, but they followed, a few more gaining on them.

Brandonin focussed on the enemy. These were flying, rather than leaping, as they often did. How did they do it? Where was that buzzing coming from?

As some of them scrambled to get out of the way of the flier, he noticed a disturbance down their backs each time they moved. Some kind of powered backpack, perhaps?

Vashta came out of her transformation and downed a sugar drink from the canisters strung at her waist. 'Do you have any forests in this direction?'

'No. They're behind the palace. Loop around.'

She banked, flying low over some nearby buildings. She weaved in and out of them, losing a few of the creatures as some mistimed her moves and slammed into the walls. Brandonin winced as he saw large chunks fall from the force of the impact. He hoped no civilians were below.

Once Vashta reached the forest, she flew within a hairsbreadth of the canopy of the trees. But it was full of thick, craggy branches that he knew would do significant damage to the flier if she got too close.

Several branches banged into the floor, just below their feet, causing Larinda to shriek. He clamped his lips to keep his fear inside. He'd always enjoyed a white-knuckle ride with their best pilots, but it had never been like this.

And was that a cliff face rushing up to them? He thought she might slow, but she slammed the accelerator and the flier leapt forward.

No! Had he yelled the word? He wasn't sure. There wasn't much time to do more than shield his eyes, but Vashta pulled back and the flier shot straight up, running parallel to the side of the cliff. He was sure he heard a scrape beneath his feet and was that a spark flying away near their wing?

One glance behind told him most of their pursuers had slammed into the cliff-face. The rest of them fled. Vashta didn't stop, continuing to fly parallel to the cliff for some time before she slowed. She drew in a gulp of air before reaching for another sugar canister. When she turned towards them, her face was normal. 'I may have cut it a bit close but at least we made it.'

'We certainly did.' He was pleased with how steady his voice sounded and he flexed his knuckles so they would lose their revealing whiteness. One glance at Larinda told him she was doing the same, although he thought it would take longer for the colour to return to her face.

Vashta flew above the trees. 'We should be all right for now.' She glanced at the flier's readouts. 'We have enough fuel to stay out here for another maxispan, I think. Then we'll have to find somewhere safe.'

'I'm not sure there is such a place.' It was rare for Larinda to sound so defeatist.

'We need to know the extent of the attack on the palace,' Brandonin said, as he tried to assess all possible alternatives based on what little they knew. 'If they got to the armoury ...'

'It's at the bottom, virtually underground,' his sister said.

'And they'll do anything to get at it if it means destroying the only weapons that have any effect on them. We need to move them out of there. You saw what they did. Also, you know that Loora is now effectively in charge.'

Vashta cocked her head. 'Your father?'

'Is a weak and feeble old man.' He hated talking about him that way. 'It's been coming on for years. It's made it easier in a lot of ways. He tends to listen to me more now than he used to. Of course, he listens to others as well.'

Larinda nodded. 'You've always been the voice of reason.'

He leant his head back against the seat and sighed. 'And I'll never convince Loora that the Vendel aren't at fault. After all, it's easier to think that way. But that doesn't change things. We need to find a way to fight this threat, even if our leaders won't.'

Vashta looked at the horizon again. 'So if we're not going back to your palace then where do we go?'

'I had thought of a place before the attack. I think it might be our best option. We'll need to contact Nestor and see if he can move his setup there … if he'll follow me at all, when Father's insisting on another way. Hopefully, Commander Lissia will come as well.'

'Where are we going?' Larinda asked.

Where indeed? There was only one place big enough and with sufficient external protection to be of use, although that protection had been put in place with something other than invasion in mind. But it would serve their purpose. And no one would think of looking for them there.

'We're going to the bunker.'

CHAPTER THIRTEEN

Once the heir had programmed the flier's pathfinder with the right destination, Vashta had to do little more than check there were no invaders on their tail.

She allowed herself a sense of satisfaction. The enemy had been unable to combat a flier of this type when it was piloted by someone as skilled as she was. True, she'd got a little too close to the canopy and the cliff, but no significant damage had been done.

The heir and his sister were quiet for most of the journey. She wondered if they were thinking about their father. Weak man though he was, if he was dead, they would react the same way she had when she'd learnt of her father's death.

'So what is this bunker?' she asked.

'For Verindal, our history is of paramount importance. A few years ago, there was a devastating fire that destroyed many precious records. We decided to build a facility for the safe housing of our history.'

'So it's like a museum?' She tried to keep her mind on the subject, rather than the thought that her people might have caused the fire.

'No, it's not open to the public. There are a few staff, but most of it looks after itself,' said Larinda.

'But it's huge, designed to house a growing catalogue of historical treasures. And it has high-rated security and is designed to withstand fire, bomb blasts ... pretty much any weapon your pe— I mean, anything that might damage it.'

So we were responsible. Well, it was a good thing if it meant they had somewhere secure to go. 'But there won't be much there that we can utilise?'

'All the right connections are there, to computer networks and such.'

'Computers.' Her people had computers. She'd even used one as part of her flight training. They'd been stolen from the Verindal, of course.

'Yes, they're—'

'I know what they are.' She didn't mean to sound so abrupt, but her people weren't clueless about technology, even if they gained it second-hand.

The heir took the hint. 'But there isn't an armoury, there isn't a garrison, and there isn't anything that will be useful in this battle unless there's some stored history on these creatures.'

'We'll have to make sure we check for that,' said Larinda.

The heir nodded. 'That can be your first task.'

If the woman was upset by him dictating to her like that, she didn't show it. 'But will you be able to get the resources you need?'

He grimaced. 'That depends on a lot of things. How bad was the attack at the palace? Who have we lost?'

'Is Father still living?' Larinda's voice wobbled over the words.

'And if he is, how many are loyal to him?'

'Are they going to remain so if he follows the lead of that woman too readily?' asked Vashta. 'What kind of power does she hold over others?'

The heir's eyebrows pulled together. 'Not a great deal over the people I need. She's been too eager to throw her weight around with them. However, she holds considerable sway over the council. While I could get the most important people to follow my lead, they would have to break away from my father—disobeying the council—to do it.'

She met his gaze. 'Would they?'

He didn't look confident, but his words proved that she'd misinterpreted why. 'They would … if they're still alive.'

Yes, this attack on the Verindal palace had been far more extensive than the last. Who had survived?

Buildings came in sight and Vashta slowed, watching every movement as they approached, but there was no sign of trouble. 'How far into the city is this building?'

'In the middle.'

That was a shame. 'It will be hard to hide as we go in.'

Brandonin didn't look too concerned. 'Patrolling fliers have become commonplace lately, so I'm not sure it will make much difference.'

'Landing will.'

Their pathfinder beeped and the heir confirmed it. 'That's it.'

He pointed to a building ahead of them. It was a squat, sprawling thing, quite ugly for the city of Intersiss. This building had been structured for purpose rather than aesthetics. She checked for somewhere to land and was pleased to note that there was a space a few blocks from the building that was big enough.

She touched the flier down on a stretch of grass, its rear engines turning the trees behind it to cinders. She hoped they weren't significant. She flipped the cockpit open and Brandonin climbed out, stretching out a hand to aid his sister—then her, to her surprise—to disembark.

As they walked up the street towards the bunker, she grew edgy as four people left it and began striding towards them. At least the one leading the way didn't look like a threat, considering the lines on his face and the bend of his back. He was dressed for service, his clothes designed for ease of movement, although still with the colour every resident of their planet loved. The three with him were broader and their hefty arms made her sure they were guards.

As they approached, the man's face changed, the lines on his face increasing in depth. 'My Lord?'

He was acknowledged with a nod. 'Tellaph.'

Tellaph bowed, as did those with him. 'My Lord, we thought you had been killed.'

The heir's face paled. 'Was the palace destroyed?'

'No, it still stands. Your father made a broadcast not long ago. He said your whereabouts were unknown. I'm sure he thinks you're dead. He must be informed—'

'Not just yet.'

Tellaph gave the heir a quizzical look but said nothing more.

'This isn't the place for a conversation,' said Larinda. 'Let's go inside.'

Vashta catalogued the building as she approached it. As she had seen from above, it was a giant sprawl coated in a dull grey that didn't seem to be any kind of paint she'd ever seen. Its surface was pockmarked and craggy. There were no windows anywhere; something that would have horrified most residents of this planet, as it cut off the view of the sky.

There were three levels, all of them flat and dull and uninteresting. However, she felt that they disguised what she was concluding—that this place could withstand any disaster the planet could unleash, including, hopefully, their new enemies.

And they'd done all that to keep a stack of historical records safe?

Even the entry was not recognisable as a door. It swung inwards as one of the guards put her hand on it, pushing with all her might, as it was as thick as a handspan. She swung the heavy structure closed after them.

The inside was not as dark as the exterior had been, artificial light illuminating every corner. They walked down a pristine white corridor with no visible doors leading from it, except one at the end. Tellaph opened it and ushered them inside. They entered a large room with several desks and computer consoles set up. An image caster was mounted on the wall and, as they entered, one of the guards hurried to program it for them.

Vashta glanced at the heir out of the corner of her eye. 'What should I call you?'

He looked like he was waking from a trance. 'What?'

'I think we're going to be in one another's company for the foreseeable future and I don't want to call you "my Lord" any more than you want to call me "Your Highness".' Titles be damned. What did they mean now?

He looked at his sister. 'You're right. All that court protocol seems a bit unnecessary. My name's Brandonin and this is Larinda.'

Vashta was surprised at her own hesitation to greet him in Verindonian fashion—her hand on his shoulder. 'I'm Vashta.' When her heart rate quickened as he returned the gesture, she didn't let the connection linger. She greeted his sister the same way. She knew what it was like to be the younger royal sibling and wasn't about to strip a courtesy from her.

Tellaph looked askance at them but was wise enough to keep his mouth shut.

The programming finally settled, revealing the devastation from the latest attack. The Verindal palace was indeed still standing, although, from the number of stretcher-bearers who were racing backwards and forwards, it seemed that there were many fatalities.

There was no sound to accompany the images, but a ribbon of words ran along the bottom of the image caster. Tellaph nodded to it. 'You see, my Lord? Your father thinks you're dead. Are you sure you don't want us to contact him? He must be distraught.'

Judging by the look on Brandonin's face, he agreed, but he shook his head. 'No, my friend. It's better that he doesn't know immediately.'

'But why?' asked the old man, gesturing for Larinda to sit in a chair. He gave Vashta a puzzled look. Perhaps he didn't think she deserved one.

The heir cast his gaze over the guards and looked at Tellaph. The man's face became grim as he answered. 'Everyone here is loyal, my Lord.'

But who to?

Brandonin didn't seem concerned about that. 'My father is getting old. You know this. He is now too easily swayed, can't think for himself and isn't making good decisions.'

Tellaph nodded. 'I had noticed that he was growing … vacant.'

'I'm sure you've realised that the enemy we're facing is greater than any we've ever experienced before.'

Tellaph glanced at her. 'Not of Vendel origin, then?'

'I see no way it could be.'

'I'd feared so myself. We,' he gestured to the guards, 'had made a study of the creatures, cataloguing their behaviour and anatomy as much as possible given our limited access to such information. We had already noted that there were enough differences in them to suspect that they did not originate here.'

Brandonin seemed pleased. 'Very good. But some are refusing to believe that the old enemy isn't the true one.' He looked at Vashta. 'People on both sides. But if we waste our time fighting each other …'

'We'll do the work of these creatures for them,' said Tellaph. 'Perhaps that's what they want.'

'I believe so. But since my father won't listen and neither will the Vendel leadership, I feel we need to set up an alternative headquarters, dedicated to defeating our new enemy.'

Tellaph stood. 'And you chose here. Very wise, my Lord. Most wouldn't think this building important, yet it's stronger than any we have. What do you need me to do?'

'For a start, don't reveal that we've survived to anyone in the royal house or on the council. Secondly, I need you to get a message to Nestor, if he's still living. Tell him what's happened and see if he's willing to move at least some operations here. Although, perhaps it would be better that I meet with him first to discuss it.

'Please also see if you can find out if Commander Lissia is loyal to me or my father. I don't know how subtle your people can be, but if you can discover that, it would be beneficial. Ivanna as well.'

Tellaph nodded. 'Do not fear, my Lord. Everyone here knows what you have done to keep our history alive all these years. We are dedicated to you. And I know my people. I know which ones will be able to carry out this action for you.'

'Excellent.' Brandonin looked at Vashta and then his sister. 'Erm, I'm not sure what accommodation you have here …'

The archivist spluttered so much Vashta thought he would never get the words out. 'Nothing suitable for any princess.'

Like she cared. 'I don't need anything fancy.' She had nothing but the clothes on her back anyway.

Larinda smiled. 'I'm sure whatever you have will do for now. However,' she glanced at her outfit. 'We need to find some clothes if this is to be an extended stay.'

Brandonin hummed in agreement. It seemed he hadn't considered that.

'Yes, my Lady. We will try to retrieve attire from somewhere,' said Tellaph.

The old man ushered Vashta and Larinda out of the room, assigning a guard to lead them to their chambers. It caused hot anger to well within her. She was sure he intended to keep talking to the heir after they'd left, and she was more interested in knowing what was going on than seeing where she was going to sleep.

Larinda glanced at her. 'Don't worry. My brother will fill us in later.'

She hoped she was right.

***

The bunker's guards had to clear rooms for her and Larinda, and that was all they were—rooms. No furniture, no bedding, nothing. A number of them flapped around trying to find something for them to sleep on or some clothing, eventually coming up with one or two items, while Larinda assured them it didn't matter, that they were doing such a stellar job, that they were so helpful, and all the other things she could never think to say.

Vashta's mother had always impressed upon her how important it was to make every worker feel valued for what they did, so she tried to mimic Larinda, but there was so much going on, she felt she was wasting time. So she went to find the heir.

Their chambers were on the second level of this strange, squat building, and she peeked in the rooms as she passed. They were all filled with large metal containers, just as her own chamber had been at first. A glance in one or two confirmed that they contained paper records. Row after row, box after box, container after container. In room after room after room.

They really did take their records seriously!

She went to the entry level and saw Tellaph relaying calm instructions to his workers. She didn't linger, especially as the man's curious gaze burned on her the whole time she passed. She wondered if he'd ever spoken to a Vendel before. Maybe he thought a conversation like that would be a wonderful addition to their history.

'My Lady?'

She turned back to Tellaph once she realised that he was addressing her. 'Yes?' Maybe he was hoping for that interview. Was there a polite way to say no?

'If you're looking for the heir, he has gone to the main records room.' He explained the route to her.

I wonder if I could wander through these corridors forever. Was that his plan? Lose her inside the maze-like interior, so that she was never found again?

She followed his instructions and opened another door, finding the heir sitting amongst a pile of documents. He looked up, blinking, as she entered, before scrambling to his feet.

She cringed. 'Please don't get up. I thought we were past that.'

He shrugged. 'It seemed like the polite thing to do.'

He settled back on the floor, papers strewn around him. 'Looking for anything specific?' she asked.

He pointed to a stack next to him. 'These papers Tellaph had already put aside. He thought they might have some record of the creatures in them.'

She picked up two bound leaves on the top. They detailed various native fauna and their habits, also relaying what happened when different species were interbred. 'That's a possibility.'

'Interbreeding?' He looked over her shoulder at what she held. 'Perhaps. I can't think of many of our local creatures who could make up these things, though. And what about the lasers?'

She sat in a corner and flicked through the pages. There were records of parcacks crossed with chummings and some lerkeks crossed with ransims and with grondals, which made her wonder how they could have achieved that without the grondals swallowing the other two whole. Reading that one was an eye-opener.

'I don't think they fly naturally.'

She looked up. Was he talking to her? 'The creatures?'

127

'Did you hear when they were flying next to us? There's a whooshing sound. Perhaps some kind of tech. I'm not sure.'

Her transformed abilities hadn't catalogued it. 'If it is, it's not a weakness.'

He gave her a curious look. 'What makes you say that?'

She bit her lip. How much did she tell him? Why not everything at this point? 'When we transform, we instinctively know our enemies' weak spots and it wasn't brought to my attention, so it's not a useful way to destroy them.'

The light dimmed on his face. 'You couldn't have been mistaken?'

She'd trusted him with this knowledge and he was questioning it? She expected him to squirm under her glare, but he just watched her.

'I know something about your transformational abilities,' he said, 'but I didn't know that.'

Perhaps the Verindal weren't as clever as they thought. 'I'm sure there's a file on it here somewhere.'

He put some papers down and stretched his arms. 'I'll dig it up later. What else did your abilities tell you about the creatures?'

'Their eyes are weaker than anywhere else, but not enough to damage them. That's pretty much it, and, from observational evidence, your new laser guns can kill them. Nothing else.'

'Yes, even your energy fields didn't seem to have much effect.'

That had surprised her more than anything. 'There's not a lot that can stand against that.'

'And that power is borne out of love, isn't it?'

She could feel her face heating up, even though his gaze seemed more curious than anything. 'Yes. If a couple has a true bond of love, they can produce energy together. The energy comes from the joining of their hands and is channelled through the woman. She's the one who releases it.'

He kept his gaze on his fingers as they flicked through some pages. 'So love is important for your race?'

It was the most important thing for a Vendel. The gift of casting energy was the most prized of all their abilities. The greatest efforts were made to find the right love matches for every couple, especially in the court, where strategic and military skills were so vital.

But there was no one for her. Erleph had assured her she didn't have to cast energy; that her skills could be enough without it. But she was unable to quell a tiny voice that shrieked she had to do it. She couldn't let her sisters shine where she did not.

It was ridiculous. It was a mirror of Mestitha's pettiness. She had to be better than that.

'It is,' she said. 'Every Vendel searches for the right person, in the hope that they will have that ability.' Just thinking about it made her depressed.

Brandonin slumped. 'I wish it was more that way for us ... or at least, for me.'

The defeated look on his face drew her interest. 'Love isn't that important for the heir?'

'No, especially since we must select from a small group. All members of the elite, of course, the daughters of people of high standing.'

So they married for political expediency. She remembered hearing something about that in her studies. It had seemed so academic then, but looking at his face, it seemed more like a life sentence. 'That doesn't seem fair.'

He looked resigned. 'That's life as the heir.'

She felt a surge of sympathy for him that made her think of Mestitha. Was being the heir to the throne—whether Vendel or Verindal—as prestigious as everyone thought? But she tried to think of what cage might hold her sister prisoner and came up with nothing. Mestitha had never seemed to do anything other than glory in her position.

This man was not like her sister. He was more like her father. Ruling well, or planning to at any rate, when he took the throne. 'Your father wouldn't allow you to make your own choice?'

'It's not unheard of, but it doesn't happen very often,' Brandonin conceded. 'Anyway, I have more pressing concerns than who I get to bond with.'

'I hope he's still alive.' The words shocked her even as they came out, but they were true.

He gave her a puzzled look.

'Your father,' she said. 'I hope he's still alive ... for you.' That was the only reason it seemed important.

'So do I.' He glanced at her. 'I know he hasn't been the best ruler, not when dealing with your people anyway, but everything ... I mean the little that was compassionate in him died with my mother. She tempered his worst impulses.'

His mouth turned down as he spoke, as if he was trying to hold in his sadness. What a terrible loss! While Vashta and her mother didn't have much of a relationship, she knew how empty she would feel if she lost her, especially if it had happened when she was a child. 'How old were you when she died?'

He cleared his throat. 'Ten. It was harder for Larinda. She was nine. And a girl and her mother ... Father did what he could, which wasn't much, I guess. It was hard.'

Vashta felt a throb of pain for what he'd endured in losing their mother, especially with a tyrannical father as their only comfort. But although hatred of the overlord streaked through her, she couldn't shake the thought of the evil her own race desired to unleash on the Verindal. How could she despise this man's father given what her sister was planning?

'Family,' she said. 'Sometimes we hate them even while we love them.'

He chuckled. 'That's true.' He stood up and reached for more files, bringing a new stack down. 'Here, you might like these. You never know, they might help.'

She opened the top one. 'What are they?'

'Battle histories. Maybe we fought these creatures long ago.'

She used to think the words 'battle' and 'history' would combine to make something wonderful, but that was before she'd been drilled on endless lists of dates, names and places. Now, the thought of reading them put her to sleep. She dropped the pile with a groan. 'I'm not much of a one for history.'

He cocked his head. 'Really? I love it.' He opened a page and thrust it before her. 'See? This is a record from one of Overlord Ardon's troops who fought in the Battle of Crestwood when he deposed his sister.'

She took it from him and cast her mind back. She couldn't remember ever having heard of that battle. 'When was this?'

'About three hundred years ago. It's a copy; the original fell to pieces.'

She picked it up again and leafed through it.

We have engaged every newcomer to Crestwood and have put them through their paces. There are few left who are able-bodied enough to fight who Overlord Milina hasn't already broken in her own vile battles. However, the Vendel amongst us brings out the best in each, once they learn to trust him.

She looked up, seeking his gaze. 'Our people were working together?'

He nodded. 'I love that story. You don't know it? It's a classic tale of our two races combining forces to end the fighting by taking on the ruler who forced them into it.'

She turned her attention back to the page, burying her mind in the battle and delighting in every detail that this unnamed warrior relayed. Why hadn't she heard of this? Or had she, and it had just been in the mind-numbing list of things she'd tried so hard to memorise? Just another name, just another place; so easy to forget. Why hadn't her teachers given her stories like this one? Even Erleph preferred to use detailed instructions on battle techniques, rather than tales from the warriors themselves. It was like a living, breathing soldier was in front of her, unlocking the secrets of a battle.

When she finished reading it, she rifled through the files for more. Brandonin handed her another. 'Ever heard of the Battle of Telleran?'

Yes, she had.

'An actual account from the overlord who fought your people. His own words, including the details of his treaty with your chief prince.'

She could feel shock pricking her. Did her people even know

about this? And the crumbling pages before her with their curled writing were original. 'He wrote this himself?'

He grinned. 'He did. I'd imagine it's biased towards our side, but you might still find it entertaining.'

He wasn't wrong. For the next three maxispans, she and the heir passed documents back and forth, breathing in the history of their planet. Although there were few accounts that painted the Vendel in a good light, Vashta was surprised at how much shared history there was. It filled her heart with joy.

Could this work? Could there be an alliance between their people? In spite of Mestitha? In spite of Brandonin's father?

Maybe there could.

CHAPTER FOURTEEN

'I'm going with you.'

Brandonin let out a weary sigh. He'd been expecting this. He'd just managed to convince Tellaph that he should be the one to try and contact Nestor, who the archivist had discovered was still alive, although his lab had suffered significant damage in the attack.

Fortunately for them, he'd moved to a smaller location outside the palace but still close enough to make everyone nervous when Brandonin insisted on going. And if that wasn't bad enough, Princess Vashta had decided she needed to accompany them.

He looked around at the three members of Tellaph's guard he'd chosen to go with him. 'Your Highness, I think we'd be better doing this alone.'

Her eyes cut into him like lasers. 'My *Lord*, I'm not going to be a burden, am I?' She pointed to the brand-new sugar canisters strapped to her belt, the belt barely holding up the way-too-large pants they'd found for her.

She wouldn't be able to fight much with her trousers falling around her ankles but the thought of telling her that made him blush … and think of things he shouldn't be thinking. Of her and him and what could happen between them … if she wasn't a Vendel. Thoughts like that had been flaring up a lot in the past few days as they'd spent time together in the archives, searching for anything that could help them win this battle. He'd spent more time fighting off his feelings than fighting their enemies.

And it wasn't like she didn't have the skills. She was a more effective fighter than anyone else in their squad. But he still resisted. 'Larinda isn't going.' He looked to his sister for support.

She gave him a laughing look. 'Don't bring me into this.'

A different tack, then. 'I haven't been seen in public since the attack and if we're seen together, people may think we're trying to kidnap Nestor for our own nefarious purposes.'

'Yes, they might.' Vashta stood, hands on hips, unsatisfied.

His desire to keep her safe battled with his instincts. He gave a shrug of assent. 'Nestor's new lab is here.' He pointed out its location on the pathfinder and looked up at Gisel, who was responsible for getting them there. 'Are you sure there's a route that's discreet enough?'

Gisel was head bunker guard—not a prestigious position—but she'd been stationed there because she'd once told Loora she was unqualified to be on the council. He was grateful that she was forthright; not only could he count on her to tell him what he needed to hear with no fear of injuring his royal sensibilities, the woman had arms like trunks.

She looked at the map. 'I can't be sure, my Lord, as we never know when or where the next attack will be, but the route I've planned should get us there. We'll take Tellaph's roller to here,' she pointed to the map, 'then we should be able to leave it and walk the rest of the way.'

It was only a distance away. 'Let's go.'

***

Tellaph's roller was a nondescript vehicle with tinted windows, a blessing Brandonin was thankful for as they manoeuvred through the streets.

It broke his heart to see how quiet this usually bustling area of Intersiss was. The people were fleeing the city, which was a good thing given the focus of the attacks. However, there were fewer defences further out; nothing to protect them if the fighting followed. And it would eventually.

They parked the roller in a deserted side street. Only a few scuttling lerkeks witnessed them leave the vehicle and make their way towards their destination.

Gisel went in front, her firearm at the ready. He wanted to go next but Mognul, another guard, insisted that he walk in front of him. Brandonin didn't like to force the issue. But he objected to Nenan, the third guard, going after him, leaving Vashta to bring up the rear.

'Nenan, I think it would be better if—'

The guard, a burly man with skin that looked weathered to perfection, jutted out his chin. 'Your safety is more important, my Lord.'

He folded his arms. 'And why is that?'

Nenan looked back and forth between Brandonin's stern face and Vashta's blazing one, his expression moving from steadfast to confused to contrite in a matter of microspans. 'All right.' He gestured to Vashta. 'My Lady?'

The heat left her face. 'Don't worry. Transformed, I'll be faster than all of you. I *should* go last.'

Brandonin fixed his gaze on her. 'Vashta …'

As expected, she wouldn't back down. 'Don't you want me to protect your backs? I'll be able to sense the enemy's movements. I'll know where to strike. I'll put my hand out and will instinctively find the closest weapon. I'll—'

Brandonin sighed. 'Yes, we all know how safe you are when you're in that zone.'

She smirked. 'A reminder doesn't hurt.'

At least Nenan didn't goad her into giving a demonstration.

Soon they could see the palace. The upper levels had toppled. The lower parts were still standing, but he could see damage on every level, some stairways left open and exposed. Was Father still there? Little had been seen of him since the attack, except in one public broadcast where his shaking form had tried to reassure his people that all was being done to defeat the menace. Brandonin had taken comfort in the fact that he hadn't called it 'the Vendel menace'. But he still hadn't dared contact his father, especially now he, the heir to the Verindal throne, was allied with a Vendel princess.

Gisel slowed. 'That's it.' She gestured to a small building that had received slight damage in one of the sorties. It wasn't much different from the other buildings that surrounded it—low and white with a flat roof—but this one was two stories, unlike most of its neighbours, which was probably why Nestor had chosen it. Unlike the other structures they'd passed, he could hear the slight hum of voices droning from within.

Gisel hurried across the street, pressing herself against the wall. They all followed, hugging the building.

'How do we get in?' Vashta whispered.

'Down here.' Gisel led them down a narrow path along the side. Brandonin felt safer there, out of the view of the main street. He wouldn't have put it past Nestor to have set up a vision taker outside. Sure enough, there was a dome on the side of the building that looked suspicious … 'I think we might be about to have company.'

Every weapon was hefted as they crept forward step by step. As they reached the door, it was thrust open.

'My Lord!' It was Nestor himself. The armourer had his arms spread open wide in greeting. 'We thought you were dead!'

'I'm on a secret mission from the overlord,' Brandonin said, hoping there were no lie detectors within range of his voice. 'Please let us in.'

'Of course, of course.' Nestor stepped aside and gestured that they pass him. They all hurried in. Brandonin noticed the armourer's gaze linger on Vashta, but he said nothing.

Just inside the door were several armed guards. They started to raise their weapons when they saw a Vendel princess, but he scowled at them. 'She is an ally helping us in our fight. I'm on a secret mission from the overlord.' All the guards were men. Good. No one would know that wasn't true.

The entryway was dark but quickly opened up into a wider space filled with artificial light, as the windows had all been blocked. Brandonin looked around, impressed.

It hadn't taken Nestor long to settle in. Weapons of every sort were laid on all available surfaces and it looked like he was adapting them all for use against their new enemy. His people crowded around the small space, working as well as they could without jostling the person next to them. From what he could see, much of the best equipment from the palace had been salvaged. That was a positive sign. Perhaps the enemy hadn't recognised the importance of it.

Or perhaps they'd realised it couldn't stop them.

He killed that thought before it could wind like a slippery snervel into his mind. Even if Nestor hadn't thought up the solution yet, he would keep going until he did.

The workers stopped, looking at him in shock and offering respectful bows. Nestor came to his side. 'My Lord, I can't tell you how relieved I am to see that you're alive and well.'

'Yes, but please don't breathe a word to anyone about seeing me.' Brandonin raised his voice to make sure no one missed his words. 'It's vital to our survival.'

Nestor blanched but nodded. 'Of course, my Lord. Anything to win this fight.'

Brandonin put a hand on the armourer's shoulder. 'Is there somewhere we can talk?'

'My office. Right this way.'

He glanced at his companions. Vashta moved to join him, but he turned to the others. 'Wait down here.'

They bowed and Gisel gave him a significant look. He knew they would be listening more than they talked.

Nestor led them up the flight of stairs and Brandonin wasn't surprised to see the side of each stair loaded with equipment. His curiosity was piqued and the armourer blushed. 'We don't have much space and left the palace in a hurry. There hasn't been time …'

He had many questions about the state of the palace, the state of the high family, the state of everything, really. But he kept his mouth shut until they reached the office and the door was closed behind them. It was a simple room with a wooden door, something that wasn't going to keep their voices in. Vashta must have realised it too, as she took up station there to listen for prying ears, he assumed. Either that, or she wanted to guard it. Fortunately, the window was blocked.

Nestor gestured to Brandonin to take his own chair, which was not cluttered with weapon parts, unlike the table and much of the floor. This time, he didn't look apologetic when he noticed the direction of Brandonin's stare. 'As you can see, my Lord, we are busy constructing as many weapons as possible.' He picked up the butt of a gun and cradled it. 'We have made numerous small-scale assembly points. I felt it would make it harder for the Arctals to find us.'

That caught Brandonin's interest. 'The Arctals?'

'Yes, my Lord. Since the attack, Ivanna has been able to intercept some of the enemy communications. From what I understand, she's still trying to translate them, but one word mentioned seems to be the name of the creatures attacking us.'

'She's safe also?'

'Yes, my Lord.'

Nestor was telling him the latest intel unreservedly, rather than assuming he already knew, as his position as heir to the throne would dictate. Did he trust this man enough to tell him the truth?

Yes. 'I am not here on any secret mission.'

Nestor's expression didn't change. 'Yes, my Lord.'

'We escaped from the palace and didn't return. I felt it was better …'

'Your father is still listening to Loora, my Lord.'

He hadn't expected Nestor to know *that* much.

'At least, we assume so. He seems … broken.' Nestor's face grew serious. 'It may be because of the absence of his children. At least, that's what Ivanna suspects.'

'I see.' The news cut him, but it wasn't unexpected. However, he could do nothing to help his father yet. The lives of everyone on the planet were at stake.

He didn't want to label Loora a traitor, so he chose his words with care. 'Are you reporting to my father?'

Nestor looked as though someone had just confiscated his favourite firearm. 'Only Loora takes messages to him.'

'You are supplying her with updates?'

'The overlord knows we are creating more weapons, but he doesn't know all.' He shot an accusing look at every section of the room as if expecting to find spies in its cramped corners. 'We don't trust that word will get to him.'

'We?'

He nodded. 'Ivanna, Commander Lissia and a few senior advisors. Everyone is aware that something is amiss.'

His heart lightened. He wouldn't need to convince everyone to join him. They were already setting themselves up as separate entities. And now he had a place to unite them. He leant forward. 'Then get word to them. I have a new headquarters.'

CHAPTER FIFTEEN

It was interesting to contrast the differences in the Verindal system with the way the Vendel did things.

Meetings, organisation, behaviour and everything else was almost identical to what Vashta was used to, just a bit more high tech. Not for the first time, she wondered why in the skies their races were at war.

She, Brandonin and Larinda were so busy they rarely used their tiny rooms. Not many people went up there, if you didn't count the guards Brandonin insisted must be stationed nearby to protect them. She passed one as she walked down the bunker stairs and he nodded to her. Although they'd glared at her as though she was an Arctal for the first week, four weeks on there was mutual respect and, she hoped, trust.

The next level down, the ground floor, was their meeting room, as well as the eating and recreation rooms (not that there was much time for either of those). Brandonin was already there, readying himself for their latest gathering. His face brightened as he saw her. 'We should be ready to start soon.'

'Is Commander Lissia here yet?'

'No, but she's on her way. We'll commence as soon as she arrives.'

'And Nestor?'

Brandonin grinned. 'He's downstairs already.'

That had been a revelation. When she'd first entered the building, she hadn't realised that, in addition to what she could see, there were more levels of archive storage under her feet. Most of the records had been crammed into other rooms to make space for Nestor's toy room and Ivanna's lab.

It had resulted in a change of venue for the almost daily exploration that she and Brandonin led, searching to see if they could find any inspiration for their battle in the dusty historical documents. Although they found plenty that was interesting, there was still nothing that was useful in this kind of fight. How could they defeat such an enemy?

She flopped down in the chair next to him. 'Do you think there'll be anything new today?'

He leant back, rubbing his temples. 'I hope so. We can't keep waiting for something to happen or we might not act until it's too late.'

Vashta looked at the tired lines around his eyes. 'Are you sleeping?'

He smirked. 'There's no time for silly little things like that.'

'There's no sense in you wearing yourself out. You're not going to be as effective a leader if you're not thinking straight.' *I sound just like Mother when she used to …*

Brandonin seemed amused. 'I think there are sufficient minds here to make up for any mental blanks on my part.'

She gave him a gentle glare. 'Nothing makes up for your mind and you know it.'

'I think your mind is its equal.'

For some reason, the look he gave her made her face heat up. That had been happening a lot lately. *Best not to let on.* But that was getting harder. She caught herself leaning towards him and drew back. 'Well, yes, but your people aren't that inclined to listen to me, are they?'

He laughed; something she'd didn't hear often from him. 'But they should.'

Again, her body drew itself towards him. 'Do you think we'll have time for some more research later on?'

'I hope so.' The look in his eyes held her fast. 'I think we need to pursue it until we find an answer, don't you?'

'Absolutely.' And even if they didn't, it was amazing how much they had discovered about their joint history. The more they could reveal, the more they could convince others that there could be peace between Vendel and Verindal.

He reached out towards her, to her hand. Hers seemed to inch towards his of its own accord. She didn't try to stop it.

They both snatched their hands away as Nestor bounded through the doorway waving an enormous firearm, which gleamed a shiny ebony in the light. She hoped Nestor was too distracted to notice the red on the heir's face.

He was. His face lit up with delight as he held out the weapon to her. 'What do you think?'

She took it from him, glad of the distraction, marvelling at how light it was, considering its size. 'How many will it take down at once?' She held it up, her vision narrowing to slits as she looked through the sights.

She was surprised and a little disgusted when Nestor dived to the floor. She lowered the gun. 'I do know how to use a firearm.'

Colour returned to his face as he stood up. 'Sorry.'

She heard a chuckle from behind her and saw Brandonin trying to stifle his laughter. 'It's an automatic reaction for Nestor to dive out of the way of an armed Vendel.'

She knew the heir well enough by now to take no offence at his words, although she gave Nestor an even more withering look.

Gisel came to the door and bowed. 'My Lord, Commander Lissia has arrived.'

Brandonin nodded. 'Then we'll begin. Call Larinda and tell her we're ready.'

***

The first part of the meeting proceeded the same way they did every time. Commander Lissia updated Brandonin on the fighting. Nestor updated him on the latest weaponry. They hadn't been expecting Ivanna to join them that morning, but she had, even though she had nothing new on the Arctals. 'Most of my studies have already unearthed all I feel is of benefit to us in our battle against them.'

'Like the fact that their ability to fly seems to be via the aid of an artificial device? Is there any more intel on what it is?' Vashta asked.

The scientist shook her head. 'No, and we've been unable to find a piece of one, even though we've gained access to more bodies through various combat situations. I believe it may be designed to self-destruct when the wearer perishes. We've found some traces of a peculiar metal, but nothing of any substance.'

'Nothing new, then.' Larinda sighed.

'Nothing useful, my Lady,' said Ivanna.

'Anything could be useful,' said Commander Lissia with a frown.

But Ivanna wasn't the vague I'm-only-interested-in-test-tubes-and-DNA type. She bristled at the commander's tone. 'Well, I've discovered that they lay eggs rather than give birth to live young and that they can only get pregnant every seventh year and none of the females I examined are close to that cycle.'

'How far out of it are they?' asked Brandonin, where he sat to her left. He was making his usual notes on a pad. She knew Larinda would type them up for him later. She was the only one who could read his writing.

'The ones I've seen are all three years away, as close as I can tell.'

'So about the middle of the cycle?'

'Perhaps they wait until then before they go into battle,' Vashta mused.

'Could they be considering this a new breeding ground?' Brandonin asked. 'Another three years would give them enough time to raze the planet for their own use.'

Ivanna's mouth turned down. 'Sorry, my Lord. I can tell you what's going on in their bodies, not their minds.'

He turned back to the commander. 'And there hasn't been an increase or change in the attacks?'

'No, my Lord. They continue to attack and withdraw. I know the palace is expecting another attack at some point.'

Vashta was about to ask the question when Brandonin beat her to it. 'Have there been any more attacks on the Vendel?'

Commander Lissia pursed her lips. 'It's difficult to tell, especially since we're so involved in our own defence. They don't appear to be suffering any more than we are, although attacks are continuing in Vendel-inhabited areas.'

She makes us sound like an infestation.

Brandonin's fingers drummed a single tattoo on the desk. 'If they're suffering as much as we are, it's enough.'

He was right about that. Attacks had continued throughout the city. They had heard, felt and seen the Arctals swooping down to the planet's surface before departing, leaving destruction behind. The only thing that had prevented them from being attacked was the apparent insignificance of this flat, grey box of a building.

But Vashta knew better than to think it would last. She turned to Nestor. 'What progress is being made on security for this place?'

'We've been fortunate with the advances in technology we've made since finishing our new weapons.' He tapped on his computer's console, revealing a picture of the building on the image caster. A faint line appeared around it. 'This is a prototype of a shield that should protect us from an attack. When it's on a low level, which we're planning to have as a constant operating procedure, it will reduce any energy or technology signatures emanating from here, which should prevent the Arctals from showing any interest in it. And should this area come under imminent attack, I have designed a stronger shield which should repel them.'

Brandonin looked around the table. 'Is there anything else?'

'There is one more thing I'd like to mention, my Lord,' said Lissia.

'Yes?'

The commander's expression hardened before she continued. 'One of our spies has brought a message purported to be for the Princess Vashta.'

There was no doubt in Vashta's mind who it was from. 'Erleph?'

Lissia's gaze bored into hers. 'It's unsigned.' She unfolded a piece of paper, handing it to Vashta.

Your Highness,

Your sister's plans are moving forward. We have no idea whether it will work. We need to find out.

'Is it from Erleph?' the heir asked.

'Yes.' She'd been expecting a message from him since she'd arrived. And it was what she would expect—it didn't say what he wanted her to do. He expected her to work it out. 'He wants to give you the plans for Blassin's device to assess whether or not it works.'

She didn't like the way the commander looked at her. Vashta was sure she'd love to find out it worked perfectly. 'But the note doesn't say that. It hardly says anything.'

She sniffed. 'Not if you know Erleph. This tells me he wants to give it to us.'

Lissia nodded. 'I presume he intends to deliver it?'

'No, he wants me to return to get it.'

Brandonin's head snapped around to meet her gaze. 'There's no need for that. He must be able to get it out of the palace and across the lines.'

'Into the hands of a Verindal? Too risky. If this device does work, how could Erleph be sure they wouldn't deliver it straight to the overlord and Loora? He will only give it to me.'

'He can bring it to the border between our two lands,' the heir objected.

'He may need my help to retrieve it.'

'Why?'

'I don't know. He would have his reasons.'

The heir's eyebrows pulled together. 'If you go back, it could mean a battle. You may need to kill some of your own people.'

She hadn't considered that. To do such a thing could be giving her sister the proof she needed to declare her a traitor. Would Erleph have thought of that? What would he want her to do?

Nestor came to her rescue. 'Actually, my Lord, before the Arctals began their invasion, I had developed a stun weapon. One blast from it will knock out an individual for up to three maxispans. I had been planning to bring these stun weapons to your attention but work on the new weapon distracted me.'

Vashta turned to him. 'But you have some here that we could use?'

'I do indeed.'

There was no doubt the armourer had his uses, although he could be irritating at times. Vashta could feel the delight on her face, even as

Brandonin's clouded over. 'It's still too dangerous.'

Oh, really? 'May I remind you that I'm a better fighter than—'

He held up a hand to silence her. 'We all know you're a brilliant fighter, but your sister is now your enemy and will think you've betrayed your people. It's not like you'll be unrecognisable on Vendel land. And if news gets to her that you've returned, you'll be arrested and probably worse. I won't hear of it.'

She was astounded by how obstinate he was being; the heir, who was the voice of reason and calm, the let's-discuss-it-sensibly leader. What was wrong with him?

He couldn't think she wanted to go. The thought of returning home made her feel empty; a realisation that hit her with the sting of a cold hand. Had Mestitha poisoned her heart against her homeland to such an extent?

To her annoyance, Larinda spoke up in her brother's defence. 'Brandonin does have a point. If you try to contact your mentor, you'll be arrested. Your sister may be expecting it and keeping him under surveillance.'

'Well, we need to find out what's going on somehow and I can't see any of my people marching up to one of your spies and saying, "Hey, random stranger who hangs around listening in all the time, do you want to know what we're planning?" Not going to happen.'

'She also has a point,' Larinda conceded.

Brandonin stared at the table, his fingers running along its edge before he turned back to Lissia. 'Commander, is there any way we could send a peace envoy of some kind under the guise of helping the Vendel and gaining aid from them? Perhaps Vashta could go with them, hidden as much as possible, and infiltrate the palace that way.'

The commander pondered that. 'I can't see why they would accept it, but it's the only way we could get her or anyone else close enough to find out what's going on. It would need to be someone of high rank, though, and we can't ask anyone from your father's court.'

'I know. That's why it's going to be me.' Brandonin declared.

Everyone else shot to their feet.

'My Lord, you can't put yourself into such a dangerous situation.'

'No, my Lord. The Vendel would take pride in capturing you.'

'Brandonin, remember that you need to rule. Father's no longer capable of it.'

'It's too great a risk.'

The heir sat still until the chatter died down. 'Are we all done?'

'Why would you risk yourself like that?' said Vashta.

His face was calm. 'Because it's the only way to get you in. Will they open the gates for anyone less?'

'They would open them for me,' Larinda said. 'What's more, it would be less suspicious if I went. We might even be able to keep it quiet. But if you go, it will get back to Father, and then what do we do? Is that what you want, Brandonin?'

His expression hardened. 'I *will* be the one to go.'

Larinda directed a piercing stare at him. 'Tell me why you think you're the best person for this role.'

He looked like a stubborn child as he folded his arms and pressed his lips together.

His sister glanced at Vashta, but she shrugged. She'd developed a great deal of respect for the heir these last few weeks. She had no idea what was making him so petulant, but she was starting to think Larinda did. And if his stormy expression was anything to go by, he knew that she knew. *Are they going to share it or is it a brother/sister thing?*

Larinda straightened. 'Can I have a word with the heir alone, please?'

Brandonin rose from the table. 'There will be no discussion. Commander Lissia, make arrangements for this meeting to go ahead. Try and keep my involvement secret if you can. If not, we'll work around it. Find us a way in and out, and a way to hide Vashta and her guard—'

'I do *not* need a guard!'

He didn't even glance in her direction. 'So they won't be discovered. I assume you can find your way once you're inside?'

'Of course I can,' Vashta spat. 'I've lived there all my life. You'll be lucky if I don't stay behind.' She pivoted on her heel and stormed out of the room. Apparently, she was not required, and if plans were going to be made around her, she wasn't going to stand there and watch.

Her fingers burned with the desire to fight something, anything. Why couldn't they have included a training room in this place? She battled the urge to revenge herself on Brandonin by mimicking his behaviour—being just as petulant as he was.

In the end, she sat on the stairs and watched as everyone filed out of the meeting room one by one until only Larinda and Brandonin remained. Vashta could hear voices coming from within but couldn't make out the words. Soon Larinda, her face as stormy as her brother's had been, moved towards the stairway. She didn't see Vashta until she nearly stepped on her. But rather than stomp past, she swung down to sit beside her. 'You should go in and talk to him.'

That was a surprise. 'You think I'll succeed where you failed? Who am I?'

Larinda gazed at her long and hard, and Vashta was at a loss to decipher what flitted across her face. Then the girl sighed. 'You're right. I don't think any of us are going to change his mind. I mean, I understand … but he should too. He's always put the people first.'

'What's stopping him doing that now?' Brandonin's dedication to serving his people was one of the things she admired most about him. It reminded her of her father.

Again, Larinda's glance puzzled her. 'It doesn't matter. None of it does. He's going to go.'

'What will you do?'

Larinda curled up just as Meeka did when she was afraid of getting into trouble. 'I'll stay here and hope I won't have to become the heir in his place.'

CHAPTER SIXTEEN

As everyone else filed out of the meeting room, Brandonin avoided Larinda's gaze.

She knew what the problem was, of course. And if she asked him, what good would it do to deny it? She could tell he was lying. But that didn't mean he was going to make it easy for her. This whole mess was a nightmare anyway. Why make things simple?

'So are you going to acknowledge the real reason you're shirking your responsibilities to the people?'

He tried not to flinch. That was low. And she was right, but he didn't care. He looked down at his notes, hoping she'd give up and follow everyone else out.

She leant over him, demanding his attention. 'Brandonin, if you're going to risk leaving me to rule, then I would appreciate it if you were honest with me.'

He refused to even consider that. 'I'm sure I'll be fine.'

She sat in her chair, swivelling to face him. 'No one would ever fall for a lie that bad. You have no idea what will happen. I mean, I'm sure you *hope* you'll be fine.'

'We'll be able to get in and out without too much trouble.'

She jumped up and walked to the other side of the table, folding her arms. 'Will you stop lying to me? Please, just acknowledge that the reason you want to go is so you can protect Vashta.'

He couldn't acknowledge it aloud. It was stupid, ridiculous. Vashta didn't need his protection. She was going to break into her home, a place as familiar to her as his own palace, seek out an intelligent mentor who was planning for her visit, and get some plans they probably had ready for her. If anything, him being there would make things worse.

But he couldn't let her go without him. Her presence beside him had been almost constant for the past few weeks, always listening, always picking up things he'd missed, homing in on the minutiae that slipped by in the never-ending stream of information that assaulted him. Then there were their times together in the archives, cramming themselves into ever smaller rooms where boxes were stacked to the ceiling, squeezing their way through the maze of files.

He didn't know what Larinda saw on his face, but it must have communicated his torment because her voice softened. 'I understand why that makes you want to go, even though it's senseless. You know she's more likely to survive than you. If anything, she'll be the one doing the rescuing.'

She sat on the table near him, trying to meet his eye. He didn't even have the courage to give her that. 'Knowing you, I'm sure you've considered the difficulties that are going to arise given that you ... care for a Vendel.'

He shot to his feet. 'I don't care for her. I mean, I do, but not in the way you mean.'

Her gaze was steady. 'Do you even know you're lying?'

'I'm not lying!'

'Yes, you are, Brandonin. I'm sorry, but your words just sounded off in my mind. I'm a lie detector, and I know you well. You care about Vashta.'

He dropped back into his chair, trying not to slump in defeat. He needed to appear in control. But that's all it was—appearance. He couldn't make it real.

She gave up and turned to the door. 'She's nice, I'll give you that. I should have guessed you'd do something like this, if only for the challenge.'

He waited until the door closed behind her.

Was she right? Did he care for Vashta? Of course he cared for her; he knew that. But he also knew what Larinda meant went beyond appreciation for an intelligent woman.

150

He couldn't love a Vendel. The thought was ridiculous. They were different species. Officially, anyway. They were still compatible in every way that mattered. But a relationship between the two of them would never be acceptable to either of their races, and that should be enough to make him clamp down on these feelings until they faded away. Nothing could ever come of it.

He marched out of the room and down the corridor, pleased that no one challenged him or presented him with reports, messages or forms to authorise.

He took a side passage to one of the smaller rooms that had once stored extra furniture and now stored priceless records—records thrust aside to make room for an armoury, a lab and countless personnel.

The room he entered was small and dark, with a musty smell that lingered over the boxes. Had he and Vashta explored this one yet? He didn't think so. He climbed up the stack of metal containers, right to the top. He lifted the lid and pulled out a wad of papers. '*The Poetry of Bantern Sonna,*' he read aloud. 'Not in a poetic mood today.'

'Then what mood are you in?'

He had to grab the side of the box to keep from falling off.

'Sorry,' said Vashta. 'I thought you'd heard me come in.'

He straightened the box and tried not to look flustered. 'No.'

'Then who were you talking to?'

'Myself. Or the ghosts.'

She looked around them. 'The ghosts?'

'Yes. The ones who live in these boxes. Ghosts of the past.'

She smirked. 'And you're not in a poetic mood today.' She pulled herself up to his level, using the boxes as a ladder. She leapt onto the top one and crawled along to get at the stacks behind.

'Careful,' he said. 'I'm not sure how stable these are.'

'You did it first.' She reached out and pulled the lid off another box.

'That's true.' He wondered how often he put himself at risk and tried to stop others doing the same. And why did he do it? Maybe because others always did it to him. It was an occupational hazard; people liked to make sure you stayed alive when you were the heir …

on his side of the line, anyway.

She handed him a file. 'This one looks interesting.'

'*The Sacrifice of Cratina Olleron.*' It could be inspiring.

Vashta settled on top of a box, her legs crossed, her head bent over a file. He crawled over to where she sat—not that there was far to go in the cramped room—and sat beside her.

She tried to stretch her legs out but there wasn't much space and the boxes beneath them moved a little. They both froze until their perch settled.

'Here, lean against me,' she said, putting her back to him. 'There's more space that way.'

The heat of her back against his set every nerve ending on fire. Suddenly Cratina's sacrifice didn't seem that important.

'So are you going to tell me what Larinda said?'

'No.' Definitely not going there.

'If it's about me, I'd like to know.'

'It's not about you ... exactly.'

He felt her shift. She didn't believe him. 'I think I deserve to know.'

'I'm sorry. I can't tell you.' There was no point. And what would he say anyway? That he wanted to go to make sure she was safe, even though there was no way he could guarantee that? Even though he'd be a prime target?

He had grown up wanting to protect people—his mother, his sister, his people. And if he was in love with this woman, then he would want to protect her too. He couldn't stop himself. It was part of who he was. Whether she needed it or not.

But she jumped to the wrong conclusion. 'I can do it, you know. I've been trained for this. I passed my hand-to-hand combat assessment with the highest marks of any of my sisters. I passed my flight combat assessment with exemplary marks, which is more than I can say for Meeka, and Mestitha wouldn't know one end of a flier from another. Even Lara's final marks paled in comparison with mine. I—'

'Vashta,' he said, silencing her tirade. 'It's not that. I don't doubt your abilities in any way.'

Silence reigned as she processed that. 'You don't?'

'No. You've more than demonstrated how capable you are. No one here could doubt it.'

'Oh.'

Her voice was small, vulnerability leaking through. Did she really think she needed to prove it? He'd never given her a reason to believe that he considered her incapable. 'Why would you think that?'

She sighed. 'I'm sorry. I'm just used to … You've no idea how hard it is, being the fifth of five princesses. No one expects very much. You talked about how you're required to bond with someone more or less chosen for you. Well, I'm expected to not be all that remarkable. There are only certain futures that I can draw on, none that are interesting. I don't want to be forced into that. I want to make a mark … somehow.'

He hadn't considered how difficult it must be to be fifth in line. He knew it was challenging enough for Larinda being second, but she still had prominence, especially because she was such a skilled lie detector. But the fifth of five women with similar talents, similar beauty, similar fates? 'Vashta, anyone who thinks you're not worth anything isn't paying attention. You've more than demonstrated how skilled you are, how intelligent, how essential.' He peeked over his shoulder at her. 'Your value shines through.'

He could feel her shoulders straighten against his back and his heart sang with the thought that he could make her feel a little lighter.

'But you still don't want me to go.'

That was the crux of the matter. 'No.'

He knew she wanted to know why but he couldn't bring himself to tell her. Having said everything he had, he would run the risk of stripping his words of the strength they'd given her if she knew the truth. They sat for maxispans in the quiet room, passing files back and forth, saying nothing. The silence both comforted and judged him.

***

Brandonin was engulfed in childhood memories when he climbed in the back of the heavy-duty roller.

He'd always loved the covered vehicles that brought goods to the palace. As a boy, he'd haunted the kitchen when a shipment was due just so he could see what delights were produced from its tray—sweetmeats, breads, milk. Or it might be new furniture, as his mother had always been redecorating. Or equipment for Nestor.

It seemed strange that he was now the goods being shipped. Lissia had insisted on using a covered roller so he would be hidden as they passed through the streets of Intersiss.

He looked over at Vashta and Gisel, who were crouched in a corner. A crate sat next to them, strapped to the wall. 'Are you sure you'll both be all right in there?'

Vashta didn't answer. She hadn't spoken much since he'd refused to tell her what was wrong. He didn't know if she was furious or disappointed. Or something else, but he didn't want to consider that. Whatever Gisel felt, she would never have dared refuse to answer the heir. 'Yes, my Lord. There is space for both of us and ample holes to allow air inside.'

He acknowledged her reply but found it hard to concentrate on it, as his eyes were drawn to her companion. Princess Vashta was wearing serviceable clothes and had tucked her hair up as much as possible to try and look inconspicuous. He only hoped they would find her mentor quickly.

He tried to concentrate on his role in this, but he was merely a distraction to allow Vashta sufficient time to do her job. He hoped they wouldn't find her. He'd already run through a multitude of scenarios where she was caught, trying to work out the best way to rescue her. It was difficult when he knew so little about their destination. She would have the upper hand where they were going. But that didn't prevent him from worrying. And it didn't stop his gaze from continuing to drift to her slender frame. He despaired at how often he had to turn his head.

He shifted his mind back to his childhood memories to distract him. But nostalgia wasn't enough to divert his attention from his greatest challenge—making sure he *didn't* fall in love with Vashta.

As they were about to leave Verindal lands, the roller stopped. The swinging door was heaved open, and Mognul peered in. 'My Lord, it's time for you to join us.'

He tried and failed not to let his gaze linger on Vashta. 'Take care, both of you.'

'We will, my Lord,' said Gisel.

He thought she would say nothing, that her head would turn away. But after shooting a look at Gisel, her mouth seemed to crumple. '*You* take care. Don't trust my sister. She'll kill you if she can.'

He put his hand on her shoulder in farewell, but instead of returning the gesture, she laid a hand over his, keeping her gaze averted.

'I'll see you soon.' His words had the seal of a promise he hoped he could deliver.

A platoon of soldiers took his place in the roller. He was moved to a vehicle that befitted a state visit, although he wondered if anyone would notice, given what was happening around them. He also noted that his new roller, although more opulent than most, still had a high degree of protection. He heard the heaviness in the door as it slammed shut and could feel the weight of the vehicle as it sped along. This was no ordinary roller for a far-from-ordinary state visit.

The effect the Arctal invasion had had on Vendel lands couldn't be ignored either. Several times Mognul had to stop so they could move debris from their path. Usually, it was rubble or a fallen tree, but once it was several Vendel males, then a family of twelve, then a group of Vendel women, all dead. And this was supposed to be the safest, least-affected road into the capital. He would have to offer his condolences to the chief princess.

How would Vashta have felt if she'd seen that?

'My Lord,' said Mognul. 'We're approaching a boundary.'

Five Vendel guards stood at a barrier. Their heavy-duty roller pulled up behind them, and he knew the soldiers in it were making a show of their presence lest anyone believe that the heir was only accompanied by a small retinue.

After a brief exchange, they were allowed through, the gate

clanging shut behind them. He hoped they would have little trouble leaving the same way. 'Do you think they were suspicious?'

'Not that I could tell, my Lord.'

'Just because they aren't suspicious doesn't mean the Vendel elite won't be,' Nenan said.

'Thank you for that clarification, Nenan,' Brandonin snapped. But he knew the guard was right.

It was still a few maxispans before they reached the boundaries of the Vendel palace, passing several more checkpoints as they did so. Each stop had an increasing number of soldiers manning it. Brandonin kept calm, at least as far as their curious eyes could see. Nothing would be helped by panicking.

Finally, the Vendel palace came in sight. He had known that an entire level had been destroyed but there was also significant damage to all four of its main towers, and several of the wings adjoining each spire had crumbling debris around them.

He drew in a deep breath as they were waved to a halt by an armed force. There were fifteen of them, which seemed inadequate, given the circumstances. Maybe the Vendel didn't have the forces to spare.

He watched as the heavy-duty roller lumbered to a stop beside his vehicle, closer to the palace wall. He didn't let his gaze linger on it; he'd only wanted to confirm that it was positioned where Vashta had requested. The soldiers who'd ridden in the roller alighted at the same time, so he pretended to cast his eyes over them. Hopefully, the official would think any lingering glance was to check on the platoon he'd brought with him.

The official, who introduced himself as Tremore, nodded to Brandonin but didn't exchange the usual pleasantries. 'We were surprised to hear you were coming, sir,' he said as they began to move into the palace. 'It seemed a trifle dangerous at such a time.'

If it was a warning, Brandonin didn't care. If he was fishing for information, he would get none. That honour would go only to Princess Mestitha, as much as he'd prefer to take her to task for her pathetic example of leadership. His blood boiled at the thought of her treatment of her own family.

Tremore didn't seem troubled by his silence, although he looked around at their company. In spite of the menacing way the two forces regarded each other, it was comical to see all the soldiers trying to fit in the dusty, mangled passages. He made no comment on the damage, noting that it was not extensive in this part of the palace. He assumed that was why the high family were using it.

He was led to a different room from last time. This one was on the level closest to the ground and was small, square and dimly lit. The only furniture within was the throne, which was unoccupied. A few Vendel stood inside, watching him carefully. He assumed they were councillors since Merlina was with them.

He moved out of the way to allow the platoon in and glared at Tremore when he put out a hand to prevent it. Gone was any pretence of civility. 'No enemy platoon in the throne room.'

He held the man's stare. 'If your chief princess was visiting us, would you allow her to enter our throne room alone?'

Tremore's gaze was unwavering but Brandonin knew a thing or two about creating a commanding presence. It wasn't long before the man's stare began to droop under the force of his, and he lowered his hand. 'Only half may enter.'

'All, or I leave here immediately.' He hoped the man wouldn't call his bluff. But it had only been a brief flare of courage on the official's part and he nodded. He wasn't sure how everyone was going to fit in that room with twenty of his elite soldiers surrounding him and the princess's guard yet to make an appearance.

A man appeared and stood to the left of the throne. 'All hail the chief princess!'

The Vendel bowed their heads as their princess entered, dressed in her full royal regalia, accompanied by her attendants, some advisors and another ten soldiers. No other members of her family were present, except her bond-partner, who looked subdued and stood to the right of the throne.

Mestitha looked immaculate, her skin polished to perfection, her clothes neat, covered with rich brocades full of rippling colour. She was the epitome of the royal who wanted her visitors to know how prestigious she was. He could feel his temper rising that she should waste her time with this kind of pointless preening when people of both races were dying on the streets. While he had made sure he was dressed well, he'd shunned the idea of any finery, not that he had much to call upon at his current location. Her extravagance was designed to intimidate him. Or else she was just showing off.

As she made herself comfortable on the throne, she turned up her nose at Brandonin. 'To what do we owe this unexpected and unwelcome visit at such a perilous time for our planet?'

The disrespect in her address did not escape his notice, but he didn't intend to stoop to her level. What's more, he was more likely to succeed if he set her at ease. It helped that he'd worked out the best way to do that. He'd seen enough similar women back home that he knew the best approach when it came to someone as shallow as this.

Flattery. Good, old-fashioned fawning. She'd swoon over it.

'My apologies, Your Great Highness, if my visit was ill-timed. I had heard you had come to the throne and would have come to pay my respects to your father and to congratulate you on securing your reign prior to this, but as I'm sure you understand, we have been trying to combat an invasion.'

Her face was stony. 'Yes, I have heard that you *seem* to be fighting almost as hard as we are.'

He chose to misinterpret the accusation in her words. 'We don't fight as well as the Vendel, but we're doing our best.'

As expected, that threw her off guard. 'You put on a good show.'

He bowed. 'That's quite a compliment, coming from someone of your impressive skills.'

It was refreshing to know that he was speaking to an audience with no lie detectors among them. The fact that both his mother and sister had been excellent at detecting lies had taught him a lot about the most effective ways to bend the truth. This was a skill, it seemed, that Mestitha had had no reason to develop. She seemed confused by his words.

'The reason I'm here is because we have discovered some details about the enemy both our races are fighting and are seeking your help to end this threat.'

She glanced at her advisors. 'Go on.'

'I'm sure you've suffered under the Arctals as much as we have, so we—'

His words caused a stir. He'd decided on the journey which details he could give away. He knew he'd have to give them something in order to hold their interest.

Mestitha's eyes narrowed. 'The Arctals?'

'Yes, Your Great Highness. That is the name of the enemy we face.'

'How do you know this?' challenged one of the advisors. Brandonin didn't recognise him from his last visit.

'We have a team of people who have managed to intercept and translate some of their communications. While we haven't broken them all yet, we're making progress every day.'

'Have you discovered their plans yet?' His words were as direct as laser fire. 'Where will they aim their next attack?'

Brandonin realised he may have made a tactical error. 'Unfortunately, we haven't discovered those details yet.'

There was a glint of satisfaction on Mestitha's face. 'The information you share seems to be selective.'

The councillor jumped on this. 'Yes, isn't it strange that the heir to the Verindal throne knows the name of these creatures but nothing useful about them, like their plans for invasion? But then, perhaps he does know this.'

'Because he *made* those plans. Don't you agree, Councillor Blassin?'

Blassin. So this man was the architect of the weapon that could destroy his entire race. From what Vashta had said, he'd thought Blassin was a low-level scientist, not one of the Vendel elite. That must have changed.

The Vendel soldiers raised their arms, as did his own troops. He signalled to the platoon with him to keep their weapons down. He needed to give Vashta as much time as possible.

'Your Great Highness, I can assure you that I came here to offer you what information we have in the hope of forming an alliance with your people for the good of the entire planet. There's no doubt you're aware of how much our own people are suffering, as are yours. I'm sure you want to spare them this suffering, just as I want to spare mine. As more information about these creatures come to hand, we will share it with you.'

'And yet we hear you've made weapons that are effective against these *Arctals*,' Blassin spat. 'Do you bring any of those for our use? How sincere can your efforts be?'

He needed to keep calm. 'I was not aware the Vendel would be interested in our weapons, given that you are such fine fighters owing to your enhanced abilities. I have seen how effective you can be without weapons. However, if—'

Mestitha rose from her throne and stabbed the air with her finger. 'Yes, when you ambushed members of my family!'

'I apologised for the loss of one of your own and returned him with the full honours of our people. I also made sure the Princesses Illora and Vashta, and Councillor Merlina and her bond partner returned safely. If what I did was not enough, bring your sisters here and I will apologise and seek to make what restitution I can.'

A muscle in Mestitha's cheek twitched. 'They will not be disturbed by someone like you.' Vashta had told him Mestitha wouldn't admit she had disappeared, although Brandonin had wondered if the chief princess might accuse him of kidnapping her.

Vendel hands slid across their weapons. His own guard watched him for the signal to act. He didn't know how much longer he could hold on.

An aide hurried into the room and ran up to Mestitha, whispering in her ear. Brandonin watched as her face turned white. She leapt to her feet. 'Arrest them!'

Vashta must have been discovered. He'd known it might come to this and so had his platoon, but as he looked around, he realised how small their chances of escape were, as every Vendel in the room went into their safe zone, transforming in front of him.

His platoon raised their weapons to fire, but shots rang out from the Vendel soldiers and some of his force began to fall. The enemy approached him, their faces dark and disturbing up close. He saw a couple of his Verindal guard move to rescue him, but they wouldn't be quick enough.

He was thrown against the wall, his head snapping back. Blinking to clear his vision, he saw a beam of light arcing across the crowd, striking down the fighting Vendel.

Meeka and her bond-partner stood in the doorway, aiming their energy at their own people. 'Vendel who were loyal to my father, Chief Prince Liffon, join us and save our kind from ruin!' she declared.

The room was now so full of people it was difficult to move. Mognul stood in front of him, one of his hands on Brandonin's chest, pinning him to the wall, while he took aim with his gun. 'Make sure you don't hit anyone on our side.'

'I'm trying, my Lord, but I can't tell who that is.'

Meeka was at his shoulder. 'Illora told me you were here. We need to leave now!'

His heart felt like ice. 'Vashta's in trouble?'

She rolled her eyes. 'She always is.'

CHAPTER SEVENTEEN

Vashta sat in their hiding place, the only sound the occasional breath from her or Gisel.

It was difficult to forget Brandonin's face when he'd left the roller and the heat of his hand still lingered on her shoulder. She hoped he'd be all right. He would be in the palace, trapped in confined spaces. The odds were against him. He shouldn't have come. But there was no point in worrying about that now. 'I think it's time we went.'

Gisel insisted on waiting a little longer, then she nodded. 'Let's go.'

The back of the roller was locked from the outside, but a trigger had been put in place so that they could open it. Gisel pushed open the door, wincing as it creaked, and peeked out. 'All clear.'

Vashta jumped to the ground and sprinted to the corner of the building, feeling its rough surface slide against her shoulder as she continued, moving on her toes as much as possible. She could hear Gisel behind her.

It had been difficult to guess where on the palace grounds they would be parked, especially since she hadn't known what new damage had been done. She tried not to look at the crumbling walls and the turret that was little more than a pile of rubble. The science lab was just a few corners away.

She reached the edge of the building and took a cautious look. As expected, there were guards in this section, and they were on high alert. She held five fingers behind her so Gisel knew how many they faced.

She had been hoping not to need one of her five sugar canisters straight away, but there was no way she could beat five soldiers without one, even with her Verindal laser pistol. Gisel would be lucky to reach them before she was shot.

At least their lasers had stun functions. Apart from the optics of engaging her own people in a deadly battle, she had no desire to kill a Vendel, especially those who were only doing the bidding of their leader.

She was ready to spring when she felt something land in her hair. She shook it out, realising it was dirt. Where had it come from? She looked up at the top of the wall to see Erleph leaning out a window on the first floor. He held up ten fingers, then disappeared.

Count to ten …

'Guard our backs,' Vashta said.

'I will fight,' the stubborn woman insisted.

'You'll be no use in this fight. Guard our backs.'

Vashta knew her mentor would be ready as soon as she moved. She could already see where he now stood—on the roof above the guards.

She went into her transformed state and launched herself at the guards, shooting as she went. She took one down before diving for cover. The remaining four transformed, but not before Erleph dropped from above and took another out. The distraction allowed her to leave cover, shooting a third as she went. He knocked another unconscious as she shot the final one.

They both came out of their transformation and drank. One can down.

Erleph surveyed their work and looked over Gisel as she joined them. He raised his eyebrows at Vashta. 'They're not dead?'

She held up the weapon. 'Stunned.'

He nodded. 'We need to move.'

He led the way but not towards the lab. Vashta grabbed his arm. 'We're here to get Blassin's device.'

'Of course you are, Your Highness. Isn't that what I instructed you to do? But the lab has been moved.'

He led them inside through a servant entryway, towards where the laundry had once stood. She was delighted to see Illora waiting in an alcove half a length ahead of them. She acknowledged them with a nod.

'We've been busy trying to find as many guards as possible who are disillusioned by Mestitha's behaviour,' said Erleph. 'Fortunately, your sister has made this easy. As soon as we heard the heir was coming, we knew you'd be the reason for that, so Illora arranged for as many of our guards as possible to keep watch over Blassin.'

'So he's now in the laundry?'

Her mentor nodded. 'It's in the middle of the complex and deep down. It's the safest place.'

Vashta sniffed. 'It's a wonder Mestitha hasn't put her quarters down there.'

'She has. But she's greeting the heir, so her rooms are unoccupied at the moment.'

Anger was always her companion when she thought of her eldest sister, but this time it was difficult to control the rising tide of fury. Father would never have hidden in the bowels of the palace like a frightened child.

As they approached the next corner, Erleph held up his hand and they slowed. He peered around the edge before waving them on. Vashta was alarmed when she saw three guards in the passageway, but they gave no reaction when they saw her other than starting with recognition.

Erleph didn't turn his head. 'Keep watch, soldiers.'

At the next corner, he paused longer and, after he'd checked it, Vashta heard a short scuffle before her mentor waved them on. As they rounded the corner, three guards lay unconscious, with two more grabbing the bodies and dragging them away.

The two guards quickly joined them. She felt stronger now, surrounded by her own kind. Had this been left to her and Gisel alone, it would have been difficult to carry out their plan.

One of the soldiers came to Erleph's side. 'Sir, Blassin is not in his lab or his quarters.'

Erleph's expression did not change. 'No, I imagine he's followed the chief princess like the obedient servant he is.' He turned back to her. 'Blassin seems delighted at your sister's faith in him and pays her all the obsequious attention she requires.'

No wonder Mestitha liked him. 'I imagine he's kept busy, then.'

Erleph signalled for silence as they crept along the final corridor.

'I will transform first,' he whispered. 'Vashta, you do the same. You,' he pointed to Gisel, 'would be better staying here. Elestin, you will transform as well. The rest of you, hold in this state unless we need help.'

He peeked around the corner once more before transforming and letting out his battle cry. Vashta sprinted around the corner, passing Erleph, hearing Elestin hard on her heels.

The three guards before them didn't have time to transform before they were taken down. Vashta grasped the door only to see that it had brand new electronic locks that required a code. She searched her transformed mind for it—sometimes information like that came to them when they were in that state—to no avail.

But Erleph was prepared. He tapped on the keypad before swinging the door open.

There were no guards inside, only lab technicians. They had already transformed, but Vashta could tell they were no danger. Her own 'safety zone', as Brandonin had called it, told her what to do to defeat the seven workers. She dived for cover, then sprayed them with stun fire. Her shots took down three of them. Their allies and Illora, now also transformed, subdued the others, dragging their unconscious forms out of the way.

Vashta changed back into her normal self and drank from one of her sugar canisters, the others doing the same.

'Do we know where it is?' Gisel said as she joined them.

Vashta turned to her sister. 'Illora, please tell me you know.'

She clapped her hands on a metal box. 'This is what he's been working on.'

'You're sure?'

She looked disgusted. 'Give me some credit, please.'

'But there'll be plans here as well,' Erleph said, rummaging through the desk.

There were computers there too. She pointed to them. 'Are they the only ones?'

Erleph did a double-take. 'They're new.'

'They aren't anymore.' She aimed her laser at each in turn, smoke and sparks coming from the gaping holes in their panels.

But Erleph was still rummaging through the papers on each desk. Vashta joined him. They found all the notes that seemed to relate to the device, keeping one copy and blasting the rest to ash.

'I think we've got them all,' Illora said.

But Vashta wasn't so sure. 'Wouldn't Mestitha have her own copy of the plans?' She had no doubt that her sister would want them for the sake of insurance, if nothing else.

The others looked uncertain, but Vashta scoffed. 'Of course she would.'

The next door was also locked and sealed with another electronic keypad. Erleph shook his head; he didn't have it. Never mind. There were other ways to get in. She raised her laser and fired.

'Vashta, wait!'

Erleph's warning came too late. As soon as her blast hit the panel, an alarm blared throughout the corridor.

Illora hissed. 'Nice move, sister.'

'How was I supposed to know that would happen?'

'How were we to know you'd want to break into our sister's room?'

'Enough!' Erleph pushed past her and went inside, throwing Mestitha's furniture right and left. 'Illora, contact Meeka and tell her to go to stage two. Vashta's right—your sister could have a copy.'

After sending the guards into the corridor to buy them more time, she, Erleph and Gisel ransacked Mestitha's room. There were no computers, but Vashta took pleasure in tossing her sister's prize possessions around, smashing whatever she could against the wall.

'Keep your mind on your job,' snarled Erleph, before he grunted in satisfaction. 'I think I have it. Let's go.'

But the corridor was no longer silent. Illora raced back towards Erleph. 'I sent Elestin to notify Meeka. Mestitha's forces are coming.'

'Who zones first?' Vashta asked.

Illora looked lost. 'Zones?'

She hadn't realised she'd used Brandonin's term. 'Transforms.'

'You and I will, Vashta. What's your escape plan?'

Not much of one. 'Get back to the roller and drive our way out.'

Illora laughed. 'That's it?'

'We had no idea what we were coming into. If you've got a better plan …'

There was no more time to talk. Several transformed soldiers appeared at the end of the corridor. However, rather than transform, Erleph stepped down a side corridor. They all followed. 'Fire at will.' His voice was deep and slurred.

Fighting in a corridor was to their advantage. The space was only wide enough for three across. She transformed and used the laser to take down all three of the first line of guards while running backwards. Erleph took Gisel's stun weapon and used it to take out a few who'd been behind the others.

They sprinted down several more corridors, Erleph regularly changing direction. She trusted that he knew where he was going and tried to keep her transformed state focused on her surroundings.

Vashta and Erleph came out of the transformation and Illora transformed instead, with Gisel to support her. Vashta glanced at her mentor. Should one of them transform too? But she only had two sugar canisters remaining. Hearing a rumble from behind her, she turned to see more Vendel sealing off their escape. Before she could despair, they transformed and began attacking Mestitha's forces.

'Help has arrived.' Erleph sounded satisfied. 'Let's get out of here.'

They weaved their way through the friendlies and headed for a damaged wall, which allowed them to squeeze their way out into the courtyard. She ran through the rubble until she found their vehicles. There was no sign of Brandonin. He must have realised they'd been discovered. And that could only mean one thing—he'd been captured. 'We need to find Brandonin!' Where had they taken him?

Erleph scowled at her. 'Vashta, calm yourself. I'm sure Meeka has—'

'You trust Meeka to save him?' Her sister had all the tenacity of a bleating ransim. She set off to look for him, diving from cover to cover through what was now continual fire between her eldest sister's forces and her allies, who were retreating. And she was heading into the fray.

That didn't matter. Meeka wouldn't be able to save Brandonin. It probably wouldn't even occur to her to try, since he was only a Verindal. And Vashta couldn't leave him behind.

Over the sound of scorching blasts, she could hear her mentor ordering her to return. She ignored him.

The atrium. I'm sure that's where Mestitha would have held court.

Three transformed soldiers appeared in front of her. Unable to keep from doing it any longer, she transformed and aimed as she dodged their shots. To her surprise, it took longer than expected to take down the three. In fact, the third stubbornly refused to fall. Then he was joined by two more. She rolled to avoid their fire, sheltering behind a statue that had lost its head. She took aim when she could, taking another down, before fleeing to new cover.

Fleeing. Yes, that's what she was doing now. She was retreating. But she had to save Brandonin!

She dived behind a crumbling wall and transformed out, gulping down another canister, before allowing her skills to direct her aim. She took a couple more down, but now there were five of them. She was forced back and realised she was being driven towards the palace, not away from it.

Then she saw Mestitha, her mouth twisted into her favourite triumphant smirk, watching as Vashta was driven towards her. But she had to save the heir. His life was—

'Give up, sister.'

Vashta answered her with laser fire, her sister scrambling out of the way. But she had to come out of her transformed state again and reached for her final canister of sugar. Unless she could find Brandonin quickly, she wouldn't stand a chance.

Her heart sank as she saw Elloran racing to join Mestitha. She saw them link hands and her sister raised her other hand, pointing it in Vashta's direction. Even with her transformed powers, she'd never be able to avoid their charge.

The heavy-duty roller barrelled through the middle of the conflict, sending enemy soldiers flying through the air. With a cry of fury, Mestitha unleashed her charge on it, pushing it towards Vashta until it rolled on its side. But typical of her sister, she couldn't resist continuing her barrage, and the second blast rolled it back on its wheels again.

The cabin door in front of her swung open. 'Get in!' Brandonin yelled.

She dived inside, slamming the door behind her, keeping her head down as he crouched low in his seat to avoid shots.

He kept driving until Mestitha's forces were behind them, the covered back of the roller shielding them from any attack. Brandonin straightened up and slammed down his foot on the pedal, the vehicle surging forward. Rather than steer around obstacles, he went through most of them. Fortunately, the roller was large enough to handle it. But he was headed for the patch of forest on the east side of the palace. She leant over and tried to take control. 'We need to rendezvous with the others.'

She looked at his face for the first time and saw the anger written large there. 'Don't you dare!' he snapped, pushing her away with his shoulder.

'You're going the wrong way!'

'I don't know if you noticed, but the other way is blocked by enemy fire.'

'But this won't work.'

'Don't tell me what to do!' he roared.

She shrank back. He'd never raised his voice like that before. Any louder, and he'd drown out a Vendel battle cry. She sat and fumed until he drove into a field just near the forest. *Like that's going to do any good.*

He stopped the roller there and, unable to stand the tension in the cab, she leapt out and slammed the door, heading back towards the road. He was right behind her. 'Don't go off like that. We've got to get out of here!'

'And we're going to make it when we're on the wrong side of the palace, aren't we?'

'Vashta, you—'

But she was sick of listening. 'Don't speak to me like that. Why weren't you where you were supposed to be? Haven't you heard of a plan?'

'I wasn't the one who tried to take your sister down rather than *sticking* to that plan.'

'I wouldn't waste my time trying to take down Mestitha.'

She could see a vein popping out in his neck. 'You headed straight for her! You abandoned our plan and ran straight into danger. Why would you do that? I told you that you didn't need to prove anything, not to me. Weren't you listening? Don't stand there and tell me—'

'I was trying to save *you*!'

He swallowed his words and stared at her. She took advantage of his silence. 'You weren't where you were supposed to be. I couldn't see you. I assumed she …' Tears came and the shame of them stung. She should not be crying, not because of a battle, and not because of …

He walked over to her, his steps measured, his arms spread apart, as though he was afraid that she'd run. 'I'm sorry.'

The last few steps before he reached her were tentative ones. When he was within touching distance, his eyes locked with hers. He stretched out his hand and ran a finger over her cheek. His touch was so light the desire for more flamed inside.

She launched herself at him, taking his face in her hands and pulling his head down so she could kiss him with ease. Instead, he wrapped his arms around her and lifted her up, cradling her to his chest as she clung to his neck, pulling him close as his lips met hers again and again.

'If you two have quite finished.'

She sprung away from him. That was Illora!

Only then did she look past Brandonin to where the roller stood. There was her sister, Gisel, Erleph and a few other Vendel, the latter looking at her with varying degrees of shock. Gisel screwed up her nose and Illora seemed mildly annoyed. Erleph was unpacking some weapons from the back of the roller.

'Where did you come from?' she spluttered.

'Where do you think?' She gestured to the roller's compartment. 'We were in there when the heir came to get you. Or did you think he's as reckless as you?'

Erleph muttered something she didn't hear.

Vashta turned to Brandonin. 'Why didn't you tell me they were with us?'

He blushed. 'It slipped my mind.'

Illora folded her arms. 'If you'd given him a chance he probably would have.'

'We don't have time for this conversation,' Erleph said, as he handed the weapons around before heading for the treeline.

Vashta tried to keep calm. She could tell her mentor would have a great deal to say about her running off to save Brandonin. 'Erleph, we need to go back to Verindal land. We need to head—'

'Vashta, one of your biggest faults is your tendency to assume no one else has a plan.' As he reached the bushes, he grabbed some loose branches and tossed them to one side, revealing a larger roller there, as well as some supplies and heavier weaponry.

'You …' Why had she assumed that Erleph wasn't prepared?

But there was no rebuke that she could see. He looked at Brandonin. 'Do I have permission to call you by your name? Calling you "the heir" is too remote.'

'Certainly.'

'Good. We have several heavy-duty rollers in here. Each of you is going to take one and drive it to …' He looked at Brandonin. 'Where?'

He told them where the bunker was and tried to describe the most direct route. Fortunately, one of them had a pathfinder and pinpointed it. Once everyone had an idea of the route in their heads, they breathed easier.

'Of course,' Erleph said, 'there's no such thing as a direct route at the moment. Do what you can to get there.' He turned back to Brandonin. 'Now, given that you're such an important figure in this fight, why you came here yourself is beyond me.'

Vashta snorted. 'He insisted.'

'You two are well suited, then.'

His pronouncement was so unexpected it took her a moment to absorb it.

'But you will need to stay in the back of the roller, Brandonin, especially while we're in Vendel land. Getting you back safely is our highest priority.' He patted the vehicle behind him. 'I will drive this one and I think it would be best if you, Vashta and Illora stay in the back together.' He turned to Gisel. 'You are?'

'Gisel.'

'You'll travel in front with me. Once we reach Verindal territory, you'll be my guide.'

The five other Vendel each took their own roller with instructions to pick up others on the way. Then Erleph bustled them into the rear of the roller, locked it, and soon they were rumbling along.

It was dark and stuffy in the back, but Vashta was glad of it because it meant she didn't have to return Brandonin's gaze, which she regularly felt on her. She wasn't sure how to deal with what had happened, especially with her sister sitting between them. She could already hear the layers of arguments she was sure she would be regaled with as soon as they had a moment.

But that brought something else to mind. 'Meeka's involved in this too?'

Illora sounded insulted. 'Of course. You're not the only fighter in the family, you know.'

'But Meeka's so … so …'

'Not like you? That's not always a bad thing.'

When would she stop putting words into her mouth? 'That's not what I meant.'

Illora seemed to tire of the game and put her hand on Vashta's shoulder. 'She's a sister who is dedicated to honouring our Father. Lara would have been there too if it weren't for the baby.'

She wondered where her mother stood in all this. But Mother had no spirit and was probably still overcome with grief at Father's loss.

So Mestitha would be standing alone in this. That would make gaining the trust of their people a lot easier.

CHAPTER EIGHTEEN

It was difficult sitting in the back of the roller not knowing what was going on.

The vehicle had rumbled to a halt twice. Both times they had hefted their weapons and held their breath, only to have the roller start up again a few minspans later. Each time Brandonin felt relief flood through him, but he knew he wouldn't be comfortable until they reached the bunker.

Not even then, perhaps.

A glimmer of light came through a crack in the roller's door and lit up the side of Vashta's face. It was as much as he could see of her. She'd said nothing about what had happened, presumably because her sister was with them, but maybe she wouldn't have wanted to anyway. He wondered if she regretted it. What would he do if she did?

Nothing, probably. If anything came of it, he knew there would be obstacles as large as the palace spire in their way. It might be better if it went nowhere. But he didn't want it to.

The rear door of the roller swung open and they brought their weapons to bear, only to let them drop as Gisel peered in. 'We're here.' He clambered out, the two princesses ahead of him, and saw the familiar shape of the bunker.

His feet had just touched the ground when he was assailed by an officer. 'My Lord, Commander Lissia asks that you come to see her immediately.'

'I'll see her soon,' he said, looking at the device Vashta was carrying. 'First I have to get this to Nestor. Bring Ivanna as well. They both need to examine it.'

He marched inside, Vashta taking up her usual place to his right. 'You don't think your commander should take priority?'

He eyed the box. 'This thing should come first. The sooner they start work on it, the sooner we find out how clever Blassin is.' And how dangerous.

She turned to face him. 'Why don't I take it to them? You can go and see the commander and find out what's happened in our absence.'

At least she wasn't avoiding his gaze. Her eyes were clear and untroubled, maybe even a little softer than usual? 'All right. Just tell them to find out if this thing works or not.'

'And you tell me what the commander says.' She grinned. 'We'll meet in the middle.'

***

Commander Lissia was in the meeting room. It looked like she hadn't slept since he'd left, and he was taken aback when she came over and bowed low before him. 'My Lord, I'm so relieved to see you're back. Was your mission a success?'

'We believe so. We have returned with a number of Vendel. Some are still on the way. One of Princess Vashta's entourage should be able to give you more details about the rollers they're travelling in.'

Lissia signalled to one of her officers to go and find out.

'What's been happening here?' he asked. 'More attacks?'

'They've been constant. We don't yet know their exact plans, although Ivanna has made some progress in her translations.'

'And?' He sat in a nearby chair because she looked like she was going to collapse and there was no way her honour would let her sit while he was standing. He nodded to another chair and she sank into it, her shoulders slumped like they carried the planet's weight.

'They intend to wipe us out. The intent is clear—no sentient being can be left alive.'

He'd thought that but it sickened him to hear the words. 'Does Ivanna have any idea why? Do they need this planet for some reason?' Surely they could dialogue. There was plenty of space if the invaders needed land. Some arrangement could be reached.

'There has been no indication of their purpose, no, but it's clear that they don't view us as beings worthy of mercy or even life, it seems. Some earlier communications that she has only now translated reveal that their first strategy was to get us to weaken each other.'

He scowled. 'Which we have been doing efficiently for years. Go on.'

'However, there are signs that they're unhappy with how long it's taking. There's every reason to believe that they're going to move to a more devastating strategy so they can complete their invasion.'

'So we need a strategy of our own to defeat them.' Not just fight back. That wasn't enough, not now. They needed to drive out every Arctal on or around their planet. They had to convince them that attacking Verindon was not in their interest.

'Yes, my Lord. But there's more.'

He'd guessed there would be.

'Your father has been appearing less and less on the comm channels. Even Loora hasn't appeared much, and she seems at a loss of what to say when she does. It's possible she may be losing council support, but we don't know what any of this means for your father.'

There could be any number of reasons for this. Could she have imprisoned him to keep him from being swayed by those who stood against her? But Father had become so reliant on her. Could he ever be prevented from accepting her counsel? And if he still favoured her, she would be using him in public appearances.

So that meant that it was likely he was unable to appear in public with her. He must be unwell.

Or dead.

One look at Lissia and he knew what she thought was true. 'Does Larinda know?'

'She has been scanning the comm channels, searching for any sign of him, trying to piece clues together.'

***

Larinda was in the comm room, which had been set up with as many image casters as they could find. She was so intent on one of the screens

175

she didn't hear him enter. It wasn't until he placed his hand on her shoulder that she leapt at his touch. She threw herself into his arms. 'Oh, Brandonin! I'm so glad to see you're safe.'

She wasn't the kind of girl to seek refuge in tears, so when he saw the trace of them on her cheeks, he held her tighter. 'It's all right. I'm here now.'

She turned back to the terminal. 'Commander Lissia filled you in? This is the most recent thing I can find on Father.'

She brought up an image that was like a laser bolt to his heart. Although his father was speaking, Loora, who was at his side, whispered in his ear constantly. He didn't stand and seemed to be struggling to hold his head up. Once his halting speech was over, he sank back into his throne, exhausted.

'That was yesterday morning,' Larinda said. 'There's been no sign of him since then. Loora's been seen twice. She said he was taking charge of the fight against the invaders, but there's no evidence of that.' He could hear the question behind her words and soon she voiced it. 'Do you think it's time to return?'

He felt a pull to go back to the place where he'd grown up, to everything that was familiar, to an ailing father who needed him, to a people he could serve publicly.

But if he returned to the palace, he would have to fight Loora's meddling, not to mention convince the council that what he intended to do was a valid course of action. And with the Arctal attacks becoming more frequent and, if Ivanna was right, more devastating, there was no time for bureaucratic entanglements. Though reassuring the people was a compelling reason to return, he knew he could serve them better where he was. 'I don't think we can go back, no. We can do more where we are.'

He saw the light leave her face at his words, but her sense of duty was as strong as his, and her conviction destroyed the desire to comfort their father. But that didn't stop the tears from falling. He took her in his arms and stroked her hair, his own heart heavy within him.

***

The fact that the Arctals seemed ready to increase the level of their attacks meant that a plan of action had to be formulated. Brandonin requested Vashta, Larinda, Commander Lissia, Nestor and Ivanna meet with him in the conference room. 'Nestor?'

The man was smart enough to know what he meant. 'My Lord, you can say what you like. This room is secure.'

He sat back. 'Good. We're here to formulate a strategy that will drive the Arctals off our planet once and for all. Ivanna, have you had a chance to examine the device we stole from the Vendel?'

She nodded. 'My people are working on it as we speak, my Lord, and I hope by the time this meeting is over we'll know whether it works or not.'

'Excellent.' Although he didn't really want to use a device like that, he knew it might be necessary. 'Nestor, I understand you've made some changes to the security in this building to protect us from attack.'

'Yes, my Lord.' Nestor stood, bowed, and turned on a display. An image beamed onto the blank wall behind him. 'As you know, other locations around Verindon have taken over the development of the anti-Arctal weapons.'

'Some of which have been discovered,' Lissia said.

Nestor was unfazed. 'That was always going to happen. Considering how many we have now and how varied their locations, it's unlikely they'll get all of them. We're also setting up new ones constantly.'

'But what about this place?' Vashta asked.

At the click of a button, an image of the building from above was projected onto the wall. Its squat shape was instantly recognisable. 'The bunker consists of three levels above ground and two levels below ground and covers three square spans. I've created a device that conceals any sign of organ function and anything else that might alert them as to how many people are now in residence. This is what I believe the Arctals have been using to identify the best places to attack.'

'So none of that registers now?' said Vashta.

'Some signals are allowed out. It's less likely to raise suspicion if some people can be detected, so I have added false signatures numbering no more than the bunker's old staff of fifteen. I think this should prevent them from identifying this as a worthwhile target.'

'But they will still see people coming and going. That should alert them.'

'They have to see it first.' Another image appeared of the surrounding buildings. 'We have now extended our operations five additional spans in each direction. We stagger entries and exits to give the impression that fewer people are here, not to mention the advantage of the underground levels.'

'Yes, what's the latest on that?' Brandonin asked.

'It was recently discovered that most of the surrounding buildings also had underground levels. We are using a holemaker from one of the mines to drill tunnels between each building. This is happening as we speak.'

Vashta was incredulous. 'And you think the Arctals haven't noticed that?'

Nestor looked affronted. 'There's no sign they have.'

Brandonin could read the scepticism in her gaze. However, she didn't argue.

Nestor seemed to take her silence as a victory. 'We're planning to extend the tunnels as far as we can, leading out from this building. I'm also developing a laser system to help defend us in the unlikely event of this building being attacked.' He walked over to the closed door of the meeting room and pulled across a metal shield. 'They're not all in place yet, but when they are, we can sit here in safety. I'll have emergency image casters so we can see what's happening outside these walls.

'When everything's done, we'll be able to view any unauthorised entries to this building.' He projected an image of all of them in the meeting room, watching an image caster, before moving to an image of an Arctal. 'We can use the vision takers that are stationed throughout the building to target and destroy these enemies before they can reach us.'

They watched a beam of light leap from a vision taker and disintegrate the Arctal. Even Vashta looked impressed. 'But it's not in place yet, is it?'

Nestor shrugged. 'Give me time, please. I have been rather busy.'

But she leant forward, both hands on the table. 'We don't have time.'

Brandonin gave Nestor an appreciative smile. 'Thank you, Nestor, for all the good work you do. I know how much it will benefit us, both now and in the long term. But we need to discuss what we're going to do next.'

***

It was a long meeting, but it was finally done. They settled into various tasks, all the time keeping watch for the latest attacks from the Arctals. There were so many now it was hard to keep track.

It wasn't until a new attack targeted the palace that Brandonin was called to view the intel. His first thought was for his father. Would this finally end his life? It was clear from what he was seeing that it was destroying so many others.

He darted from monitor to monitor, trying to get a firm grasp on what was happening. Then he noticed a gasp from Vashta, who was squinting at a screen displaying a grainy image of a section of forest near the palace. His eyes blurred as it went in and out of focus.

Then it solidified and he realised what he was seeing. Vashta realised it at the same time. 'Is that a *ship?*' she asked.

That caught Nestor's attention. He bolted over to the screen. 'We *must* have it!'

Vashta was already heading out of the room. 'Nestor, have those fliers been fitted out yet?'

'Yes, they're in our landing bay.'

Brandonin almost launched himself over the monitor. 'Vashta, you can't beat them by yourself. Wait for help!'

But she had gone.

He followed her out of the room, searching through the many officers clamouring for his attention, but it was no use. He dragged his mind away from her and returned to his duty. Troops needed to be organised and action begun. For Nestor was right—they needed that ship.

CHAPTER NINETEEN

Vashta tried to put Brandonin out of her mind. She knew he was concerned for her safety. But she also knew he needed to be a leader and ready his people for battle. And she needed to prepare as well.

As much as she didn't want to sell Brandonin's people short, she was sure they would be of little use against an Arctal. She needed Vendel. She raced around the bunker, searching for Illora and Erleph.

'Vashta!'

Relief flooded her as she turned to meet her sister's confused eyes. 'What's happening?'

'The Arctals are attacking the Verindal palace and they've brought a ship with them. We need to get it.'

As she'd hoped, Erleph and Meeka were hard on Illora's heels, as well as a number of other Vendels. 'Which of you can fly well?' Every hand shot up except Meeka's. 'Be honest. These aren't like our fliers. Who has studied jet flying?'

Hardly any hands dropped. She looked at Erleph and he pointed to some of the pilots. 'You five come with us. Meeka, take the rest of our people and see how you can help the heir's forces.'

There were seven people following her when Erleph's next question came. 'How many fliers do we have access to?'

'I know there's more than one.'

'And they're proper fliers?' Illora sounded as excited as a child coming of age. 'No propeller engines, no projectile guns?'

'They'll be the latest, and they've recently been armed to fight Arctals.'

Because the fliers stood out, they'd been stationed in a damaged block spans from the bunker. As they burst into the makeshift hangar, several Verindal were preparing eight fliers. When the Verindal saw them they raised their weapons. Vashta could see no one she knew, so did the only thing she could think of. 'The heir sent us!' She held up her hands, revealing them empty. The others did the same.

The pilot who'd been prepping the nearest flier clambered to the ground, his weapon still pointed at her. 'You're Vendel.' Fortunately, they looked confused, rather than aggressive.

'I'm sure you're aware that Vendel have been working with your leaders, or don't you recognise the princess who hasn't left your heir's side?' She didn't care how that sounded.

The pilot passed a calculating glance over them. 'So, have you come to guard us while we prep the fliers?'

'No, we've come to fly them.'

That went down like an injured grondal. 'You don't have the skills to fly a machine like this!'

'The Vendel only have propeller fliers. They can't fly these ships.'

'Enough!'

Every head turned as Larinda strode in. All the Verindal bowed.

'Verindal, stand down,' she said. 'These are the pilots who'll be flying today.'

'But my Lady!'

'No buts. As much as I'm sure it pains you to hear it, they will fly them better than you.'

Vashta turned to Larinda to spare the Verindal soldiers the triumph that flushed her face. 'Thank you.'

She nodded. 'Brandonin thought you'd need help.'

'Where is he?'

'Doing his duty, the same as the rest of us.'

She was right. Vashta snatched a helmet as she raced to the flier, jumping into the cockpit. To his credit, the pilot continued to prep the ship, even though she could see mutiny in his eyes.

It was still another several precious minspans before he nodded and she revved the engine, delighting in its rising purr. Verindal fliers were much quieter than theirs, something they could use to their advantage. Illora commandeered the next flier. She flashed her an excited look as she slipped on her helmet.

Without waiting to see how anyone else was faring, Vashta took to the air. No sooner had she sailed out of the hangar than she heard Erleph's disapproving voice on her headset. 'Vashta, wait for your squadron to join you. Going into this fight ahead of us will weaken everyone.'

She wished he could see the glare she gave him, although she knew he was right. She slowed until the other seven fliers pulled up beside her. 'We're heading for the Verindal palace. That's a setting of one zero six. Confirm?'

A chorus of voices came back to her.

To her surprise, Erleph let her lead. She had expected him to take point. But he hung back, taking a place on her left wing. Illora was on her right.

Already the palace was in sight. What was left of its spiral wobbled under the bombardment raining down on it. Smoke rose from its base, where she could see Verindal forces engaging the enemy, their newly built weapons flashing out constant barrages of fire.

'What's the strategy?' Illora asked.

Illora was asking her? Vashta's gaze slid to her mentor's flier out of habit, but his voice disillusioned her. 'What's your attack plan, Vashta?'

'Um …' Why was Erleph doing this to her? This wasn't the time for a lesson in strategic warfare! But she could hear his usual reply in her head. *There's no better time.*

She took a deep breath and surveyed the scene below her. 'Flier number four, you take numbers five, six and seven and support the ground troops. The rest of you, come with me. We need to destroy any defences protecting their ship.'

As four fliers peeled off, Vashta checked her readouts for anything unusual. 'Do we even know what to look for?' She should have asked for the ship's position.

'You should have a feed going to the command post,' Erleph said. 'Use it.'

There were two highlighted channels on her control panel, so she switched over. 'Hello?' *That sounded professional.*

An officious voice sounded in her ear. 'Bunker Command Post.'

'This is Princess Vashta. Can you give us the location of the enemy ship?'

'Copy that, my Lady. Set course for zero eight three from your current position.'

She set course and her flier diverted around the palace over the fields of debris that had once been the beautiful garden where she'd walked with Brandonin. She sailed past the palace towards the forest.

The ship was undercover. Her mind raced with fractured ideas of how to get to it when she noticed the obvious—it had punched a hole in the canopy when it had flown amongst the trees. She dived towards it to get a better look, pulling up as she spied the ship. She could see several Arctals in front of it, shooting the forces engaging them. They were more than holding their own if the Verindal corpses were anything to go by.

But her view was impeded by the trees curling around the battlefield. 'We need to get a clear shot at their troops!'

'What's your plan?' came Erleph's calm voice. How many times had he used it before, waiting for her to state her ideas, to receive his quiet nod of approval?

'The hole they punched in the canopy is only going to give us a direct line on the ship,' said Illora. 'And that's not what we want to hit.'

'No. But we need to prevent them from taking off again.' That gave her their first action. 'Illora, aim for the trees surrounding it. Do what you can to hem it in.'

'They'll just punch another one through.'

'Then we need to make it as difficult as possible.' She switched her comm back to the command post. 'Can you contact the forces fighting near the Arctal ship and tell them to fall back?'

'If they do, the enemy will escape!' the voice on the other end spluttered.

Not if we can help it. 'Unless you want your forces to die, do as I say!'

She gripped the controls tighter, waiting to see how much weight her commands had. She was about to scream in the receiver when she saw the soldiers start to move away. 'Illora and … who's in the other flier?'

A voice rattled back to her. 'It's Elestin, Your Highness.'

'Illora and Elestin, start your attack when we start ours. Erleph, you know what I'm planning to do?'

'Yes, Your Highness.' She could hear the trepidation in his voice, but he must have known there was no other option. 'I'm ready to follow your lead.'

The Arctals didn't chase the Verindal forces, disappearing back under the cover of the trees. 'Illora, now!'

Her sister dived for the canopy, blasting branches that rained down on the ship. Vashta could see little from where she was but hoped that the Arctals weren't on board yet, as she needed to take out as many as she could. And there was only one way to do that.

She went into the safety zone and swept as low to the ground as possible. Her transformed abilities catalogued everything about the ship and its surroundings in the moment it took her to inhale. By the time she'd exhaled, she'd already fired her shots and pulled up. She almost cut it too fine. She could feel the branches thwacking into the bottom of the flier as she passed by. One strike was so hard she thought she was going to lose control. She knew Erleph was behind her, having copied her manoeuvre.

No sooner had she burst up above the treeline than she looped and came back down, aiming for the scattering Arctals. They returned fire. But this time she wasn't aiming for them. Her powers had got a decent read on the ship and she knew where to shoot to disable it, but not destroy it. Her flier was buffeted by shots, but she managed to get a blast off exactly where she needed to, climbing after letting loose.

A shot struck her hull and she could feel the power disappearing from her flier. She moistened her lips, drawing on all her skills to keep it in the air until she could find somewhere to land, sweeping the Arctals with fire as she turned. Hopefully, she'd got them all because she was out of the game now. Her nose tilted down and she lowered the landing gear, which still worked. But instead of hovering to the ground as it should have, the flier skidded along the grassy plain before her, tall, thick-trunked trees racing up to meet her.

She pulled back, but the flier slowed so gradually she was sure she wouldn't make it. She could feel the trickle of sweat down her face as she waited for the final impact when she slammed into the treeline.

It never came. The flier shuddered to a halt half a span from the nearest tree. *That was a bit anticlimactic.*

Erleph's flier was beside her in a flash. 'Vashta, are you all right?'

She came out of the safety zone. Once she'd taken a restoring gulp of liquid sugar, she hoped her voice would be steady enough to answer. 'Yes. That last pass was a little too damaging.'

Erleph didn't stop to sympathise. 'Now that you're on the ground, you can go and supervise the Verindal forces as they take charge of that ship. I'm going to help Illora and Elestin take out any remaining Arctals.'

She popped the canopy and jumped out, surprised to see several distant figures racing towards her, legs flying, arms pumping. Their looks of relief were plain when they saw she was in one piece. 'My Lady, are you injured?' demanded one.

'I'm unharmed. Thank you.' She could see another talking into her comm, and it wasn't hard to guess who'd sent them to check up on her. However, there were more pressing things to worry about. 'Is the Arctal ship intact?'

'This way.'

The smoke was drifting away in grey swirls by the time she got back to the site of the battle. She examined the charcoaled blast points on the trees as she walked into the forest. Gisel and a platoon of troops were swarming over the ship by the time she reached it. A pile of Arctal carcasses had been thrown to the side while the Verindal ones were being removed more respectfully.

She turned her attention back to the Arctal ship, noticing the panel in the front where her strike had hit. A light stream of smoke issued from it. Hopefully, the damage she'd done was repairable. The ship was oval and about a length and a half long with a square panel on the side that lay open. Its surface was like metal, but not one she was familiar with. It was cool to the touch.

An officer was jabbering on his comm as he came out and saw her. 'Don't touch that.'

'Don't tell me what to do,' she snapped back.

His nostrils flared, but Gisel spoke up. 'You would do better to respect our Vendel allies.'

In addition to her rebuke, there was a buzz of noise from his comm. The officer listened and his expression cooled. 'My apologies, my Lady.'

She sighed. 'Is that your heir?'

When he nodded, she held out her hand for the device. 'Brandonin?'

'Vashta, are you all right? They told me about the crash. Do you need—'

'No, I don't need anything. Your flier took care of me. No reason to worry.'

Reassured, his voice turned to business as she and Gisel stepped inside. 'What do you make of it?'

'The metal is unfamiliar. It feels too thin to be of any use in space.' Not that she knew what was required out there. 'It must be tougher than it looks.'

There were no seats in the main section, although there were ten large clasps on the wall—five on each side. She wondered what they were for. Storing weapons? Did they hold whatever these creatures used to fly? There was a pipe coming down from the ceiling in front of each clasp. A power source?

She moved into the cockpit, where there were no seats, only four indentations in the floor. The front two indentations were in front of the controls. There were no levers or switches of any kind. Instead, there was a series of round panels.

'Be careful,' Gisel cautioned from behind her as Vashta reached out to touch one of them. As she hesitated, her hand hovering over it, it lit up and some strange symbols passed over its surface. Writing of some kind? Could Ivanna translate it? She waved her hand again and more symbols appeared. She poked her finger into one and heard a hum of power beneath it.

Gisel looked around, startled. 'Your Highness, stop it.'

Brandonin's voice sounded from the comm. 'Vashta, don't take any risks with that thing. You don't know how it works.'

Yet. 'These are the controls.' As she drew her hand away, the purr of the engine drifted into silence. 'You know, if we can get these symbols translated, I think I could fly this.'

The voice became authoritative. 'Under no circumstances are you to try and fly that thing.'

That drew a laugh from her. 'You need to spend more time with Erleph. He'll tell you that the sure way to get me to do something is to tell me not to do it.' She ran her hands over the surface of the console, letting it speak to her.

Now he was frantic. 'Seriously, Vashta. Please don't try it. You don't know what might happen.'

His concern made her feel warm. It was odd, because she'd always hated that kind of fussing, but she didn't mind it from him.

'Ask Gisel to deliver the ship to Ivanna. I'll get her to go over it,' he said. 'It could be what we need to end all this.'

Stepping back onto the forest floor, she looked at the carnage around her. The Arctal carcasses had been moved into the field. Ivanna would want to examine them. 'Is the fighting over?'

'I think they have withdrawn … for now,' said Brandonin.

'How much damage was done?'

His silence spoke volumes even before she heard the change in his voice. 'We believe the palace has been destroyed. Our forces are moving through the remains, looking for survivors.'

She could hear his pain, even feel it inside herself. It echoed the death of her own father, something he was likely about to experience. 'I'm so sorry, Brandonin.'

She couldn't believe the hope his voice held. 'We don't know the worst yet. There could still be some survivors.'

She felt his optimism was painting a brighter picture than most would see, but she hoped for his sake that he was right.

CHAPTER TWENTY

Brandonin gazed at the pile of rubble that had once been his home.

He pushed away the guilt he felt in all its different facets. Guilt for walking away from the bunker while Ivanna was learning all she could from the Arctals' commandeered vessel. Guilt for delaying the decision-making essential to defeating the menace that had invaded their planet. Guilt that he'd walked away from helping build on the fragile unity that was growing between his people and Vashta's.

But worst of all was the wracking guilt as he realised what he'd left his father to face alone.

'Brandonin.' Larinda touched his sleeve. Her eyes were rubbed red. She swayed as she tried to find steady ground where she could stand. His hand extended to help her.

A platoon had accompanied them and refused to let either of them out of their sight. Although the Arctals had withdrawn from the palace, there were still pockets of fighting in some places. And there was the ever-present danger of those at the palace—or what was left of it—who considered him a traitor. Not that many of them had survived.

'Have you seen him?'

'Yes,' she said. 'He's asking for you.'

Succumbing to the tug of her hand, Brandonin was led out of the crumbled concrete and stone. The platoon followed them as they headed half a span away to the only building that had survived the barrage more or less intact. It had been storage for maintenance equipment, all of which had been thrown out so that a triage could be set up for the survivors.

A medic he didn't know was waiting at the door. Her gaze was wary but respectful as it fell on him. 'My Lord.'

He slipped into his official role. 'Thank you, on behalf of my people, for what you've been doing.'

A myriad of emotions flickered across her face. He thought there was resentment, but it flew away before he could latch onto it, leaving nothing but a professional mask in its place. 'I'm afraid nothing can be done to save your father. He was already bedridden before the attack. The injuries he sustained will be fatal.'

That's what happened when you were trapped in your bed, screaming for help, while the walls of your room disintegrated around you. 'How many others survived?'

'Of the council, I believe three will survive. Two others still live, but they won't last much longer.'

'Loora?'

'Dead, sir.'

'She died trying to save Father,' Larinda put in.

The guilt washed over him again. Loora had refused to leave his father, trying to shield him with her own body, and had been killed in the process. They'd found her draped over Father, him trying to push her out of the way. 'She was loyal to the end.'

No one commented on this pronouncement, but the silence was heavy with accusation. Or maybe he was the only one who would dare label himself a traitor and a coward now.

The interior of the building smelled of dust and rot, both from the still smouldering sections of the walls and the flesh on the survivors. At least the equipment was clean and crisp. He could hear the beeps of medi-regulators and the pump of breathing masks.

They led him to a curtain that looked like it had been torn from the palace walls. The bottom-left corner was blackened and some of it burnt away. He pushed it aside to see an old man lying before him, his face pasty white, the beeps of the regulators steady, although they seemed to be counting down the beats to his end.

Father was conscious. His eyes met Brandonin's, and he didn't know how to feel when delight blossomed in them. 'My son, I'm so glad to see you safe and well.'

He held out his hand and Brandonin knelt by his bed. 'Father.' He tried to keep the sob out of his voice. 'I'm sorry.'

'No, there is no need for that. No need.' He let out a breathy chuckle. 'Leave that to your mother. She will have enough sorrow for all of us.'

Brandonin turned to Larinda and the medic. 'My mother?'

The woman shifted her feet. 'He has been speaking about your mother frequently, my Lord. He's waiting for her to visit.'

Tears trickled down his sister's cheeks.

Perhaps it was better. If he was to die, it would be a blessing if he didn't remember the estrangement, the battles, the mistakes that had been made. He gripped Father's hand tighter. 'Yes, I'm sure she will.'

'We will comfort her,' Larinda said.

'My two loving children. It lifts my spirits to think of you taking my place. Especially you, Brandonin. You have your mother's soul. You have her quest for justice and the mercy that tempers it. I know you will lead our people well.'

'I will follow in the footsteps of a truly great leader.' He felt Larinda flinch beside him; the only thing that made him aware he'd just lied.

His father sighed a smile. 'So many mistakes. You will make them too. Just do your best to see beyond them. Promise me you'll never give up.'

'I promise.'

His eyes closed and his breathing slowed.

Larinda put a hand on his shoulder. 'You should return. I'll stay with him.'

He turned to the medic. 'How long has he got?'

'I doubt more than a couple of maxispans.'

That was all he needed to hear. 'I'll stay.'

'But you need—'

'I've been away too long, Larinda. This is my chance to redeem that choice. To say goodbye.'

She didn't argue further. Instead, she fell to her knees on the other side of Father's bed, holding his hand.

The medic was right. Father passed away with both of his children beside him in just under two maxispans. No sooner had they covered his body than the woman was on her knees before him. 'Hail, Brandonin, Overlord of Verindon!'

The other workers echoed her words and the few patients who were conscious croaked it out, some with terror on their faces. After all, they'd supported Father over him. Some overlords of the past wouldn't have let that go unpunished.

But Father had been their ruler. They'd been following him, as they should.

Even Larinda bowed before him, something that made him uncomfortable. He signalled for everyone to rise. 'Thank you so much for your homage. Please see my father's body is embalmed as per our protocols. Unfortunately, the passing service will need to be postponed until our planet is more settled.'

And now Father was gone, it was time to return his full attention to the fight. They needed to find a way to win this war; a struggle greater than any they had ever faced on their planet.

He was determined that Verindal and Vendel alike would face it together.

***

When he returned, he was heartened to hear that Ivanna had requested his presence in the hangar where they'd housed the Arctals' ship. He and Larinda went there immediately.

Nestor was hovering beside Ivanna—she was concentrating on the scientific, he the militaristic. They were chattering as he entered. They didn't notice him at first, although Vashta did. She was prowling around the vessel, taking in everything she could about it, Erleph shadowing her. She muttered something to her mentor before heading towards him and Larinda as Commander Lissia led them in.

She held both hands out to Brandonin as she approached. He

191

took them without hesitation. 'I'm so sorry to hear about your father.'

Her voice was heavy with sincerity. She knew the pain of losing a parent. 'Thank you.'

At the sound of his voice, Ivanna and Nestor's heads popped up like ransims peeking out of their burrows. 'My Lord,' said Nestor, as they hurried over. Then he screeched to a halt and gave a deep bow. 'My Overlord.'

Ivanna copied him and Brandonin bid them stand. 'What is the news?'

'My Lord,' Nestor said, 'we've been working hard together—'

'Passing information back and forth,' put in Ivanna.

'Breaking down all the functions of this ship.'

'Dissecting every detail.'

'And fixing the damage that Her Highness did to disable it.'

His neck was getting sore as his head snapped back and forth between the two of them. 'Can we get to the details?'

He began to walk towards the ship as Nestor and Ivanna continued their commentary. 'It's definitely from off-world, my Lord.'

'The interior has maps of the stars surrounding Verindon, giving detail we've never been able to obtain from here. There are no seats, presumably because the creatures didn't need them. We think they stabilised themselves in flight using several clasps on the wall.'

That made sense. 'If we're going to use the ship, I guess we need to add some, then.'

'That's easily done. The ship's weapons seem to mimic those that are part of the Arctals' own bodies, firing with ten times the intensity.'

'That must be what caused the more significant damage,' he mused, as he looked through the doorway. The craft seemed innocuous, but so had Loora for a long time. 'Have you checked it for traps? It seems unusual that they would risk a ship like this.'

Nestor held out his hands, revealing a small metal box. It was scorched and broken, the metal on the front of it gaping like an open wound. 'There was a homing device onboard, my Lord. Well hidden. Fortunately, not well enough. We found three other similar devices and destroyed all of them before bringing the ship here. I believe they intended to use it to find our headquarters.'

'Good work.'

'But be wary,' Vashta said. 'I doubt they've only planted one kind of trap.'

Nestor nodded. 'We have continued to sweep the ship, but it's been difficult at times to work out what some of the tech does.'

'Although I have made inroads in translating their language, my Lord,' said Ivanna. She directed them to a corner of the hangar, where she had set up some of her equipment. She positioned herself in front of the computer console and pointed to text that looked indecipherable to him. Clearly not to her. 'This was information that we found onboard. Unfortunately, it seems to relate to using the controls on the ship, which has certainly helped. But there's nothing to tell us their plans.'

Vashta snorted. 'If there was, we should be suspicious. Traps, remember?'

Ivanna shrugged off her criticism. 'Of course. But this has allowed me to translate more of their communications.'

'Anything interesting?' asked Larinda.

'Nothing pertinent, but it has helped with one thing.'

She and Nestor gestured to an image caster showing a squat object hovering beyond the clouds, up in space. 'Is that another ship?'

'Yes, my Lord,' said Nestor. 'We believe it is their mastership.'

'The control centre,' said Ivanna.

Vashta ran her fingers over the image. 'That's what we need to destroy.'

'Now, hold on,' Brandonin said. 'I can't imagine it being as easy as all that, even with a stolen ship. They'd recognise it, wouldn't they?' He looked to Nestor for confirmation.

Vashta smirked at him. 'We've thought of that.'

He felt a scowl form on his face. 'We?'

She looked satisfied. 'We had to do something in your absence. Formulating a plan seemed a good idea.'

This can't be good. 'Such as?'

Erleph stepped in. 'You're right, sir, in saying that it would be dangerous to use this ship. It's likely they intended us to do so.'

'But something we don't think they've realised is that it's a great practice craft.' Vashta's face was full of confidence.

Nestor took over. 'And they also didn't realise that this ship has a particular signature. I'm running a new program over the entire planet, seeing if they have any others here. If we can find where they keep them and steal one …'

'Anything they've done to this one will be irrelevant,' finished Vashta.

'That's a lot of ifs,' Brandonin said, glaring at them. 'I'm sure you know how dangerous it is to base a military operation on too many assumptions.'

'What else can we do?' Vashta said. 'The only alternative is to stay here and continue to fight them off, but that's not going to happen if Ivanna's translations are correct. It's only a matter of time before they decide to just wipe us all out.'

'The fact that they haven't done so yet tells me that they need the planet for something and are reluctant to damage it too much, but more drastic action is bound to follow in short order. And we need to act, striking them at their heart, before things get any worse. And remember, no matter how hard you've tried to hide your bunker, they will find it eventually,' said Erleph.

Nestor pouted but didn't argue. And it was a point he also had to concede. The Arctals had wiped out the Verindal palace and most of the Vendel palace. They were attacking every point of significance, every area where those in charge might gather, where weapons could be stored, where troops would train. Soon they would get sick of waiting and abandon all restraint. 'So you train in this ship and steal another one. Then what?'

Commander Lissia spoke up. 'We can destroy the Arctals both here and on the ship with this.'

He didn't fail to recognise the device she held in her hands. His blood ran cold. 'That's Blassin's tech.' He heard Larinda gasp. 'It works?'

'We believe so, my Lord.'

He looked at the device. It was nothing more than a square metal box with a primitive-looking panel on the side with some switches and readouts. So basic, so innocuous. Yet it could wipe out an entire species.

Could they justify this kind of action? What would the Arctals do to Verindon if they didn't? Only Nestor's weapon had been effective against their new enemy and even that might not work forever.

Perhaps that's what the Arctals were hoping for. That might be why they hadn't increased their attacks. Did they know it was only a matter of time before they had an answer for Verindon's only line of defence?

So Blassin's box of death might be the only way.

He didn't realise that Lissia was still speaking, only catching up as she drew her sentence to a close. '… but it would be best to test it.'

'No.' Testing it meant destroying an entire species. And what if it did more than that? 'How can we be sure that it will only destroy one species? How is it even possible to do that?'

'There are enough differences in the DNA of every species on this planet to target a single species alone, and enough similarities to make sure it wipes out every member of that species.'

'What if Arctal DNA is different?'

Ivanna shook her head. 'I've carried out tests on the tissue samples we have from their corpses. There is DNA there we could use to target them. But I believe we should test it first to see if it will work.'

Just pick a species and hope the planet could survive without it? 'Ivanna, you of all people should know the problems this could generate. I can't warrant that kind of destruction. Analyse the plans Vashta retrieved and confirm whether it will work or not.'

Vashta looked shamefaced. 'That's just it. The plans are incomplete.'

His mouth ran dry. 'What?'

Erleph nodded. 'The two copies we obtained were missing different pages. It seems Blassin's the paranoid type.'

But that meant … 'He could still have a complete set of the plans.'

'No,' Vashta assured him. 'We went through everything. And while there may have been a copy on his computers, we destroyed them.'

The Vendel have computers? Stolen, probably. 'You can't be sure of that.'

'No, we can't, that's true.' She seemed annoyed at his insistence. 'But this was the only assembled device he had. At the very least, he'd have to make a second, which would take time.'

That made their deadline more important. Not only did they have to stop the Arctals, they had to make sure they did it before Blassin could build a new device. But that wasn't the only problem. 'How can we be sure it works without endangering the entire planet?'

'We've thought of a way,' said Ivanna. 'Over here, my Lord.'

She led him over to where Nestor was checking a transparent cube. It was about ten handspans squared, see-through and made of heavy-duty plastic. 'And this is?'

Nestor looked through it from the other side. 'According to Blassin's notes, the field of destruction can be limited to a certain location. We have worked out how to calibrate it.'

'We intend to put a couple of lerkeks inside and program the box to destroy them,' said Ivanna, 'with some remlings put in as a control.'

He looked over the cube. They wouldn't be suggesting this if they felt it wasn't going to work. But … 'Are you sure the charge from the box will be contained?'

Ivanna's face showed no doubt. 'It will, my Lord.'

Could she be wrong? What would happen if she were? Lerkeks would be wiped off the face of the planet. But did that matter? They were small scuttling rodents, slightly bigger than the remlings. They regularly raised screams around the palace when they managed to gnaw their way into bags of food. More than once as a child he had slipped a lerkek into the kitchen just to watch the servants run around trying to bash it with their brooms.

Even the smallest, most annoying creature could prove essential to a planet's natural balance, but if their planet was overrun by Arctals, lerkeks might be the only creatures that survived. Perhaps not even them, if the Arctals found them as pesky as the servants had.

It was worth the risk. 'Do it.'

***

He felt sorry for the rodents as Ivanna loaded them into the cube. They sniffed around, some of them attacking the remlings as they were added.

Ivanna winced as she watched a lerkek move in for the kill. 'Maybe they weren't the best mix. Nestor, we'd better hurry.'

'Not to worry,' Nestor said, slipping some food scraps in opposite corners of the box. The creatures retreated to separate areas; the food too tantalising to ignore. Then he put Blassin's box in as well.

'Can you set it off from out here?' Brandonin asked.

'Yes, my Lord.' Nestor pulled out a small electrical device. 'I programmed this for remote function.' He waved everyone back, not that it would make any difference if the box decided it was a little more potent than his advisors had anticipated. If that was the case, lerkeks would drop dead all over the bunker.

Or maybe they all would.

Flexing his fingers, Nestor pressed a control.

There was no sign that the box did anything. It didn't move or light up, there was no smell or sight or sound. But every lerkek inside the cube curled into a ball, writhed, scrambling its little feet, and died.

The remlings sniffed at their corpses. One started to gnaw on a still twitching lerkek.

It worked.

Who would have thought a Vendel could do it? By the look Vashta gave him, he thought she almost wished it had failed. Brandonin wondered what she read on his face. Because it was good that it worked. It was also appalling.

Nestor and Ivanna whooped and hugged each other, opening the side of the cube, where Nestor extracted the box and Ivanna a lerkek corpse.

But Nestor's face paled as a thin curl of smoke arose. 'No. No, no, no!'

Racing over to one of the benches, he began to pry one side of the box away.

Ivanna followed him. 'What's wrong?'

'I think a circuit has shorted out. I can't be sure. I'll—' He winced as everyone pressed in around him, trying to see. 'Please, give me space!'

They drew back, Nestor muttering behind them as he rummaged through the device, prodding, poking, investigating. Ivanna stood beside him, the two of them like parents wringing their hands over an ill child.

Didn't they realise what it was? This genocide-in-a-box could destroy all their enemies with the press of a single button. Yes, the Arctals were invading, but …

His eyes landed on Vashta. There was a wariness in both her and Erleph. They knew full well he could unleash this on them if he decided to. Vashta's sister had been prepared to do that to his people.

But as unsettled as they were, they were still warriors. 'We should wipe out the Arctals here first,' said Vashta. 'Then a force should try to penetrate the mastership.' Her face puckered as she said it, the words racing out.

'It may be better to destroy the ship first.' Erleph's face was grave. 'Then deal with the remainder on the planet.'

He couldn't bring himself to respond. Yes, they had to do it. Their people had to be saved, but to kill all the invaders? Swiftly, neatly, like brushing unwanted parts off a workbench.

Nestor's muttering became more intense, his grumbles louder, his cursing more distinct. Brandonin looked at Vashta to see if she was offended.

'I didn't think Nestor's vocabulary was so broad,' she commented.

'Only when there's a problem,' he replied. And it was a significant one, by the sounds of it. Should he be glad about that?

Furious whispers flew between him and Ivanna, but it was some time before the armourer straightened up. 'My Lord?'

He went over to the workbench, careful not to crowd him. 'What's the problem, Nestor?'

'It seems that Blassin wasn't as clever as I'd hoped. The wiring he used in the circuitry isn't able to function the way it's intended. Given the energy curve required for the box to work, and how it has to be constructed ...'

Vashta peered at the exposed cables. 'You can't fix it?'

'I can, to some extent, but since I don't have the full details of what Blassin did, I don't want to do too much in case I affect the device's functionality.'

So one false tweak and this box could destroy everything near and far. But one look at Erleph made it clear that he didn't want to give up on it. 'So, it's unusable?'

'No,' Nestor said. 'I have tricked it up with wiring that *should* hold ... once.'

'Only once?'

Nestor's face puckered. 'I *think* so.'

Brandonin had heard enough. 'It's too dangerous to use.'

'No, my Lord, I think it would work again.'

He turned to his sister. 'Is he lying?'

Larinda fixed her gaze on Nestor. He shuffled. 'Eighty percent? Not beyond one more charge, though. I think the whole thing will burn out after that.'

'He's telling the truth,' confirmed Larinda.

Erleph nodded. 'It'll do.'

Brandonin looked at him in shock. 'It's too risky.'

But Vashta's mentor was firm. 'Sir, we have seen that this can be effective. And if we're going to go out into the sky, beyond where we have ever travelled, we need something that will work with devastating speed and efficiency. We can be sure of nothing out there. Any advantage must be taken. We know what they're about to do. It's only a question of time before they do it. We must defeat them now, and swiftly.'

Vashta nodded. 'Use it on their ship and destroy the Arctals here in battle?'

'You would have to be on board their ship,' Nestor said. 'I doubt it would work through the vacuum of space.'

'We'll find a way,' said Erleph. 'And confining the blast to their ship will lessen the effect if the box does malfunction.'

Brandonin shook his head. They couldn't do this! The risk was enormous. They wanted to gain access to this mastership and set off a charge that might not work at all, in which case the Arctals on board would wipe the invading squad out. Or the box could malfunction and wipe everyone out.

But he had no other answer for defeating the Arctals. How much longer could they hold out? 'So, you will gain access to their ship, set this off and destroy them.'

'It will work,' said Vashta. It wasn't hard to see that she would fight to be included on this elite attack team. Could he stop her going? Should he try?

Would he hesitate to put himself in danger if it meant saving the planet?

***

After maxispans of discussion, they reconvened in the conference room.

Commander Lissia displayed an image of Intersiss. All of it was derelict.

She didn't comment on the devastation. 'The Arctals have been attacking here, here and here.' She pointed to some battlements, storage areas and, of course, the palace. 'They have attacked similar Vendel sites. Based on this assessment, we think we can anticipate where their next attacks will be directed.' Three sites were highlighted on the image. 'Our stores at Cressin, the weaponry at Falight and battlements at Metosiss.'

'Unless they step up their attacks or find the bunker,' said Vashta. 'If they do, that's their next target.'

Nestor rubbed his hands together. 'Let them try.'

Although Brandonin wanted to have unwavering faith in the systems the armourer had set up to keep them safe, he doubted anything would be enough to keep the full force of the Arctals from destroying the bunker if they wanted to.

Commander Lissia brought up another image showing the captured Arctal ship. 'We feel a three-pronged attack is best. The attack on the mastership is first. For the second, we'll use the heavier, long-range weapon Nestor has developed.' Her gaze slid to the Vendel. 'Our people will use these to take the Arctals out at long range. While we do that, the Vendel army Princess Vashta's sisters are assembling will attack any who escape it.'

'Take care you don't hit us.' Erleph's voice was heavy with menace.

Commander Lissia rewarded that with a glare. 'We'll do our best, but you know the dangers of warfare as well as I do. Some of your people will fall. So will ours.'

Vashta had told him what an experienced fighter Erleph was. Brandonin knew he would accept that.

His thoughts turned to the assault in the sky above them. He had already guessed that Vashta would be on the team venturing into space. Time to confirm it. He turned to Erleph. 'Have you picked a team?'

'Yes, we have. I will go, as will Vashta and Illora. The others on the team are soldiers who are fighters of the highest order. I assure you, sir, that if it is possible for us to do this, it will be done.'

His eyes were drawn to Vashta again, and he let a glance of concern rest on her before he looked away. There was no point in agonising over a decision that had already been made. 'Very well. I suppose the first order of business is to find another one of these ships.'

'We're already searching, my Lord,' Nestor told him.

Of course they were.

CHAPTER TWENTY-ONE

Vashta powered down the simulator. They didn't have enough space to use the Arctal ship itself and they were concerned that igniting its engine might reveal their location, so Nestor had mimicked the workings and movement of the craft in space as much as they could. Vashta had been surprised at how much the Verindal knew about space, having never heard of the unmanned ships they'd sent up to study it.

She and her mentor had been familiarising themselves with the simulator for the past week. The controls were tricky. She found rolling her palm around on the panels was the best way to steer it, and fortunately, firing its weaponry was as simple as lining up a target and pressing a panel. It clearly suited Arctal stumps better than their hands.

It was not unusual for Erleph to be quiet, but as the hum of the simulator faded, the silence felt overwhelming. Although she didn't know where his thoughts were, she could almost see him working through them. 'What's wrong?'

'You do realise this whole thing could be a trap.'

She wasn't that naïve. 'Of course I do. We find this ship so conveniently, after never seeing one before? That's why we're trying to find another one.'

'But they would have thought of that too. They will probably be prepared for it. And then there's Blassin's device. Will it work?'

She locked her gaze on him. 'What other choice is there?'

He didn't flinch. 'Are you prepared to die for this fight?'

'Is there another option?'

It wasn't normal for compassion to flit across his features, but it was there as he spoke. 'Vashta, you could do so much good for this planet.'

'I'm not chief princess.'

'You could be more than that. You could be someone great, with another great leader by your side.'

'Brandonin?' She had never allowed her ideas to cement when it came to thoughts of him. He was the leader of his race, her eldest sister the leader of theirs. Any bonding between their two races was unprecedented and would usurp Mestitha in a way her sister would never forgive. But there was no doubt it would be the best thing for the planet.

And there were positive signs that their two races could work together. The level of cooperation between Vendel and Verindal as they'd joined forces to defeat a common enemy had amazed all of them. A bonding between their two races could align them forever.

But there was one problem with even daring to think of this kind of future. 'There's no hope of that if the Arctals destroy us all.'

He nodded. 'I know. I think this plan will work. However …'

'Most likely at the cost of our lives,' she finished for him.

As they heard Nestor approaching, Erleph rushed through the words. 'You need to ask yourself if you could do more by staying behind.'

She didn't want to consider it. What if she didn't go? What if their team all gave their lives for this mission? Illora and Erleph would both die. Could she stand staying away, thinking of the greater good and reassuring herself that her survival was the best thing for the planet?

Wasn't that what Mestitha did? Was that how she justified sending others out to battle while she hid inside? Vashta didn't want to do that. Such a mindset … it would be nothing more than the slippery slope to cowardice.

Brandonin wasn't going with them, but he would still be doing whatever he could on the ground. His life would be in danger too. There was no excuse for her not using her abilities to help them win this fight.

She gave Erleph her sunniest smile. 'You know I'm the best pilot we have for this mission. That gives us the best chance of success.'

He must have seen the decision on her face and accepted it without a blink. 'Careful, girl. You know I'm better than you.'

She laughed. 'Whatever you say, old man.'

As Nestor entered, he looked over the readouts from their session. 'You two are getting better every day.'

'I'd hope so.' Erleph's tone dripped with sarcasm, not that the armourer picked up on that.

'A good thing too,' he continued. 'Because guess what?' He put a mini image caster in front of them. At first, Vashta was distracted by it. Yet another wonderful innovation the Verindals had created! Even on such a small device, she could see an Arctal ship. 'We've found one.'

She looked up at him. 'How do we get our hands on it?'

He snapped the caster shut. 'Already done. I didn't realise your sister was such a good pilot. I guess the trait runs in the family.'

Vashta scowled. 'You found a ship and you got *Illora* to steal it for you?'

'You two were busy training, and she offered.'

Since when had Illora been practising with the simulator? Erleph must have been sneaking her in for sessions. 'Is it still in one piece?'

Erleph gave her a warning look. Nestor didn't notice. 'It's fine. We found it in a section of the forest. It was hidden in a cave at the base of a cliff. I went with her and managed to disable its sensors so the Arctals wouldn't notice when it went offline. Hopefully, they won't miss it anytime soon. We're sweeping it for traps and will remove anything that looks suspicious.'

Vashta tried to fight back her irrational envy at missing out on all the fun.

'So, we proceed as planned?' Erleph asked.

Nestor grinned. 'We proceed as planned.'

***

Vashta checked her supplies for the fourth time. She had five functioning and loaded sugar canisters. She had a laser pistol that would take down an Arctal. She had all the skills she needed to pilot the stolen ship. And she had the right codes to arm and fire Blassin's weapon.

She still couldn't believe one of their own technicians was responsible for creating such a thing. She was glad a Vendel had had greater technological skill than a Verindal for a change, but she wished it had been in the creation of something nobler. But she felt a sense of righteous justice when she thought about deploying the weapon against their invaders. She tried to kill the thought every time it flourished in her mind.

Then there was the ship. Nestor had practically disassembled and reassembled it to check for anything that looked suspicious. Five traps were found. While it was a relief they'd been discovered, their very presence made Vashta nervous. Did the Arctals do that to all their ships or had they done it to this one because they knew it would be stolen? Had they left it at the base of that cliff, so conveniently quiet and empty, just waiting for a force of Vendel to board and fly it to their deaths?

It was possible.

She checked the strap that secured her sugar canisters to her jumpsuit again. It didn't move. Without them, she wouldn't stand a chance.

She could hear someone outside her room coming and going, walking up and down. She opened the door, sure who she'd find. His hand was raised to knock.

She gave him a curious look. 'Did you think I wouldn't have time to see you?'

Brandonin's face was creased with lines that hadn't been there a week ago, but he was still every bit as handsome as he had been the first time she'd seen him. 'I wasn't sure if you'd like being interrupted when you're preparing.'

She stood aside to let him enter. She was sure everyone, including him, would be shocked at him entering her room unchaperoned, but the corridor was not the place for this conversation. There was only a slight hesitation in his stride as he stepped inside.

He looked around her scant room. There was barely enough space for the small and springy bed they'd found somewhere, and he stood awkwardly before it. 'Everything's ready?'

'I believe so,' she said. 'How about you? Are our forces in position?'

His face relaxed a little. 'They are. The combined Vendel and Verindal army are getting on well now we have two commanders who can talk to each other without snarling.'

Rallace, Meeka's bond-partner, was leading the Vendel forces. He and Commander Lissia had butted heads at first. 'That's progress.'

'I'm amazed that they're getting on as well as they are. We let them have a bit of friendly sparring in groups and it was astonishing how much that bonded them. I think our races have always had mutual respect.'

'We've spent years trying to defeat one another with no one ever getting the upper hand.'

He considered that. 'Yes, I guess that helps. And so has that flight simulator that Nestor created. I didn't realise how much better our ships would fly when piloted by your people.'

'It's the speed of the reactions.'

'Yes.' With a huff of air, his small talk ran out. 'How do you feel about all this?'

That was the question. Was he thinking like Erleph? Would he ask her to stay behind? 'I think we have a good chance of success.'

'That's not what I meant.'

No, his questions never just skimmed the surface. They always cut deep to get to the sinews below. 'Do you mean do I think I'm going to live through today or am I worried about destroying an entire species?'

He was serious now. 'Both.'

The last thing she needed was to appear unsteady. 'There are risks with every mission. Yes, this one has greater challenges because we're launching into the unknown, but I'm confident that we've done everything we can to ensure success and get us home.'

'And the other question?'

That was the troubling thing about what they were setting out to do. Because of what it meant. Because of what it turned them into. 'I think it's necessary.'

'But you wish it wasn't.'

'In some ways, yes, but in others, I don't think that.' She may as well let him see the worst of her. 'The Arctals want to destroy us. They spare no one. Why shouldn't we deal with them the way they're dealing with us?' She looked at the ceiling. 'What if there are other races out there that they've destroyed? What if they do this to other planets? What if, by destroying all of them, we save lives, and not just our own?'

He looked uncomfortable, and she was stricken with the thought that she'd disappointed him. But instead, he took her hand and drew her down on the bed next to him. Her face felt like a blazing fire sitting where she was, so close to him. If her mother knew, she would hear her screams of outrage from Matarsiss.

But this could be the last day for both of them, for the whole planet. She clenched his hand in hers.

He seemed more disturbed by where he was sitting than by anything she'd said. 'It's hard not to think like that. But there's always another side; another argument.'

And this one was obvious. 'I know. Those reasons are why my sister wanted to use it on you.'

He dropped his gaze, drawing her hand to his chest. The warmth of his touch was soothing. It expressed an acceptance of her, of her words, of her thoughts. She moved closer to him.

'It's different, isn't it, when you know the race you're targeting?' he said. 'We only see the evil of the Arctals.'

'To be fair, they haven't let us see anything else.'

'No, that's true, but each of our races would have said that about the other once upon a time.'

'So perhaps we need to understand the Arctals.' Her voice was flat.

'Unfortunately, we passed that stage a while ago. And you know, it's unlikely all their people are on that ship. They may have a world where there are more of them. They could live on.'

'Only to come back.'

'Let's hope this discourages them.'

He toyed with her fingers. Her lips burnt with the words she wanted to say—*What about after? What about you and me?* But how could she say that when such a future might not even exist? Better not to say it, not to think it, unless she clung to a life she might never have. That would be too distracting given what she had to do.

His eyes explored her face. She didn't know what he saw there, if he saw anything. Maybe there was another reason he drew her towards him and kissed her. Maybe there was no reason at all.

Whatever it was, she didn't care, forgetting everything as she wound her arms around his neck and lost herself in the sensation of his mouth moving with hers, something she'd never experienced before him and didn't care to experience with anyone else.

He drew back from her, his hands cupping her cheeks. 'You're beautiful.'

I love you. The words were on her lips, but she bit them back, even though they were true. She didn't want to say it, not in the face of everything that was about to happen.

But the smile that radiated on his face was more glorious than anything she'd ever seen, even the skies of Verindon. Maybe he knew anyway. Maybe those words didn't need to be spoken between them. She hoped so, because the moment was over.

'I'd better go,' she said, drawing away.

'I know.' He stood with her, led her to the doorway and they walked down together, close enough that she hoped everyone would see them as one unit. Because that was what they were.

She left him at the door of the control room before heading down to the lower levels and into the tunnels Nestor had created. She travelled down the dank, dripping pathway, rarely moving aside for anyone— they did that for her—until she emerged in the hangar containing their stolen Arctal ship.

Erleph was doing safety checks. Illora chatted with Meeka and Rallace. The other members of their team milled around, checking their gear, going over safety protocols. At least none of them looked nervous.

Ivanna was in the corner, her head bent over Blassin's box of death. They'd decided that Erleph would be responsible for it while they were on their mission. He stood in front of Ivanna. 'Is it ready?'

The scientist nodded and held it up, like an offering. 'You remember how to activate it?'

'Red, green, then the alpha sequence.' He ran his fingers over the keypad embedded into the squat device.

'There's no need for you to be out of range when you set it off. It will only harm those with Arctal DNA. You shouldn't notice anything at all, except the Arctals dropping dead, of course.' Ivanna had assured them of this so many times Vashta wondered who she was trying to convince.

Meeka and Rallace stepped up. Meeka threw her arms around Vashta. 'Do well, sister. We need to take charge of the ground forces.'

As she stepped back, Rallace put her hand on Vashta's shoulder. 'Fight to win, sister.'

As they left, Illora came up to them. 'We need to be ready to leave on the control room's signal.'

Ivanna's confidence belied the danger they were about to fly into as she touched their shoulders. 'You'll do well, I'm sure of it. And when this is over, we'll be a united people.'

'I hope so.' It was true that there were many encouraging signs of that, perhaps more than she'd realised if someone as closeted as Ivanna had noticed.

Once all their team was seated, Illora sealed the door and she and Erleph headed for the recently installed chairs in the cockpit. He glanced at Vashta. 'Are you ready?'

'I hope so.'

His expression hardened. 'Are you ready?'

She set her mouth. 'Yes.'

CHAPTER TWENTY-TWO

The control room was abuzz with activity. There must have been fifty image casters set up along its side walls, each manned by a Verindal relaying instructions to this unit or that, their consoles tied to comm-feeds carried by unit commanders.

Brandonin looked up at the ceiling, comforted by the fact that they were under the ground. Hopefully, even if the bunker's main building was destroyed, they would be secure. In the middle of the room, Nestor had set up a three-sided image caster that put everyone in its shadow, beaming live from the three locations they expected the Arctals to attack.

'The stores at Cressin, the weaponry at Falight and battlements at Metosiss,' Brandonin muttered. Would Lissia be right?

Nestor appeared at his shoulder. 'Everything is ready, my Lord.'

'Has Larinda been secured?'

'She is in the barracks at Retin, my Lord.'

It had been difficult to get Larinda to agree to lie low at Retin, but she knew as well as he did that they couldn't be in the same place. If he died …

'Is there any sign of an attack?' he asked, glancing at Ivanna as she walked in. She must have finished handing over the device to Vashta's team.

Nestor also looked her way. 'We've had some indication of an impending attack from the Arctals' communications but it's overdue.'

'That worries me.'

'I know, my Lord, but Commander Lissia has calculated their most likely plan carefully. There's no doubt in my mind that she's right.'

He heard a rumble from above them. The image casters flickered off, then came back on. 'Nestor …'

Another rumble sounded, louder this time. Nestor leapt up before Brandonin could. 'They're attacking here!'

'What happened to those shields you put up?' Brandonin scanned the room. The image casters all seemed operational.

Another blast sounded, then another, then another.

Brandonin snapped into action. 'Find where we are being struck. Identify the source of these blasts and their distance from us. Transmit this intel to our forces. You know what to do.'

A babble of dialogue bubbled up from all around him, an ever-increasing rumble of noise that combated the enemy's strikes. Nestor ran from image caster to image caster, trying to assess details. 'My Lord, Commander Lissia is contacting us.'

'Put her through.'

There was a crackle of static, then the commander's voice. 'My Lord, they're attacking the bunker!'

'Thank you, Commander, we've managed to work that out.'

'Are you all right, my Lord?'

The rumbles came again. 'We can hear a lot of noise but nothing more so far. Our position below ground is helping with that. What can you do to stop them?'

'The gunners are changing positions, but it means firing through the city itself. Our troops are preparing to storm the streets.'

Brandonin's chest tightened at the thought of the collateral damage that would result even though many people had fled, but it was either that or the destruction of their headquarters. 'Tell them to fire without delay.'

'Yes, my Lord.'

Nestor began rewiring his image-casting masterpiece, the images changing every time he made a new connection. Finally, he grunted in satisfaction. 'I think that does it.' The image casters now showed three Arctal ships hovering above them, firing at the protective shield Nestor had created.

The armourer nodded with satisfaction. 'At least it's holding.'

Another blast sounded; the largest yet. The room trembled. 'Let's hope that doesn't change.'

'Oh, it will hold, my Lord.'

At least he could always count on Nestor's confidence in his creations. 'Where are our forces?' Brandonin demanded. 'Let Commander Lissia know what's happening.'

'They're on their way, my Lord.'

They could see the Arctal ships as they turned to defend themselves. But that meant that many of the shots designed for the Arctals hit them too. 'Nestor, please tell me your shield will hold against our own fire.'

This time Nestor looked a little less certain.

At least they could see the Vendel forces coming into view. However, he could also see the Arctals' ground forces going to engage them. But the sight of wave after wave of invaders didn't deter the Vendel. At an unseen command, the front line went into the safety zone.

The Arctals paused and that provided enough opportunity for the Vendel. They raised their weapons and fired, each shot taking down one of the enemy. Brandonin could also see a number of bonded pairs shooting energy towards the invaders. While it didn't destroy them, it frequently drove them into the fire of other Vendel in what became a deliberate strategy.

Some Vendel fell, but there seemed to be more Arctal dead. There also seemed to be a surprising number of Vendel troops. He knew a few platoons had arrived in the past few days, but that many? They were pouring in from all directions. He hadn't thought to ask Vashta about it.

The barrage of shots started up again—closer blasts from the Arctals' ships and a rattle as the shots from the Verindal forces ricocheted onto them. He licked his lips. They needed to hold.

***

As the sound of battle began, Vashta knew it was time to move.

She was about to nudge the ship out of the hangar when Erleph put a hand up to stop her. 'Those blasts are way too close.'

He tapped on the console and brought up a feed from the same intel that Commander Lissia was getting. Vashta gasped in horror as she realised that, contrary to what Lissia had predicted, the Arctals were attacking the bunker.

'Not good,' said Erleph.

'How do we get out now? They're right on top of us.'

He looked out at what little they could see from their position. 'There's nothing blocking our way. Leave now.'

'But they'll see us!'

'Leave now, girl.'

'What's wrong?' demanded Illora from where the rest of the team sat in the main hold.

'We're under attack. Strap in.' Vashta revved the engines and put them at full throttle. The ship lifted from the ground and shot out of the hangar, heading up towards the beautiful Verindonian sky. She didn't let up on the engines, climbing as far as she could as quickly as possible. As she'd feared, fire began raining around them.

'Ignore it. Keep climbing.'

She did as she was told, trying not to dwell on the fact that she'd never flown this high before. The further they went, the more pressure she could feel against her, something that Ivanna had warned her about. It was far worse than it had been in the simulator.

'The internal equaliser,' Erleph said, nodding at a control.

That's right. Once she'd put her fist on the equaliser, the pressure in the cockpit normalised. But fire still came from behind them. 'We're being pursued.'

Her mentor checked the readouts. 'They're not close enough to hit us. Keep going.'

She kept her attention on the route Nestor had programmed, based on the information Ivanna had gathered on the Arctal mastership's location.

Their craft kept climbing, shaking under the pressure of their atmosphere, as they headed into space. It was awe-inspiring and terrifying, and her hands shook at the controls as 'what ifs' fractured her mind in a million different scenarios.

Would they die? Had the Arctals tricked them?

But the ship kept its steady pace, its rattling rising to a crescendo which made her sure it would break apart. Then the vibration drifted away and all she could hear was the engines.

It was hard to stay focused on her job at the sight of stars, sprinkled against a field of black on every side of them. She could see Verindon's moon to her right, growing ever larger. It was not as beautiful as she would have thought, with surrounding planets appearing as little more than distant dots of light.

Erleph checked the controls beside her.

'Everything all right?' she asked.

He scowled at what was in front of him. 'What did Ivanna say this indicated?'

She looked at a dial that was flickering, heading towards a reading of 'empty'. 'I think that was oxygen.'

The dial continued to drop. Why, she didn't know, but she could guess. It was the Arctals' final trap. The one she'd expected. The one that Nestor hadn't been able to find.

She felt like laughing. It bubbled up in her, forcing its way out. Erleph relaxed back in his seat as well. They'd feared a trap and had been waiting for it to descend and destroy them.

The poor Arctals. How were they to know? 'I guess they assumed we breathe the same way the Verindal do.'

Erleph chuckled. 'Obviously, any autopsy they made of us didn't make that clear.'

Their misguided enemy. They had made a fatal assumption that many Verindal had also made over hundreds of years of battle. For while Verindal needed oxygen to breathe, Vendel did not. 'So there are no other problems?'

'The equalisers seemed to have handled the pressurisation. I can't see anything else that could cause a problem.'

A burst of fire drew her attention. 'Except for that. How many?'

'Five, so far.'

'And it's not like I can keep outrunning them.' They were approaching the mastership and there was no point in going beyond it. Perhaps this was why their pursuers hadn't bothered catching up to them before now. They knew where they were headed. And there was another obvious question. 'So how do we get on board to set this thing off?'

They had discussed it earlier with Nestor, who had cautioned them about a possible shield. Erleph looked at their console, which portrayed the ship as an out-of-focus blob. Even at this distance, she could see it better through the cockpit window than on the image caster.

'The distortion must be their shield,' Erleph said.

As he spoke, a section of the haze dissolved around a dark protrusion on its surface and three smaller ships exited. Coming to greet them, no doubt. 'That must be their hangar,' Vashta told her mentor. 'That's where we need to get in.' But the haze returned to the image. 'No way in now.'

The mastership's outer shell was marked with long rectangles that looked like viewing platforms. A couple more ships emerged from the hangar and headed for them.

'Your Highness,' Erleph said, 'it's time to fight.'

'Right.' She'd been surprised to discover how much easier it was to manoeuvre their ship once they'd escaped her planet's gravitational pull. She'd been worried about evasive action with this machine, but now it felt light under her hands.

Illora appeared at the cockpit doorway. 'Status?'

'We've arrived at the mastership but need to avoid fire while we find a way inside.'

She nodded. 'You need to transform, then.'

As their craft shuddered under what was almost a direct hit, Vashta switched into her other state. Erleph did the same, manning the weaponry. Vashta's senses, heightened by the safety zone, told her to veer left, make a pass and then a half-loop. The mastership tumbled around them. Bank right. Roll.

She tried to keep the enemy fighters in scope but with seven buzzing around them like pests, her attention was drawn to every angle at once. And each time, a blast made their ship shudder. It wasn't as easy to manoeuvre as a fighter, something that she hoped wouldn't mean the end of them. At least their attackers were using the same vehicles, though they'd been flying them for years.

But they also weren't Vendel.

Erleph had success with his strikes, disabling one and destroying another, the debris pelting their ship, giving her something else to avoid. She swooped close to their target, using her senses to locate any weak points that could gain them entry. There were none.

She glanced down at the sugar canisters on her belt. She would soon need another one. At this rate, she would go through all of them before they accessed the ship.

As she continued to evade their pursuers, she dived and made a pass, seeking anything that could help them. Erleph directed two well-targeted blasts on the enormous vessel, which barely trembled at the impact.

That's useless, she thought. And Erleph couldn't keep wasting time on it when he was their only line of defence.

The need for more sugar forced her out of her transformation. She quickly downed another canister, despairing that it had to be so soon. She went straight back into her transformed state.

Illora approached, gripping the side of the doorway to keep her feet with the buffeting of fire around them. 'How many times have we been hit?'

'Does it matter?' Erleph said as he downed his own drink. 'We're still flying.'

Illora looked at their belts. 'You're going to run out of sugar.'

'No joke,' Vashta said, knowing her voice sounded even more menacing in that state.

Illora took a canister off her belt and put it beside her chair. Vashta objected. 'You need it.'

'You need it more.' Illora disappeared, returning a few moments later, rocking and moving with the ship, more canisters in her hands. 'There are thirteen of us back here. We can all spare one each.'

***

Vashta downed another canister, still no closer to gaining entrance to the ship. At least Erleph was making more progress in destroying their enemies.

'Watch it,' she said. 'They're aiming—'

She banked to avoid the zap that exploded against their side, narrowly missing their weaponry.

Erleph's face snapped back to normal. 'Keep your mind on your job!' he spat as he downed another drink.

Another ship was blown out of the sky the following moment. At least the Arctals didn't seem to be launching too many. Maybe most of their troops were on the planet. She scowled. Would the box of death make any difference if that was the case?

On the image caster, the haze surrounding the ship lessened as two more ships came towards them. She had to find a way to slip in as they came out. But there would hardly be any time or space and if she failed the first time, the Arctals might stop sending them.

But now there were two more ships to battle.

She looked at the empty canisters surrounding her. They couldn't waste any more sugar trying to get inside. But she needed to be at her strongest. She dived, looping around behind the mastership as she waited for the best opportunity. It had to be just after re-entering the safety zone and before they realised what she was doing.

A ripple of fire hit them. Alarms blared as the ship shuddered. Erleph emerged from the safety zone, drank more sugar, then was gone again. It wasn't yet time for her to do the same, but she saw the tell-tale lines of the ship solidifying. They were preparing to open the hole in the shield again.

She forced herself out of the zone, guzzled her drink, and zoned again. No sooner was she fully transformed than two more ships appeared in the entrance to the hanger.

There was barely a ship's breadth between them, but it made no difference. She aimed for the narrow space, her senses alerting her as they took evasive action, widening the gap to get out of her way. She switched to full throttle, hoping she would have enough time to make it through and still prevent her craft from slamming into the wall on the other side of the hangar.

She felt a blast of heat sizzle over her skin and was about to shriek, but it was over in a microspan. Light dazzled her as they flew into the hangar at full speed. The Arctals hurried about as she flew across the length of it, but she paid them no attention as she leant on the console as hard as she could, throwing her weight against it as if the force of that alone would prevent the ship from crumpling into the fast-approaching wall.

Her senses told her they wouldn't make it and she leant back in her harness and braced for impact.

They struck it with a deafening crack, and she was thrown forward, her head slapping into her chest. A searing pain rippled up her back as she exited the safety zone and unstrapped herself. She knew she couldn't succumb to pain now, ignoring the spreading throb that wracked her body.

The hatch was already open by the time she and Erleph reached it. Illora was ready to lead the first wave of Vendel, all transformed, as they exited the ship to the waiting fire of the Arctals.

Almost instantly, six disappeared, moving to various points of cover throughout the hangar.

Two already lay dead.

Vashta didn't even acknowledge the fallen fighters. There would be time to honour their sacrifice when the job was done. She stood with the remaining soldiers, including Erleph, ready to exit.

They all returned to the safety zone and, with the Vendel battle cry, exited the ship.

Fire blasted all around her as she raced for the nearest cover—some unidentifiable equipment spewing cables. She looked around, ensuring that Erleph was still alive. However, his cover wasn't large enough to shield him and he looked around for better shelter.

Vashta looked down at her belt. Two canisters remained. They needed to finish this. 'Cover Erleph!' she cried as she saw her mentor make his move.

Despite their extra fire, he fell as a shot struck him. It was so powerful it blew him in one direction and the box in the other. Vashta was about to scramble for it—it was essential that the Arctals didn't lay their stumps on it—but one of the Vendel soldiers scooped it up, only to be shot down herself.

Another soldier grabbed it, diving behind a screen with it, but he too had been hit. He fell and moved no more. Another took the box. He began keying in the sequence and was shot. The Arctals must have realised the box's significance. It flew out in front of her and she reached for it when she heard Illora. 'No, Vashta!'

She dived out, but she was peppered with shots and felt pain shooting up her legs. Numbness gripped her and she felt her eyes closing. She fought the agony with all her strength.

CHAPTER TWENTY-THREE

'My Lord, they have gained entrance!'

Brandonin reached for his weapon. He'd insisted that everyone in the control room be given a means of defending themselves in case the Arctals broke through. Even though they were underground, there was still every reason to think that the enemy would make it down to them.

He looked at Nestor, who didn't seem concerned. 'The beams will destroy them.' The armourer adjusted the image casters so they showed the top floor of the bunker. A gaping hole had been blown in the wall right near Brandonin's quarters—he doubted that was a coincidence—and the creatures were creeping down the corridors, heading for the stairway to the lower levels.

As they passed the vision taker, a beam of light shot out from it, striking the lead Arctal and reducing it to dust. Amidst the gasps of surprise, Nestor chuckled. 'Knew it would get them.'

Two Arctals behind the leader shared the same fate, the ones further back retreating out of sight.

'You do realise, Nestor, that this kind of defence won't be as effective if the entire force comes charging into the building.' This laser guard would not be able to handle one hundred Arctals at once.

Nestor didn't seem fazed. 'There are more on the next floor, my Lord. If they survive that level, they will be destroyed on the one below.'

Looking at the faces around him, Brandonin was sure some were hoping the Arctals would give up, but there was no doubt in his mind that an enemy of this calibre would not. They would have worked out that this was the command centre. They would do everything in their power to silence it.

Uncertainty settled on the room as a new force of Arctals entered. The first five were destroyed by Nestor's laser guard, but three more slipped through, as did more behind them. At Brandonin's count, fewer than half the force swarmed through the level above them.

There was still hope on Nestor's face. 'There are more laser guards on that level. They won't make it.' He brought up the vision taker's feed and they found it was covered with bodies.

But more made their way through the remains of their comrades. A good number of them joined the growing pile on the floor, but they kept coming, shooting at each laser guard once they'd located it. One by one, Nestor's weapons were destroyed.

Even the armourer hefted his firearm. 'Where are our forces?'

'Fighting off other Arctals.'

Nestor looked nervous. 'We should have unleashed Blassin's box here. We should have wiped them off our planet and not worried about the ones left above!'

He knew as well as Brandonin why they had decided otherwise—it was better to cut off the head than a few limbs.

The bombardment seemed to have stopped. Hopefully, that meant their ground forces were coming to aid them. But the scuttering in the corridor outside the control room didn't sound like Verindal or Vendel. He could hear the laser guard striking again and again, and smell the reek of ozone as each Arctal fell, but soon Nestor's laser was silenced. The door began to buckle as shot after shot was fired against it.

'My Lord,' said Ivanna, her face white, 'what do we do?'

There was only one thing to do. 'Everyone get into the tunnels.' He raced to the panel in the side room, triggering the mechanism so the door slid aside. 'Go!'

Minor technicians leapt from their chairs and raced to the tunnel entrance, fighting each other to get in. Ivanna took Brandonin by the arm, something she would normally never have dared to do. 'My Lord, your own safety.'

He armed his gun. 'Get in there, Ivanna.' She hadn't been trained in fighting. He had.

The soldiers in the control room lined up in front of him and a chorus of whispers pleaded with him to escape, but there was no way he was deserting his post. He pushed Ivanna through the entrance before glaring at Nestor. 'Off you go.'

Nestor's face was stubborn. 'My Lord, would you deny me the opportunity to wield my own creation in combat?'

He knew that the armourer was better at making weapons than he was at firing them. He also knew he didn't stand a chance of convincing him to go and he didn't feel like making it a command. If Nestor wanted to fight, let him.

He sealed the tunnel behind those who had escaped. Several serious faces trained on him before turning back to the door, which was now flaming under the barrage of weaponry being brought against it.

He checked his weapon again. *Larinda, you'll make a great overlord. I hope you get the chance. Vashta, we might both fall today. If we do, we know we did everything we could to save our people. I love you.*

The door exploded inward, killing a soldier standing too close. All thirty of Brandonin's force opened fire on the smoking hole that was left, taking down the Arctals that were trying to enter. That caused a delay for the others, who had to remove the bodies before they could fit through the opening. It made them easy targets.

But it wasn't long before the hole was enlarged and Arctals began shooting at them, making them dive for cover. Those who didn't fell to the floor, dead. There was so much smoke in the room that Brandonin couldn't see anything through the haze. He just kept firing at the doorway, knowing it would be the enemy he hit.

Another of his soldiers fell. Then another. Then another. The ones left crowded around him, trying to shield him, even as he tried to get off shots between them, desperate to take down as many of the enemy as he could.

Nestor shrieked, his face blanching in pain, and fell beside him, clutching his chest. Brandonin could see the man writhing in agony.

He dragged his gaze away from his fallen comrade and turned again to the door, only to find himself thrown back against the wall by some unseen force. His head felt like it was exploding, so great was the pain of it, but he couldn't tell which had hurt more—the power that had hit him or the crunch when he'd slammed into the concrete.

His weapon fell from his hands and he scrambled to find it, to continue his onslaught. He wouldn't stop fighting until he was dead.

'Will you stop shooting already?' came a voice that sounded familiar.

A vision of beauty came through the smoke. 'Vashta?' Had he died and gone to be with her?

But as the smoke lifted and the woman picked her way over the dead Arctals around her, he realised it wasn't Vashta. This woman flicked her blonde hair out of her face and released her bond-partner's hand, the energy they'd produced still buzzing as they separated.

Everyone stopped shooting as the Vendel force flooded through the door, armed and in the safety zone. They stood down when they saw the only living still in the room were Verindal.

The woman who looked like Vashta approached him. It wasn't Meeka, and he knew Illora was still in the skies with her sister. There was no way this could be Chief Princess Mestitha. Therefore …

She bowed before him, a smirk on her face. 'Princess Lara at your service. I'm sorry I'm late to the party, although I hope you don't mind the company I've brought.'

***

'Vashta!'

It was Erleph and by his tone, she knew she was in trouble. He only used her given name when she'd *really* messed up.

She was surprised to find that the world was swirling. Which way was up? And her legs weren't working. Pain shot up them, into her back, into her head.

A wave of noise struck her. It was as if invisible hands had been removed from her ears. The sounds of battle echoed so loudly within them that she wanted to scream. She could taste blood in her mouth and noticed she was crawling, dragging a box with her.

Then she remembered what had happened. She was in the hangar of the Arctals' mastership and she had possession of the one thing they hoped would destroy them—Blassin's box of death. She didn't know where everyone else was. It was impossible to tell from her hiding place how many of the force she'd arrived with still lived, so there was no time to lose. She needed to activate the box and destroy the Arctals.

She snapped open its console, her addled brain trying to recall the sequence. But she couldn't do it. Her transformed mind dragged her attention in a hundred different directions, none of them focussing on the most important thing.

Illora appeared beside her, also transformed and firing shots over the top of the crate where she'd taken shelter. She looked up at her sister. 'I can't remember it.'

Illora's fingers flew over the console. 'I do. Let's finish this.'

Before Vashta could reply, a blast sent them flying in opposite directions, the box sliding to a stop out in the open. Both dived for it and Vashta could feel the sensation of the enemy approaching, her abilities warning her to duck for cover. She ignored them. They had to activate the box before it was rendered useless, or worse, turned against them by the enemy.

Her fingers reached it first, her sister firing over her head. 'Have you got it now?' Illora demanded.

She did. Her sister had started the sequence and the rest of it flowed through her mind.

Vashta's fingers sped over the console, keying in the sequence and slamming down the 'activate' panel. As she did, another blast exploded beside her. She didn't know where it had come from, only that it left her lying on the ground, unable to move. A screech sounded; a wail of sound that she tried to block out, but she couldn't raise her hands to cover her ears. Bravery fled and she choked back sobs.

It was death coming to claim her.

Nausea threatened to overtake her. She fought against it, trying to regain her feet, but the blast had forced her out of the safety zone, and she was helpless to rise.

Her ears rang and her head spun. She lay there … for how long? A minspan? An eternity?

Erleph's frantic face was before her. 'Your Highness, are you all right? Speak to me!'

'Ugh,' was all she could manage.

He looked her over, assessing her injuries. He pushed her down as she tried to rise. 'Don't get up.' He gestured over the top of her head.

There was a swarm of activity around her, one of their people bringing the foldout medic stretcher they'd put onboard the ship. Three of them lifted her and put her on it.

'But what about the—'

It was only then that she noticed the quiet. Had she been unconscious? She must have been because all around her were dead Arctals. And judging by their contorted forms, they hadn't died peacefully.

She looked for Blassin's box. One of their team was carrying it, holding it out in front of her to avoid the smoke pouring from cracks in its casing.

As she followed it, her eyes passed over her sister.

Illora was gathered in Verindal arms, but unlike her, there was no stretcher brought to help her. Instead, the two weeping soldiers covered her with a blanket and carried her towards another of the Arctals' ships, which sat waiting in the hangar.

She turned her frantic gaze on Erleph, seeking something, anything, that would make a lie of what she had just seen. 'No. No, she can't be.'

'I'm sorry.'

Her father and her brother-in-law, and now her closest sister.

She lay on the stretcher, weeping, as she was carried to the waiting ship, dead Arctals everywhere. The only beings left alive in the hangar were eight Vendel.

She had to behave like a soldier, like the fighter her father had been. 'I will pilot the ship.'

'You will do no such thing,' said Erleph. 'I am capable of getting us home.' He tore a strip from his jumpsuit and tied it around a wound on his arm.

'What about our fallen?' she asked as she was deposited in the hold. Her mentor used the clamps to fix her stretcher to the wall.

'They are being gathered by our remnant. They will be with us shortly. Then we will leave.'

He was about to go into the cockpit when she put out a hand to stop him. 'Please at least tell me we've won.'

He drew in a breath. 'As soon as you initiated the sequence on the box every Arctal in sight fell down and died. We have seen none alive since then, so we assume this ship is now their tomb.'

The two carrying her sister's body laid it with the others. There was little space for them and no way to strap them in, but Vashta could see how her people tried to show respect for their dead.

The six remaining soldiers stayed in the hold with her while Erleph piloted the ship alone. The one they were flying home in was almost identical to the one she'd slammed into the wall—same hold, same cabin, same power, no seats, of course, but her compatriots used the clamps to keep their feet, although that was hardly necessary as the trip back to Verindon was smoother and quicker, probably because no one was shooting at them.

She tried to be brave, but the tears leaked out as she kept from looking at her sister's still form. Illora. Her closest friend. She was with Brexin now. Vashta knew she should be glad about that, but it didn't lessen the sobs.

And what had happened on Verindon? Was Brandonin still alive? The Arctals had been attacking the bunker when they'd left. While his people would have tried to protect him, she knew he wouldn't run and hide.

What would she do if he was dead? She had lost her father and now her dearest sister. Could she stand losing the man she loved?

***

226

Brandonin tried to block out Nestor's cries of anguish.

As soon as he'd realised that reinforcements had rescued them, he'd dropped to his knees at the armourer's side. Fearing the worst, he'd lifted his shirt.

Lara peered over his shoulder. 'Looks like a graze to me.'

Relief was followed by annoyance as Nestor refused to be reassured. 'Nestor, I'm telling you, your wound is superficial.'

'But my Lord, it burns!'

'That's what weapons do,' Lara told him.

'Yes, if you don't like it maybe you shouldn't make them anymore.' He had greater things to worry about than Nestor fainting at the sight of his own blood, although it would be convenient and quieter if he did.

Trying to ignore the armourer's moans, he helped reset the image casters and activate them. At least this activity made Nestor's contribution more constructive. 'Try the reboot trigger on the left-hand side, my Lord.'

The image caster flickered to life, if a somewhat lopsided and blurry one.

'Much better,' Nestor said, before returning to his groans, as Ivanna and the others who had hidden in the tunnels appeared.

Ivanna raced to his side. 'My friend, are you injured?'

'Yes, the heat of battle was too much for me.'

The princess moved to Brandonin's side. 'Is he always like that?'

'Not when he's building weapons.'

She sniffed. 'Then give him a corner and some parts.'

Three image casters showed smoking remains in various places with soldiers milling around. 'When did you get here? What was happening when you came in? Did you pass our forces?'

'We joined them, actually. We'd let them know we were coming in, but we couldn't get a message through to you. We think the enemy was blocking transmissions. Once we realised that, Rallace sent me to aid you.'

He looked at the soldiers under her command. There were twenty of them in the room, and more could be seen clearing away the Arctal corpses through the still-smoking hole in the door. 'How many did you bring with you?'

'Our entire army.'

But that couldn't be right. 'Your sister ...'

'Which one? Meeka? Illora? Vashta? I have four, you know. I suggest you be more specific.'

'Mestitha.'

'Ah, yes. Mestitha.' Her mouth twitched. 'She didn't have much say in the matter, I must confess.'

'But she leads your people.'

Her eyes darkened. 'Not anymore.'

Mestitha had been dismissed from her position as chief princess? 'What happened?'

She seemed annoyed at the question. 'Our people are not fools, Overlord. We can see when we're being led by a coward. Mestitha made the fatal error of ordering our forces to fight against her own sisters; against our people, not yours. If she'd continued to direct her ire only at your race, she might have stood a chance.

'But she was always blinded by jealousy. It's ridiculous when you think about it. She was the heir to the throne. She never walked behind us. She never allowed us to shine.' A satisfied sneer slid across her face. 'But she still hated it whenever any one of us outshone her in any way.

'She couldn't endure the sight of *her* people, the ones *she* commanded, listening to any of us over *her*. Especially Vashta. I'm afraid my little sister's betrayal left her unbalanced, not to mention without her greatest weapon.' As if awoken by its memory, her fierce gaze pierced the haze around them. 'Where is Blassin's DNA Destroyer?'

That brought his mind back to what he hoped was happening above. 'Destroying the Arctals, if your sisters have anything to say about it.'

An aide came rushing in and bowed. 'My Lord, are you all right?'

'Yes, I'm fine. What do you have to report?'

'The enemy is fleeing; we presume back to their ship in the sky. Many are dead. They were unable to overcome our long-range guns and the Vendel presence was more than enough.'

'I told you the guns would work!' Nestor put in, groaning again when he noticed Ivanna was distracted by the conversation.

'What about the ship that was sent to the sky?' He turned back to Ivanna and Nestor. 'We need to know what happened to them.'

Another soldier ran in. 'My Lord, there's an enemy ship approaching!'

He raced out the door. There was only one reason an Arctal ship would be approaching when the others were fleeing. He could see it heading for their hangar ... or what was left of it. Meeka was out there, conferring with Gisel. He picked up speed. They were going to shoot it out of the sky! 'Wait, it's Vashta! Don't shoot!'

At the sound of his voice, they both turned, their features losing some of the strain as they saw him. 'My Lord,' said Gisel. 'We were so relieved to hear that you're still alive.'

He didn't waste time with congratulations. 'Vashta's on that ship.'

'We know,' Meeka said, her tired face collapsing into a frown. 'Erleph sent a signal to let us know they were coming in.'

'My Lord,' said Gisel. 'We believe we've been successful in fighting off the Arctal menace. The only ones left on the planet are dead and, according to the messages we've received from the special squad, they were successful in destroying those aboard the mastership. We believe the number of Arctals who escaped alive would be fewer than one hundred.'

'Let's hope they don't breed quickly.' Brandonin looked around, relieved to see that Meeka and Gisel had survived. But who had they lost? 'Where are the other commanders? Where's Lissia?' It was a stupid thing for him to ask. Given the battle they'd just endured, there could only be one answer.

'She didn't survive, my Lord,' Gisel said.

'I have to give your commanders credit,' Meeka said. 'They fought on the front line with their troops, often where the fighting was the worst. I didn't realise that your kind was like ours in that respect.'

He felt a bond of comradeship form between them, tightening as the ship came into view. 'Our officers would be forever shamed if they didn't lead by example.'

'As would ours.'

Their attention was now drawn to the approaching ship, the throb of its engines rising to a steady whine as it came closer. Brandonin hurried to the hangar as it came in to land. He was impatient as he waited for its struts to settle on the ground and for the noise of the engines to die away with a long wheeze.

Just because they'd been successful in their mission didn't mean they'd survived unscathed. What price had they paid for their victory?

He had to restrain himself from striding to the door to end the agony of waiting, but if she was dead, it didn't matter how quickly he got there. And it was likely that some were injured, so it was sensible to allow the medics to enter first and assess the situation.

'Sensible is overrated,' he muttered.

But his progress was halted by a familiar hand on his arm. 'Patience.' Larinda gestured to the medics. 'Let them do their work.'

He did as she commanded. 'I hope they're the best.'

The look she gave him would have struck down a herd of parcacks. 'Would I trust her to any less than the best?'

As much as he wanted to look at his sister, to glory in the fact that she was alive and unharmed, her words struck him. Did she know something about those within the ship? Was that why she'd hurried from Retin to join them?

The medic team emerged; a stretcher borne between them. At first, it didn't register that Vashta was lying on it. Her body was battered and bloodied, her jumpsuit hanging off in strips that revealed torn flesh and burns underneath. Her face was ravaged by sweat and soot and streams of red, her hair so coated in filth it looked almost black.

Erleph was beside her and held Brandonin back as he moved towards her. 'She suffers from nothing that can't be mended.'

He barely heard those words, so intent was he on following her. The shriek of grief from her sisters was the only thing that drew his attention, and he turned to see Princess Illora's body being removed from the ship. Lara and Meeka fell to the ground, weeping over her and kissing her broken limbs. Larinda approached them but didn't interrupt their mourning. He knew she would be ready to give them whatever they needed to put their sister to rest.

He turned back to Erleph. 'Does Vashta know?'

The man gave a sharp inclination of his head.

At least Vashta's recovery could move forward with no renewed suffering from discovering her sister was gone.

Everything in him wanted to stay with Vashta, but their city had been torn apart, their planet was in tatters, and both races ravaged. He knew that he had to re-establish order before they sunk into anarchy.

His sister was by his side. 'Go and do your duty. I will sit by Vashta and be you for her.'

Part of him rebelled against her words. *I need to be with Vashta. I need to be there when she wakes up. I need to comfort her as she grieves for her sister.*

'You wouldn't be the man she loves if you put her before our people.'

Again, she was right. 'Yes. Our people.'

'The people of Verindon.'

Her thoughts were tandem with his. '*All* the people of Verindon.'

CHAPTER TWENTY-FOUR

Vashta leant on Brandonin as her sister's body was lowered into their crypt.

He bent over her, his lips almost brushing her ear. 'Are you all right? Do you need to sit down?'

'No. I can stand.'

If the set of his shoulders was anything to go by, he didn't believe her. The glance from his sister cautioned him. He angled his body against Vashta, taking more of her weight. She tried not to look like she needed it.

She had no idea why she thought it necessary to deceive him. This was Illora's passing service. Meeka was weeping in Rallace's arms and even Lara was dabbing tears away, Ostin's hand on her shoulder. But Vashta couldn't allow herself to cry. It seemed too much of a defeat to do so, although she was sure Illora would have understood. Perhaps she would have wanted it.

Since Illora was only—if she could ever be *only* anything—the fourth child of the previous chief prince, her farewell was not a state occasion, not that there were many elites left to attend. As the formal proceedings ended and the blessing was announced, she counted those who'd farewelled her sister. No more than thirty.

Brandonin continued to support her as she went to the edge of the crypt, looking down at her sister's multicoloured coffin. She heard a sniff from beside her and her eyes sought his, expecting to find tears in them, but there were none. She cocked her head.

His look was sheepish. 'I was just reflecting on another similarity between our people. We must be laid to rest in colour as well.'

'Yes, her gown would have been bright, her hair filled with coloured ribbons.' She swallowed against the choking sensation. 'She would have been beautiful.' She had let Meeka and her mother prepare Illora for burial.

Her two sisters and her mother came to her, holding her, although Vashta found she was the one supporting her mother. 'To lose Illora, Brexin and your father within such a short time,' Mother said. 'It's such a great loss.'

'Many have lost more.' She looked around at the cavern that had once been the crypt of the High Families of the Vendel. Set in a vaulted building with a glass ceiling so that the colours of the sky would always shine on its occupants, it was several spans long and almost as wide, the walls inlaid with the finest wood in Verindon.

Or at least it had been. It was close to the Vendel palace and the ceiling had been smashed, with holes in every wall. Many of the crypts themselves had also been damaged, but repairs had started.

Brandonin put his hand on her shoulder. 'We'll return it to its former glory. Your family will have a beautiful place to rest.'

She marvelled again at the fact that he was there at all. 'You know, I think this is the first time a non-Vendel has ever been present at one of our passing services.'

'I'm honoured to be included.'

Mother skirted around him, but both Meeka and Lara paused to let him speak.

'My sincerest condolences to all your family.' His voice was loud enough to make Mother pause, but she didn't stop, intent on speaking to anyone else she could find.

Lara was never one to avoid an issue. 'A family you will soon be joining?' Meeka elbowed her and received a hostile glare. 'What? Are you one of those naysayers who insist it will never work, like Mother?'

Meeka gave their mother a fond look. 'She'll come around.'

But Vashta was out of patience. Mother had been cold and distant to Brandonin at every opportunity. 'I doubt we'll need her approval.'

'Keep your voice down,' cautioned Meeka.

'I don't see why.' But Vashta did as she was told.

'It's the leadership you have to convince,' Lara said.

Vashta looked left and right. 'What leadership? Our leadership is in tatters—many dead and most confused.'

'That's because they're still uncertain about how to handle our other problem.'

Yes, and that needed to be addressed before anyone could move on.

The problem of Mestitha.

***

It was bizarre to look around the conference room. It had survived well compared with other rooms in the palace. Debris from a small gap in the ceiling had been cleared away and the hole covered. Apart from that, it was as it always had been unless Vashta looked at the drapings or noticed that the mud-brown table they sat at was not the rich red one that used to be there.

It was the company that was the strangest. She, Meeka and Lara sat at the head of the table, with her in the middle. Mother, Brandonin and Erleph had taken up positions nearby, then alternately around the table were a mishmash of surviving councillors from both the Vendel and Verindal races. The buzz of conversation was not as polite as she would have hoped but they were doing their best, given what they were there to decide.

The door opened and Mestitha was led in. She walked with her usual air, treating the guards on either side of her with the same disdain she'd always given anyone she ranked beneath her.

But as she turned to face the table, the mask of indifference slipped as she scanned those present and found so many she didn't know. Her eyes were like lasers when she saw Brandonin and by the time they reached Vashta, they were blazing with a fire she'd never seen. 'Sister,' she sneered, 'I see you haven't hesitated to commit treason.'

There were gasps from the other Vendel but Vashta didn't flinch. 'Sister, I see you haven't managed to think about anything beyond yourself.'

Mestitha's poise as she took her seat was as regal as if she were sitting on her throne. 'I have no need. *I* am the ruler of the Vendel.'

'You were Father's heir, yes. But, unlike the Verindal, whose line of descent always goes from ruler to eldest child, I'm sure you're aware that we've long had ways of doing things differently.'

Mestitha's mouth dropped open. 'That ruling hasn't been used for centuries!'

'Nevertheless, it still exists.' Vashta waited until her sister's face turned purple with rage before continuing. 'You know that in times past, the ruler of the Vendel could be decided by trial by combat.'

Mestitha spat the words through her teeth. 'You wouldn't dare!'

Vashta remained unruffled. 'This was considered a fair way to decide the ruler when younger siblings challenged for leadership. It was honourable to engage in battle.'

She could hear her sister's nails digging into the arms of her chair as she left her place and walked towards her. 'I have discussed this with our remaining sisters.' She didn't flinch at the thought of Illora. 'They have decreed that they have no desire to claim the throne of the Vendel as their own.'

Mestitha scoffed. 'But you would, wouldn't you? It has always irked you, hasn't it, being the youngest. Being the last and the least of us. Being the one who walks behind with no one because you *are* no one.'

Vashta heard a chair pushed back and was in no doubt as to who was rising to her defence. 'Anyone who has seen your sister's skill in battle couldn't fail to doubt her worthiness.' Brandonin's voice rang out across the room.

His words might not have mattered to Mestitha, but her head turned at the sounds of agreement from the others at the table, Vendel and Verindal alike.

Their support was enough to soothe the sting of Mestitha's words. 'I think you'll find that your opinion is in the minority in this room, amongst the only real leaders we have left. I have already expressed to them my intention to challenge you and they're all supportive.'

Vashta could almost hear her sister's thoughts. Mestitha had never had the slightest interest in combat; Father had forced her to learn. It was much more congenial to sit on a throne with people bowing before her. She was obviously trying to come up with some alternative; something she could win. 'You can't do that. I am the ruler of our people!'

Was that the best she could do? 'And I am challenging that, as is my right.'

Mestitha glanced around the table once more, seeking support. Eventually, she reached the only person who would have any sympathy for her. 'Mother, please. You know it was Father's dearest wish that I succeed him.'

Vashta watched her mother carefully. Of all the people in the room, her support was weakest. Would she yield to her favourite daughter?

'You're right. For many years it was your father's dearest wish that you would succeed him. He wanted you to rule in his place. He did everything he could to ensure you would be a good and decent leader of our people.'

Mestitha's face gained strength at Mother's words until she heard the fatal 'but'.

'But he'd told me lately how concerned he was. You showed no desire to lead, only to celebrate your greatness. You showed no desire to learn from him, thinking your way was best. And when it came to battle,' Mother rose to her feet, her gaze piercing her firstborn, 'you chose to hide inside while your father waged war, losing his life in an attempt to save us. How could you be worthy of this honour?'

Tears began to roll down Mestitha's cheeks. 'But I would have died as well had I fought with Father! Is that what you want?'

Mother's back straightened. 'Better to mourn a daughter who honoured her father than a coward who refused to. And perhaps if you'd fought by his side, you would have saved him. But nothing was worth that risk, was it?'

Mestitha's shoulders shook. 'Mother …'

But their mother collapsed back into her chair, leaning into Lara's shoulder and sobbing.

'Enough of this,' Vashta said. 'Mestitha, I challenge you to trial by combat. You may choose the place of this combat and the weapons we'll use. Erleph has been elected to decree the winner. This will take place—'

'Silence!' The others around the table leapt to their feet as Mestitha launched herself at her sister, Brandonin already halfway there.

But Vashta threw her back into her chair.

The heat on Mestitha's face was redder than a flame. 'You will stop at nothing, will you? Have your throne. Just leave me in peace.' She scrambled to her feet and raced out of the room, her guards shadowing her.

Brandonin came to stand beside Vashta and she smirked at him. 'I told you she'd back down.'

'You don't think she might change her mind?'

There was no doubt about that. 'My sister hates to lose. She especially hates to lose publicly. And she knows all too well who'd win if it came to that.'

Lara joined them; her arms folded. 'I know you think this is for the best, Vashta, but there's a reason why these fights used to be forced, and why they were to the death.' Vashta shuffled at her words but didn't cut her off as she continued. 'She will always be a threat to your reign.'

Vashta had already thought of that. But she had no desire to watch another sister die, regardless of the reason. She and Brandonin had discussed it and it was he who'd made her realise how unnecessary it was for them to fight to the death.

'If this was a normal reign, I'd agree with you. But this is more than that.' She took Brandonin's hand. 'This is a uniting of two races. The more our people work together, the less likely she is to cause trouble.'

'Your sister is right to be cautious, though,' said Mother, as she and Meeka joined them. 'She could try and draw the Vendel away.'

'She could *try*,' said Erleph from behind them, 'but she would fail. You don't know how little respect there is for your eldest daughter. Even before the war, she was unpopular. Now that animosity runs even deeper. I can't see her ever mounting a successful campaign.'

Mother pursed her lips. 'I hope you're right.'

'But there are more important things to discuss,' said Kenon, one of the surviving Vendel councillors. '*If* you are to bond—' he looked between the two of them, '—we must be sure of fair treatment. Our cities and buildings have suffered greater damage in this war than the Verindal ones.'

Lady Mirkana of the Verindal rolled her eyes. 'No one believes that, not even you.'

Kenon stiffened. 'How would you know?'

She met his gaze. 'Because I'm a lie detector.'

Kenon reclaimed his seat with a scowl as Mirkana turned to Brandonin. 'My Lord, we're in desperate need of help.'

Their overlord raised his hands to calm the room. 'I'm aware of that. There has been suffering on both sides. Vashta and I will be joint rulers, each ensuring the best outcome for our own people, who we soon hope will be regarded as one.'

'But where will the bonding be held?' said Mirkana. 'And whose ceremonies will we use?'

'Our bonding ceremony must be observed,' said Kenon, punctuating each word with a tap of his finger against the table.

'So must ours.'

'Ladies and gentlemen!' Erleph roared. 'Don't disgrace your races by this petty squabbling in front of our leaders.'

Vashta felt it was time for her to speak. 'Brandonin is right. We will rule jointly, we will distribute aid fairly, and we will make sure each race is treated the same. If you can't assist us in that goal, then we will find Vendel and Verindal who will—true leaders of our people.'

But even that couldn't stop Mirkana. 'But where will you be bonded? Every sacred building is damaged!'

'We have plans to rebuild the bunker,' Brandonin said, 'making it a combined museum, art gallery and meeting place, complete with an open-air auditorium that will seat thousands. I don't know if we could wait until then to be bonded?' He looked at Vashta. 'Maybe not, but it will be a wonderful gathering place.'

Kenon brightened. 'We could call it the Place of Meeting.'

'I hope we can come up with a better name than that,' Lara muttered, her face growing dismayed as the councillors began to talk about it.

'Never mind,' Brandonin said. 'The name's not that important.'

Vashta looked up at him. 'I notice you didn't mention the security we're planning inside. Or the tunnels underneath.'

He grinned. 'No need to mention everything at once.'

He was probably right. 'At least they seem to accept the idea of us. Do you think the people will—yours and mine?'

He took her hand. 'I think so. We're all sick and tired of war. Our races have never united like this before—under a joint rule. It could be what makes the difference.'

She glanced up at him. 'I think you're right. We'll see, anyway.'

He must have sensed her doubts because he put her arm around her. 'Don't worry, we'll convince them, whatever it takes.'

***

It wasn't long before the councillors drifted away to make arrangements. Her family lingered a little longer, but Vashta had had enough of meetings and long-running conversations. Brandonin must have tired of the talk as well, as his exhausted eyes sought her own. 'Shall we?'

They wandered out of the conference room, through what was left of the palace and into the gardens, or at least, where they used to be. Now there were piles of rubble and stripped trees, the beautiful pathways and copses she'd explored as a child buried under devastation.

'This used to be my favourite place to explore,' she said, feeling tears welling up in her eyes. 'I ran through mazes of shrubs, playing hide and seek with my sisters.'

She took his hand and led him down the only path that remained, through still-smouldering tree trunks along uneven paving stones.

He stopped and bent down, picking a lonely skyflower from beside the path. Unlike its companions, it had survived unscathed, its petals unfurled to reveal all the colours of the rainbow, just like their awe-inspiring sky.

He held it up to her. 'Vashta, you know I love you.'

She was startled. 'Of course. You know I feel the same.' Where was this going?

He must have noticed her confusion because a sheepish smile appeared on his face. 'I'm sorry. I suddenly realised I hadn't even asked if you would agree to be bonded to me. I just sort of assumed.'

She didn't realise how tightly wound her body was until she felt herself relax with relief. She could feel her face going red. 'That's all right. I sort of assumed too.'

He held out the flower to her, and she examined its perfection, the colours darkening in the fading light. Then he tucked it behind her ear, pulling a wave of her hair over her shoulder to hold it in place.

He took both her hands. 'So, will you?'

She smiled at the trepidation on his face. Did he really think she would say no? 'Yes, my love.'

He bent to kiss her, but she stopped him. 'Wait.' Doubt flitted across his face until she took his hands. 'I want to try something,' she said. 'I'm not sure this will work, since you're a Verindal, but here goes.'

She pushed up one of his sleeves, exposing the crease of his elbow, and pressed her thumb into it. He gasped; a clear indication he'd felt the heat that had passed from her hand into his arm.

As she pulled her hand away, he looked at the imprint of her thumb where it now lay, marked on his arm. 'What's that?'

'It's called a promise mark. We Vendel exchange them at our bonding ceremonies. I wasn't sure that would work with a Verindal, but it seems to. It won't last forever now because this isn't an official bonding ceremony. We'll have to wait until the day for that.'

Brandonin looked thoughtful. 'I wonder …' He took her sleeve and pushed it up, placing his thumb against her skin.

Nothing happened. It drew a sigh from him. 'I guess it's a Vendel thing.'

She took his hands. 'It doesn't matter. We'll make new traditions that show the love a Verindal and Vendel can share together.'

He kissed her in earnest, the shine in his eyes undiminished even as dusk fell and the colours faded from their sky, taking the remaining light with it.

CHAPTER TWENTY-FIVE

Brandonin flung on his cape, adjusting it so it sat neatly atop his uniform.

Larinda reached for the clasp and fastened it, setting it in place across his shoulders. 'There. I think you look decent.'

He dissected his reflection, checking every detail. He was in the formal uniform of a Verindal Overlord—a loose-fitting tunic of blue with a sash of bright red across it, complemented by indigo pants. His scarlet cape had an underlay of every colour of the rainbow to represent their beautiful Verindonian sky. 'I hope she likes it.'

A chuckle escaped her lips. 'You know she's not bonding with you for your looks … although I'm sure she doesn't object to them. She's certainly not bonding with you for the uniform.'

'That's true.' He felt weary. The past six months had been exhausting, as they'd done their best to rebuild Verindal and Vendel lands as one instead of two separate entities. Vashta had been by his side for every decision, always trying to represent her people and their interests. But with so much to be done, the bonding ceremony had been pushed back and back.

Larinda must have guessed his thoughts. 'At least the day has arrived.'

'Yes.' He took in his appearance again; at least it was something he could control. He'd found it necessary to take a behind-the-scenes role in most of the decisions relating to the styling of a new joint bonding ceremony. 'I just hope Vashta doesn't come to blows with her mother or sisters before we even see each other.'

Larinda shrugged off his worries. 'I doubt she'd want the day marred by the sight of any family members nursing injuries. It wouldn't present the most harmonious image for the people.'

Erleph entered Brandonin's quarters, bowing. He still wasn't used to having a Vendel as his closest advisor but the most trustworthy Verindal council members had been killed in the fighting, leaving him without any counsel during the rebuild. Erleph had stepped into the role and was now indispensable. Brandonin loved his calm and wise advice. It was the way he'd always wished Father had been.

Erleph was wearing a Vendel commander's formal uniform—a golden tight-fitted tunic with lapels. He looked Brandonin up and down. 'My Lord, are you ready?'

With one last look in the mirror, he repositioned his cape. 'I believe so.' He looked back at Erleph. 'It's time?'

'Yes, my Lord.'

A sleek new roller was waiting for them outside the partially reconstructed palace entrance. It had that fresh-off-the-line smell he loved. He stroked the plush seats as he settled in the back with Larinda next to him and Erleph on the other side of her.

Vashta's mentor looked back at the palace as they pulled away. 'We should do some more work on your home, my Lord.'

That drew a frown from him. 'Not until the rest of the planet is restored.'

'That could take years.'

'Well, after some restoration then. I refuse to live in luxury while the rest of our people are waiting for their homes to be rebuilt.'

He and Larinda waved at the people lining the streets, his heart lifting at the sight of their support, with both Verindal and Vendel mixing freely. *Well, mostly freely*, he thought, as he noticed a shove between a Vendel and a Verindal. The security detail had already quelled the disturbance by the time they'd passed. He sighed. There was still so much to be done.

Erleph shuffled and looked away from the street. Larinda leant across him. 'Smile, Erleph. The people want to see you.'

He shrank into his seat. 'I find it unlikely they want to see *me*, my Lady.'

Larinda laughed and made sure to wave at those standing on his side of the street.

As they turned the next corner a shadow passed over their roller and Brandonin gazed up at the structure they were approaching. The bunker, now called the Place of Meeting, was still only partially reconstructed, but he could see how much progress had been made even in the past week.

Erleph looked up at the building with disdain. 'I believe the auditorium and the balcony have been completed, my Lord, although the interior of the building is still in development.'

'As long as there's room for the ceremony and the balcony holds us up,' Larinda said.

'I believe Nestor made it his business to ensure it would be suitable.' Erleph almost groaned as he spoke.

'You're unhappy with his decisions?' Brandonin asked.

'I'm unhappy with the projected cost.'

That was understandable. 'You have my permission to rein Nestor in if you think he's going too far.'

Relief spread across Erleph's face. 'Thank you, my Lord.'

The roller pulled in at the base of a wide staircase. The last time Brandonin had been there, it had been freshly laid, but now it was clean and decorated, with a wide blue carpet running up to the doors above.

He alighted from the vehicle and turned to help Larinda out. They waved at the waiting crowds while Erleph joined them, although he proceeded straight up the stairs, most likely to find Vashta. Brandonin knew she'd already arrived and was waiting in one of the inner rooms. They gave the crowd a final wave at the top of the stairs, where they were greeted by officials and ushered inside.

Nestor met them there, bowing from the neck. 'My Lord, my Lady, this way.'

The area they walked through smelled of fresh construction and fittings and Brandonin was impressed by the plush carpet and colourful hangings. 'You've done a creditable job at creating something special,

Nestor. Quite an achievement for someone whose field of expertise is weaponry.'

Nestor seemed pleased with the praise. 'It's not that different, my Lord. While I admit most of the armoury ideas come out of my head, I still deputise others to complete the work, under my direction. All I needed was additional expertise to create what you see here.'

'So it seems.' Although he knew some of the wall hangings hid unpainted walls and disassembled fittings, he didn't mind. Better that they take the time and prioritise the people rather than this place. He'd had no problem with them completing enough of it to accommodate the ceremony, more for the people's sake than his and Vashta's, but the rest of it could wait.

They were led to a side room, with various couches set around for them. Brandonin refused to sit in case he crumpled his uniform. Instead, he paced at the long window, looking at the room beyond. No noise came through from the gathering hall where they were to be bonded. He could already see family, friends and dignitaries from both the Verindal and Vendel races taking their seats. He was thankful for the aisles that would keep them apart, just in case there was a conflict.

He tugged at the catch on his cape. Vashta was in the room across from him. It too had a window, but he could see nothing through it. 'She can't see me either, I assume.'

Brandonin hadn't been speaking to anyone in particular, but Nestor answered. 'No, my Lord. It's one-way glass.'

Erleph came from Vashta's room, heading towards them. That could only mean one thing. Larinda leapt to her feet and went out to meet him. After they'd conferred, she returned, peeking around the door. 'They're ready to start.'

'Right.' He straightened his uniform one last time and went to the door. As he appeared, the Vendel listophonists raised their instruments to their lips and let out a blast. He could see every Verindal reacting to the sound, some with interest, some with their hands over their ears. Music of any sort wasn't customary at a Verindal bonding, but he liked it. It made the occasion grander.

The tone of the instruments became lighter as Vashta appeared at the other end of the room. Her dress flowed along her body, the delicate colours swirling down from where it met her hair, half up, half down. He preferred it down so he could see its beautiful golden waves cascading over her shoulders.

He drew a deep breath and began to walk towards her. She did the same as the listophonists began softly before increasing in volume until Brandonin and Vashta met in the middle to a rising crescendo of sound. He took her hands in his and marvelled at her smile, which beamed up at him with a confidence he couldn't believe she bestowed on him.

Two masters of ceremony, elders from both races, came forward.

The Vendel elder put his hands on theirs, one on the top and one on the bottom. 'May the hands here joined today be joined together forever in the service of our people.' He intoned. He muttered on for a little longer and Brandonin tried to concentrate on what he was saying, but whenever Vashta's blue eyes fell on him he lost track of everything else.

Once the Vendel had unclasped their hands, Vashta gave him the promise mark again, and the elder ran his firming seal over it, fixing it in place. Now Brandonin would always have it.

Then the Verindal elder stepped forward. She turned to him and said, 'Brandonin, Overlord of the Verindal, do you decree to bond with this woman and rule jointly with her, for the sake of all Verindonians?'

'I will do so.' He was pleased with how the vows sounded. They had adjusted them from the traditional ones considering the joining of the two races.

The elder then turned to his bride. 'Vashta, princess of the Vendel, do you decree to bond with this man and rule jointly with him, for the sake of all Verindonians?'

'I will do so.'

Both the elders stood shoulder to shoulder. 'Then we pronounce in the name of our people,' the Verindal elder said.

'And in the name of ours,' droned the Vendel elder, 'that you are bonded, according to the ancient rites of our peoples.'

As the gathering cheered and clapped, Brandonin leant down to kiss his bond-partner. He could feel the curve of her lips as he did and felt her drawing him closer as they sealed their bonding before the congregation.

Vashta's mother was the first to reach them, embracing and kissing her daughter, and then him, which took him by surprise. It seemed she was surprised also as she looked at her hands on his arms.

'Thank you,' he said.

Her gaze was one of understanding and she withdrew as Lara and Meeka also embraced him. They fought Larinda for the honour, although his sister quickly sought out Vashta. 'At last I have a sister!' she said.

Vashta's face faltered, and Larinda looked horrified as she realised she'd reminded her of Illora, but Vashta shook her head. 'I'm used to four sisters. I think I would like another by my side in the future.'

Family gave way to councillors and advisors. Brandonin could see Erleph hanging back and wasn't sure he intended to congratulate them at all. Then Vashta spied him and snared Brandonin's hand, dragging him over. 'He'll never come to us. He doesn't know what to do at these events.'

It took some time to make their way through the throngs of well-wishers, but Vashta was not one to be dissuaded from any course of action, and soon she was by Erleph's side. 'In the absence of my father, you are the man whose approval means the most to me.'

Erleph's face crinkled into a gruff grin. 'You have it, Your Highness. You are where you're meant to be. And strangely enough, I don't think there's a man better suited to you.' Erleph put his hand on Brandonin's shoulder and he returned the gesture. 'It occurred to me that Vashta might meet her match in a Verindal, but I never thought it would end like this. Congratulations.'

The two of them were then led through an adjoining room which ended in glass double doors. Through them, they could see the auditorium and the cheering throng.

Erleph came to their sides, motioning to four highly trained

Vendel to flank them. 'Just for security reasons, my Lord and Lady, although Nestor set up enough laser responders to take out anyone in the crowd who looks like harming you.'

He opened the doors, admitting the chorus of cheers. They increased to a thunderous roar as Brandonin and Vashta stepped out, hands joined and raised, and acknowledged their people, Vendel and Verindal alike.

Brandonin watched Vashta as tears crowded on her lids. 'I can't believe they're standing together.' From where they stood, they couldn't see anything but unity.

He hoped it would last. 'We must make sure it does,' he said aloud. He expected his bond-partner to turn to him with a questioning look, but she nodded. 'We'll keep them unified and tie them together so firmly that their unity will last long after we've gone.'

How could anyone looking at her doubt it would come to pass? He didn't. They had been born for this. He was not a Vendel, so they would never be able to produce energy together like her sisters could with their bond-partners, but he knew that there was still strength in the joining of their hands.

The energy of their joining would be seen in more permanent ways.